chivalry makes a comeback

old fashioned

a novelization of the motion picture by

rene gutteridge

based on the screenplay by

rik swartzwelder

Tyndale House Publishers, Inc.
Carol Stream, Illinois

Visit Tyndale online at www.tyndale.com.

Visit Rene Gutteridge's website at www.renegutteridge.com.

For more about *Old Fashioned*, check out www.oldfashionedmovie.com.

TYNDALE and Tyndale's quill logo are registered trademarks of Tyndale House Publishers, Inc.

Old Fashioned

Designed by Dean H. Renninger

Edited by Sarah Mason

Exclusive representation by Working Title Agency, LLC, Spring Hill, TN.

Published in association with Books and Such, Inc., Attn: Janet Kobobel Grant, 5926 Sunhawk Dr., Santa Rosa, CA 95409.

Library of Congress Cataloging-in-Publication Data

Gutteridge, Rene.
  Old Fashioned / Rene Gutteridge ; based on the screenplay by Rik Swartzwelder.
    pages cm
    ISBN 978-1-4143-7933-3 (sc)
1. Love stories. 2. Christian fiction. I. Swartzwelder, Rik. II. Title.
    PS3557.U887O43 2013
    813'.54—dc23   2012043071

Printed in the United States of America

20	19	18	17	16	15	14
7	6	5	4	3	2	1

In memory of Don and Helen

R. G.

For Amber

R. S.

acknowledgments

Rene Gutteridge:

In reading just the first few pages of Rik Swartzwelder's fabulous script for *Old Fashioned*, I knew I wanted to be a part of this project. Like any woman, I love a good love story, but this story held so much more than that. It spoke to my heart. By the middle of the script, I was crying. I was also laughing. It doesn't get much better than that! I knew we had a strong script from which to work, which makes my job easier and fun. It's a little shameful when a guy can beat a girl at writing romance, but Rik outdoes me in this department—I fully relied on his beautiful telling of two souls connecting through a journey of hope and redemption.

I'd like to thank Rik for trusting me with his "baby," as we liked to call his story and script. It is quite an act of faith for a writer to turn his work over to another writer. Rik was gracious and enthusiastic, with great insights that helped make this book the best it could be. He was also really easy and fun to work with. That's a plus in any collaboration! Finally, I'd like to thank Rik for dropping the *c* off his first name so both of our names would fit on the cover. With names like Swartzwelder and Gutteridge, there's no telling how small the font might have been had he not made this tremendous sacrifice. . . .

I'd also like to thank the team at Tyndale—Karen Watson, Jan Stob, Sarah Mason, and the entire crew—for seeing the brilliance of Rik's script and believing in the book. It's always such an enjoyable, fun, and inspiring experience to work with the Tyndale team, and I'm grateful for any chance I get to be a part of your vision for publishing. Thanks so much for including me in this and for helping steer the novel to its fullest potential.

Special thanks also to Brandon Tylka, who spent hours sorting through stills from the film to send to me so I could get a good idea of locations and scenes. Really couldn't have done it without you, Brandon. You were right on top of every request I sent. Thank you! And also thanks to Nathan Nazario for helping make this whole project come to life.

Last but not least, I have to especially thank my family, Sean, John, and Cate, who willingly gave up some of their summer fun to let me do this project. I appreciate the sacrifice you each make so that I can continue to write. I am so thankful for a family who supports and loves me in all I do and keeps me grounded and secure in all aspects of my life. And as always, I thank Father God, who took me on an amazing spiritual journey that included the writing of this project. Thank You for the loud and clear message You have sent my way, that I never have to rely on my own righteousness, but through Jesus I have the assurance of the Father's love.

Rik Swartzwelder:
I don't even know where to begin. No kidding, writing the screenplay for *Old Fashioned* was relatively easy in comparison to this—my first official "acknowledgments" section. How can I, in just a few paragraphs, possibly do justice to all of the people and divine graces and years of struggle that led to this movie being made—or this book? Like a toddler taking his first steps, I feel unsteady and unsure. Yet I'm also inspired and grateful to those who have held

my hand and taught me how—how to dream, how to try, how to walk on. . . .

Since these are indeed my very first steps, I am compelled to—first and foremost—thank the Father, the Son, and the Holy Spirit for not giving up on me or this idea. There is no question: *Old Fashioned* (the movie, this book, etc.) exists not because of my faithfulness, but because of the Creator's. All glory, honor, and praise to "The Butterfly Maker" for seeing nobility and hope and colorful wings in places where proof is yet absent or wanting . . . for transformation, for new life. You alone are worthy.

Special thanks to the entire Tyndale House team for seeing something unique in *Old Fashioned* and for having the remarkable insight to know that Rene Gutteridge was the perfect author to work on the novelization. Rene, you are a brilliant writer and such a joyful spirit. Thank you for your patience with this rookie and for wonderfully translating the screenplay into something that stands on its own and illuminates the story in exceptional ways. That said, I'm still trying to forgive you for adding scenes that were so good I wish I'd thought to include them myself in the movie. But I digress.

Thanks and appreciation also need to go out to Gordon and Susan Toering for their belief and steadfastness; you are truly my patron saints and I thank God for you. Also, thanks to Bryan Zervos for getting the *Old Fashioned* ball rolling all those years ago. God's timing, my friend. Thanks to Nathan Nazario for stepping out in faith and for being the steady influence this project needed and to Dave DeBorde, Jeffrey Stott, and Rachel Dik for helping connect the dots. And likewise, to my diverse collective of other friends and cohorts (too many to mention here, unfortunately) who shared wisdom and perspective as I developed, wrote, and polished the script—I remain much obliged.

To all of our investors and supporters who believed in this story (and us) and had the vision and courage to risk, to throw in, to roll the dice on an independent film—thank you. To the entire cast and crew (and to all the friends and families) of *Old Fashioned*—thank you so much for the long hours, sacrifice, and immense effort. To my own mom and dad, siblings, and various members of my blended and beautifully overextended family—I cherish you all. Thanks for the love, for instilling the confidence and conviction in me that all things are possible, and for being the kind of safety net that I wish every vagabond/starving artist/dreamer could have so that they all might leap boldly.

In addition, for being there year after year and keeping the light of hope alive, even during the darkest of moments, I must pay due homage to Jim and Mary Seldenright, Benjamin Hershleder, Rajeev Sigamoney, Jeffrey Travis, and William and Donna Romanowski. Proverbs 11:25.

To my old hometown and our primary shooting location— Tuscarawas County, Ohio—so many of you opened your hearts (and in some cases, homes and more) to us that our modest budget was able to multiply like loaves and fishes on a hillside in Galilee. You are surely "The House That Built Me" and I am so grateful for that. Thank you.

To the Spirit-filled churches and small groups and believers who nurtured my soul along the way—there cannot be thanks enough.

And finally, to all those who ever tried to show love to a damaged heart long before it was ready to receive it or return it—this one's for you.

Dream. Try. Walk on.

CHAPTER 1

HIS DAY STARTED OUT quiet and ordinary, the way he liked and assured himself of. The morning light of early autumn rose in the east and filtered through the old, cracked windows of the antique shop, carrying with it smells of dust and wood shavings and varnish.

Every morning for nine years, before the sun fully slipped from its covers, Clay had unlocked the old shop. The store was tidy and presentable, like a perfectly tailored suit, showcasing the uniqueness of all the antiques. Everything, as it always did, had its place.

This morning he stood in the midst of them, carefully surveying the room and inventorying what he might need to acquire this week. Some items he found at estate sales.

Others, the more unique pieces, George brought his way. Most needed, at the very least, a good buffing; typically they needed much more. They came to him as trash. But with hard work—tried-and-true elbow grease—there was rarely anything that couldn't be restored. There was no magic in it, but sometimes when he was finished, it felt otherworldly. A piece would arrive at his doorstep hopeless and pathetic and leave him one day treasured and beautiful.

Wax did wonders. So did sandpaper. And paint.

But the truth was, not everything could be fixed.

It was this early part of the morning that he loved so much, before the busyness of the day began. At the back part of the shop, through the swinging doors, was his little slice of heaven, where the smell of sawdust stirred in him a delight he'd never been able to fully explain to another soul.

Clay set his keys and coffee mug aside, keeping the front lights off because Mrs. Hartnett had a bad habit of dropping by before the crack of dawn if she saw a light on. He knelt beside the small rocker he'd been working on the last several days. An elderly man had dropped it off, hardly saying a word, paying for it in advance even though Clay insisted he didn't need to do that.

"What's your story?" he murmured, his fingers gliding over the now-smooth wood. The chair was a hard-bitten thing when it came in, chipped and cracked and neglected, smelling vaguely of smoke. Whenever he worked on an old piece of furniture—or anything else, for that matter—he found his mind wandering to possibilities of where it once came from and how it had gotten to where it was now. Most pieces had spent dark days in attics and basements and back rooms that never heard footsteps. Somewhere in their lives, they'd served a good purpose. The lucky ones stayed in the house but sat invisibly in a corner or by a couch, an annoying place to have to dust, a thorn in the side of someone who wished it could be thrown away, except for the guilt attached because it belonged to a great-grandmother who'd spent her very last pennies to acquire it, or some such story.

Yesterday he'd cut and whittled the rocker's new back pieces and today he would stain them. Clay grabbed the sandpaper and walked to the table saw where the slats waited, lined up like soldiers. As he ran the sandpaper across the wood, he could practically hear the creak of the rocker and the laughter of delighted children in another century.

He sighed, rolled up his sleeves, and sanded more quickly. Sometimes he thought *he'd* been born in the wrong century. There was hardly a kid today who would care about sitting in a rocker on the edge of a porch and watching a spring storm blow in. The world that he once thrived in had become a noisy, clangoring, messy place. But here, in the shop, with sawdust spilling through shafts of dusty light, he found his peace.

The sandpaper soon needed replacing, so he went to the corner of the room where he kept his supplies and reached for a new package. Then he snapped his wrist back at the sudden and sharp pain in his hand. It hurt like a snake had bitten him. Blood dripped steadily from the top of his hand

and he cupped his other hand beneath, trying to catch the droplets.

Clay searched the corner, trying to figure out what had snagged him.

There, on the old wooden gate he'd found in an abandoned field: barbed wire. The back side of the gate was wrapped in it when he'd found it, and he hadn't had time to cut it off yet. He looked at the wound as he walked to the sink. It was bleeding so fast that it was actually seeping through his fingers, dripping on the floor.

What a mess.

He ran it under the water. It was more of a puncture wound but mightier than it looked. The blood poured, mixing with the water. And it didn't want to stop, even for the phone.

The shrill ring cut through the still air, coming from the rotary phone he had mounted on the wall next to the sink. Keeping his wounded hand under running water, he answered it.

"Old Fashioned Antiques."

"It's me."

"Lisa. Hi. I'm kind of—"

"I know, I know. Busy. As you always are. Why don't you answer your cell? Do you even carry it with you? Don't you text? People need to get ahold of you sometimes, you know. What if it's an emergency? What about that kind aunt of yours?"

"She finds me through the postal service."

"Anyway, I need to drop off the stuff for the thing."

"Okay."

"Are you going to be there this morning? Silly question. Where else would you be?"

"The hospital."

"What?"

"I might be. You never know. Maybe I got tangled in some vicious barbed wire. I might be bleeding out even as we speak, and here you are completely oblivious."

Lisa sighed. She never got his humor. "I'm being serious. Can I bring it by?"

In the background, Clay could hear Lisa's daughter, Cosie, screaming at the top of her lungs. "She okay?"

"She's throwing a fit."

"So she's in time-out?"

"You know we don't believe in punishment."

"I know. I just keep thinking you'll change your mind about that."

"So I'm coming by later, okay? And remember, this is a total surprise. Not a single word to David about it."

"I'll make you a deal: I won't tell David if I don't have to come to the party."

"Clay, he would be crushed."

"You know I'm just there to boost your numbers, fill in the empty space."

"True. But you're still coming. And not a word. I'll see you later."

She hung up and Clay raised his hand toward the light.

It had finally stopped bleeding. He put a Band-Aid on and started mopping up the blood droplets all over the floor.

It was a lesson every person learned one time or another in their lives—never cross paths with barbed wire.

♥

"Look at that, would you? Look at it!" Amber let go of the steering wheel with both hands and put her knee underneath to keep it steady. She gestured, glancing at Mr. Joe. "Nobody gets this. I realize that. I do. But see how the road winds, and then off it goes, through the trees? You don't really know what's around the bend, see?"

Amber put her hands back on the steering wheel, then gave Mr. Joe a quick scratch behind the ears. She'd temporarily let him out of his carrier, though he tended to get carsick if left out too long. "You're unimpressed, as usual. But there's something beautiful about roads. They're so full of possibilities. . . . Of course, you can always die in a horrific crash, too. But mostly, it's just about going somewhere. Anywhere. It's about what's around that bend, Mr. Joe. What's there?"

Amber's Jeep whizzed around the curve, clearing the trees as the road straightened. Her windows were down, the wind tearing through her hair so fiercely that it was going to take a good hour to comb it out, but she didn't care. She turned the music up. "Lovely Day" was on the radio, and she nudged her cat like he might sing along with her.

Then she saw it. "Whoa." She slowed and craned her neck out the window for a better view. "Mr. Joe, look at that!" Large stone buildings seemed to rise right out of the earth, sprawled across several acres. White concrete sidewalks disappeared into rolling hills and hazy light illuminated the branches of all the trees, like a scene out of some kind of fairy tale. The entrance read *Bolivar University*, but it looked like medieval England.

She leaned toward Mr. Joe and gave him a wink. "Apparently we've stumbled across Camelot. I told you I knew what I was doing when we hung a left back there."

Mr. Joe meowed in agreement.

As she drove on, Amber squeezed the fingers on her right hand. Her wrist was starting to throb, probably due to the cast more than the injury. It should've healed up fine by now. On the top of the cast was Misty's name, scrawled in red with little hearts.

She focused her attention back on the road. She couldn't spend emotional energy missing those friends left behind. But as she passed Camelot, she had to admit, it was always hard not to glance in the rearview mirror.

Still, she had to be resolved to press forward, find whatever was around the bend. She kissed Misty's name and left it at that.

This was beautiful country, and having spent much of her life on the road, she knew it when she saw it. Amber gazed at the trees. Some of the leaves were starting to turn that fiery-red color she loved so much. Soon, a cool wind would sift through them, lifting them into the air and then cradling them to the ground.

Ahead, a sign said, "Welcome to Tuscarawas County." *How did you even pronounce that?*

The speed limit indicated she should be going much slower, so she let off the gas. The last thing she needed was a ticket, and small college towns were notorious for planting police officers everywhere. It was probably how they made half their annual budget. Past the university by only a mile was the beginning of the town attached to it. It looked like something out of a Norman Rockwell painting. She was probably somewhere near Amish country too. She'd have to look at her map at some point, but her best guess was she was in eastern Ohio.

"Charming little place . . . like old-Coca-Cola-sign charming."

The car lurched and lurched again, throwing Mr. Joe off-balance. His ears flattened. Then the engine sputtered and gurgled. Amber smiled but kept driving.

She made it through the town square, going less than twenty-five miles an hour, in ten minutes. A small gas station ahead had a flat, yellow carport extending over only two gas pumps. It looked like it had been built sometime in the 1950s and seemed to be the last stop before the road stretched ahead and turned out of sight.

She deliberately drove on by, her gas light glowing yellow.

Then the engine died. With the momentum she had left, she pulled to the side of the road and let go of the steering wheel. The gas station was a five-minute walk behind her, no more.

Mr. Joe was purring again, wrapping his body around the

empty glass jar he shared the seat with. Amber took the keys out of the ignition and relaxed into her seat just a bit. The temperature was so perfect. It reminded her of Monterey in April. The sky, bright and blue, was totally cloudless.

"What do you think, Mr. Joe? Home?"

The cat blinked slowly like he was fighting a nap. Amber got out and looked around. The trees were still lush and dense, so she couldn't see far.

At the back of her Jeep, she opened the hatch, careful not to let everything spill onto the ground. Boxes of clothes, gently packed dishes, bins full of photographs. And on top of it all sat a huge bulletin board, the colorful pushpins she'd bought somewhere in Michigan still stuck into the cork. It amazed her that her whole life could fit into the trunk of a car. She grabbed her purse from under her travel bag, found her red plastic gas can, and closed the hatch.

Through the open passenger window, she picked up Mr. Joe and put him in his carrier. "All right. You know what to do. Don't be afraid to bare your fangs if you need to. Try not to look so sweet, okay? That's not going to keep anyone away."

As she walked toward the gas station, Amber tried to take it all in. She didn't see any stoplights. She liked towns that were more partial to stop signs. The buildings had character but also had an air of vacancy to them. Over the tree line, puffs of factory smoke rose like ascending, transparent jelly-fish. Toward the east and across a small field was an area that looked a little more developed, with some houses and restaurants, as best she could tell.

At the gas station's convenience store, a bell announced her arrival. It smelled like coffee and motor oil with vague hints of diesel. The man behind the counter wore a stained blue mechanic's jumpsuit with a patch that read *Larry*. He smiled pleasantly, setting down his newspaper. "What can I do you for, young lady?"

Amber put a five-dollar bill on the table. "Just need some gas."

"Five dollars ain't gonna get you very far," he said. "There ain't another town—gas station either, for that matter—for sixty-seven miles."

"I'm staying here for the moment."

Larry grinned. "Is that so? Well, welcome. We got a great catfish place—serves it up all you can eat—just around the corner there."

"Sounds fantastic. I'm looking to rent a small apartment."

Larry pointed to a stack of newspapers by the door. "That's our little publication round here. It's got a section for renters."

"Thank you." Amber grabbed the paper and walked outside to fill her gas can.

When she returned to her car, Mr. Joe's face was pressed up against the wires of his cage, his unblinking eyes staring her down for leaving him behind. She popped the gas tank open and stuck the gas can's nozzle in. Then she spread the newspaper across the hood of her car.

She had two criteria—cheap and furnished. "All right, boy. We're gonna go see if we've got a place to sleep tonight."

♥

"There you go—good as new," Clay said, rocking the chair back and forth. "Well, maybe not *as* good, but look, you've been through a lot. I've given you a pretty good face-lift. Let's face it: you're never going to be twenty again. But ninety is the new forty."

Clay stepped back. The varnish would need twenty-four hours to dry, but it looked really nice. He checked his watch. Ten minutes until time to open. He sighed, sipped his coffee, and drew stick figures in the sawdust with a scrap piece of wood.

Sometimes he attributed it to caffeine jitters, but other times he knew it was nothing of the sort. There was a restlessness scratching him from the inside. Not even a quiet workday in the back of the shop cured it. He worked hard to be content, happy even, where he was in this world, making a simple living and being a simple man. It was, however, the slightest tickle of discontentment that edged him into unwanted thoughts about the state of his life.

The quiet of the shop that usually tamped the needling hum of his thoughts was suddenly undone by . . . blaring music? That was nothing new in this town but unusual near the town square. The college kids were more likely to go down the strip, where the bars and restaurants were. At *night*. Clay checked his watch again. It wasn't even 9 a.m. Who would be blaring their music at this hour?

The bass rattled the more delicate items sitting around

the shop. The little figurines that usually stood perfectly still, frozen in their poses, looked to be dancing ever so slightly.

Then, as if it had been blown away by a breeze, the music stopped.

Clay lifted the rocker, carefully placing his hand underneath it to avoid the new varnish. He wanted to put a few screws in the bottom to make sure it was secure, but he could do that at the front of the store, where he needed to be during store hours.

He was headed for the front counter when he saw her. She didn't notice him at first. She was browsing, her fingers delicately brushing over a lamp, a frame, and then a pile of old books. Her attention moved to the hand-crank phonograph that he'd estimated to be over ninety years old. She stood for a moment looking at its detail, and he stood for a moment noticing hers—curly brown hair, a little wild, like she'd just blown in with a tumbleweed. Bright, playful eyes. Beside the phonograph, in a square, woven basket, he kept two dozen 45 rpm EPs, sometimes more if he hit a good garage sale. Her fingers walked the tops of them, flipping them one by one, before she slipped one out of its black cover and gently guided it onto the turntable, then gave it a crank or two. It came to life, warbling and slow at first, but then a light and pretty piano solo began to play. Dave Brubeck, easy to spot for his unusual time signatures.

Without warning, she turned toward him. For a reason he couldn't explain, Clay raised the rocking chair up a bit.

The woman smiled. "You look like you're in prison."

He blinked. Then realized he was looking at her through the slats in the back of the rocker. He quickly lowered it. Why was she staring at him? Her big brown eyes searched him like he was some interesting antique. He felt like an antique, so it was fitting.

"I like your little store," she said. "Old Fashioned. Cute."

She gave him one more long, concentrated look as though something entertaining might happen, then continued to explore the shop.

"Can I help you with anything?"

And then he heard the scream. So familiar, yet it always made him cringe and clench his teeth. Two seconds later, the door flew open and the pint-size tornado blew in, her arms whirling, her face wild with excitement.

A second after that, Lisa came charging after her, carrying something plastic under her arm and a great deal of exhilaration on her face.

The screaming stopped as Cosie leeched herself onto Clay's leg. She looked up at him and grinned, scrunching up her nose. "Hi."

He patted her head. "Hi, Cosie."

"You gotta see this!" Lisa said.

Clay sighed. That sentence was almost always followed by something that he not only didn't have to see but usually didn't want to see either.

Lisa set the plastic thing down in the center of the shop.

It was a training toilet. Pink and white. Shaped like a castle. Some princess character on the side looked inflamed with an enthusiasm that was apparently supposed to encourage peeing on ancient structures.

Clay knew from experience that once Lisa set her mind to something, there was no use fighting it. He gave the woman standing in the store a sheepish grin and an apologetic shrug. Weirdly, she seemed unaffected and totally interested in what was about to happen. Maybe Clay was missing the extraordinary part of this moment.

Surely not.

Lisa had now squatted on the floor and was beckoning Cosie over with gestures big enough to get an elephant's attention. Her voice rose three octaves, a technique supposed to induce compliant behavior in a two-year-old.

"Come on, Cosie. Go tee-tee." She tapped the potty with her other hand.

But as usual, Cosie stared at her, completely disinterested in the event.

"Do it for Mommy. Go tee-tee. Go tee-tee."

Clay glanced down at Cosie. She wasn't budging. For some odd reason, it made him smile inside. He kind of liked that she balked at the unusual way her parents were raising her and instead preferred the status quo of peeing in private.

Lisa's voice was rising by the second. Her eyes were growing large. Real large. Large enough that if there weren't a potty and an antique shop involved, one might think she was about to be killed in some horrific manner.

"Cosie! *Go tee-tee!*"

Apparently Cosie was also going deaf.

Then movement. Cosie took one step, setting off the strobe lights in her tennis shoes. If Clay watched them too long, he got a headache.

Another step. Clay swore he saw tears in Lisa's eyes. Lisa clapped precisely twice and nodded.

Another step. Then another. Cosie stood over the potty now, gazing into the plastic hole. A smile slight enough to be mistaken for a gas bubble caused Lisa to beam like a searchlight.

Then Cosie lifted her leg, and for a second Clay thought she might be going the way of the dog. But instead she kicked the potty. And kicked again. The castle tumbled across the wood floor. Now the small smile had broken into a full-fledged grin. And Lisa's had dropped off her face.

She rose and gasped. "Cosie! No!"

Clay couldn't resist. He walked over to Lisa and put his arm around her. "I am so proud."

She shrugged his hand off, clearly wrecked. Her whole life's worth at this moment hinged on whether her kid could use a castle potty in public. Clay wasn't about to say it, but the fact that the kid had enough sense not to go in the middle of an antique shop made him think Cosie was going to do just fine in life.

Cosie finally noticed the woman who'd come in, recognizing her as unfamiliar. She gave the potty one more nudge with the side of her shoe, clasped her hands behind her back, and grinned at the lady.

Lisa grabbed the toilet with a huff, acknowledging for the first time that there was someone other than Clay in the shop. "Who are you?" she asked.

"I live in the apartment upstairs."

Clay's mouth dropped open. "Wha . . . ?"

Lisa glanced at Clay, gave him that same old look: *You never tell me anything.* Clay scratched his head, equally perplexed. Cosie ran to him and he picked her up. She mindlessly combed the back of his hair with her fingers, like always, as they all three looked at the woman.

Lisa was gesturing that he should explain himself, but he wasn't sure what to say. Nobody lived up there. He would know. He was the landlord.

"Just needed to get the key," the woman said. There was a childlike quality to her, a mischievous twinkle to her eye that reminded him of Cosie. She looked to be about thirty, but he was never good with ages.

Clay cleared his throat. "The key?"

She only smiled, gave Cosie a wink, and walked out of the shop. Clay hurried after her, handing Cosie to Lisa.

"What's going on?" Lisa said, a hand on her hip, but Clay just went out the door, trying to figure it out himself.

The woman stood on the sidewalk outside. She took something out of the bag over her shoulder. A pen. Then she held out her hand and he saw the cast on it.

"Sign, please."

"Um . . ." Clay's face suddenly started itching—a sure sign he'd landed out of his comfort zone. He scratched it lightly, hoping it would go away. She just stood there with her arm out. And she was smiling at him. Blinking with those awestruck eyes.

So he signed. There seemed to be plenty of space. He glanced at her Jeep and found a cat perched on the passenger window, watching him closely, its tail twitching with sharp disapproval.

When he looked back, she was studying her cast. "Clay what?"

"Walsh," he said. "Clay Walsh. . . . You have a cat?"

She held out her hand to shake. It was awkward with the cast, but they managed. He gestured to it. "What happened?"

"Amber Hewson." And then, without another word but still with that engaging smile, she got her cat from the car, tucked it under her arm, and walked toward the stairway that led up to the apartment.

Clay stayed where he was, trying to get his bearings, blinking in the sunlight, realizing that the loud music earlier had come from her car. He watched her climb each stair, wanting to look away but not able to. He swallowed. Not enough spit. Then too much. And why was he blinking so much? He stuffed his hands in his pockets because that's what he did when he didn't know what to do with them.

Amber was at the top now, staring down at him. "The key?"

"Oh. Yeah. Of course." Clay pulled his key ring out of his pocket. And then he started up the stairs, trying to twist the apartment key off the little circle, trying to get her brown eyes out of his head.

CHAPTER 2

WELL, HE WAS CUTE, but he wasn't exactly a bundle of excitement.

Amber stood at the top of the stairs, waiting. She'd just asked for a key, not his soul.

Her new landlord seemed to be thinking. Seemed to be wearing nothing but caution. Seemed toned enough, but all at once fragile. He had a kind, if withdrawn, disposition. He didn't appear to smile much, but his eyes had a sparkle to them while also lending a certain heaviness to the crisp, light autumn air.

Hmm. Quite a paradox, this Clay Walsh.

She leaned on the rail, examining him in a way that brought about a fidgety scratching of his face. It was kind of fun to watch. And then, after what was apparently very careful consideration, he started up the stairs.

When he approached, she stepped aside, but he still stiffened as he unlocked the door for her.

She already liked this apartment, perched on top of the quaint little antique store, a set of old, creaky stairs leading up to the door. It had a lot of character. She'd peeked in the windows for a glimpse and it was nothing short of perfect.

"See what you think," he said, and this time he stepped aside, holding the screen door for her.

Amber walked in and knew it was right. It was already furnished with minimalist decor, just how she liked it. The windows on both walls let in a nice amount of light too. The kitchen was small, but she didn't need big. She just needed comfortable and cozy, a place where she felt safe. It had been a long time since she'd felt safe. Too long.

Mr. Joe was performing his usual inspection, concentrating less on decor and more on dark corners and spaces between the furniture.

"It's perfect!" Amber said. "It's exactly what I need. I really like the—" She turned, but nobody was there. Where'd he go?

She walked backward to find Clay still standing outside the screen door.

"I'll need some references, of course." He smiled politely. But there was something odd about this guy. Not stalker odd. Just a little damp to the fun of life.

"Aren't you coming in?" Amber asked. It was, after all, officially his apartment. Said so in the ad.

She walked closer to see his expression better. His eyes looked so . . . worn with mundaneness? But in a blink, there was a flash of . . . something. He was hard to read—especially through a screen door.

"I don't bite." She smiled as gently as she was capable of. Maybe she was the one coming off stalker-like.

"How do I know?" He smiled back at her with a relieving hint of ornery playfulness. And then she got it. She knew what she'd seen in his eyes before. Resolve. But resolve to do what?

Amber walked away from the door, just out of his line of sight. "Hey! Cool! Wow! Amazing!" She glanced at Mr. Joe, who was splayed on the couch like he should have a beer and a remote, and put her fingers to her lips. "Shh. It's just a method I'm using with this guy. He's kind of . . . different." She didn't hear anything from the door. "Whoa! What's this?"

"What's what?"

"Come here and I'll show you." But the door didn't open. Apparently he hadn't budged.

Sighing, she walked back to where he stood. As deadpan as she could manage, she said, "I feel like there's something between us."

Clay laughed, boyishly glancing to the ground.

She put her hands on her hips. "Seriously. What's your deal, stress boy?"

He didn't even falter. It was like he knew the questions were coming. "What happened to your hand?"

"Fishing accident."

He nodded, but she knew he wasn't buying her story. The question was, what was *his* story?

He had turned, brushing a few leaves off the balcony railing.

"Fine. I broke it hitting my previous landlord in the mouth for being too nosy."

He smirked. "I knew it wasn't safe to be in there alone with you."

Well. Now he was just getting on her nerves.

With a small sigh, he let down his guard a bit. "Look, don't take it personally. I just . . . I made a promise . . ." He was scratching his face like he was anticipating hives. And then it seemed he'd lost all the words in his vocabulary. But she waited. Whatever game this guy was playing, she wasn't impressed.

Then Clay stood up tall like he'd found his way. He gave her a small, gentle smile, the kind that looked genuine enough to be followed by true words. "I made a promise to never be alone with any woman that's not my wife."

"Oh . . ." Amber tried to nod, but it came out as an awkward rolling of her head and scrunching of her brows. "That's, um, sweet. I think. She the jealous type?"

"I'm not married."

Amber pointed down to the woman with the potty dangling from her hand, who had come outside to watch all this nonsense. "That's not your . . . ?"

"Heavens, no."

"Oh. Um, okay. Engaged?"

"No."

"Living together?"

He shook his head.

"Dating?"

"No. I don't date. I have a theory . . ." His words trailed off into silence as loud as a freight train.

"So," she asked finally, "who'd you make this promise to?"

He only shrugged again.

Amber looked him up and down. This guy, she thought, was as perplexing as Latin. She'd seen the world and traveled to many places. Yeah, she'd made a few mistakes along the way. And paid for them too—she had the cast to prove it. Still, she considered herself fully able to read people.

But this guy was sending off all kinds of signals. And she was having a hard time interpreting any of them.

His hair was shaggy but not in a haven't-taken-a-shower-in-days way, like one of her former boyfriends, Mac. Clay came across more laid-back. Kind of cool. Honestly, he seemed far too secure and casually seductive to possibly be this peculiar and uptight.

And, man, those swimming blue eyes . . . destiny in motion.

"Okay. Well, that's different," Amber said.

"Yeah, I know."

"Clay!" the woman with the potty hollered at him. "We gotta go! Cosie's Chinese lessons." She held up a paper sack. "Here's the stuff for that shadow-box thing. Don't forget. And keep it to yourself, got it?"

Then she stepped out of Amber's line of sight. She apparently made some sort of gesture that Clay waved off. When he turned back around, he had a bit of pink glowing from his cheeks.

"What?" Amber asked. *"Keep it to yourself"*? He was getting more mysterious by the minute.

"Nothing."

"So. Old Fashioned, huh?" The sign that hung over the door of his antique shop seemed more appropriate hanging around his neck.

"Yes."

"It's a little on the nose."

"What can I say?"

"You are a very, very strange man."

He only smiled, like that wasn't the first insult he'd chosen not to dodge, and then he held up the key. "It's yours if you want it."

"What about references?"

"I usually have a pretty good feel for people."

"Ah. You won't trust me alone in a room but you're completely sure I'm not going to bounce hot checks."

He laughed. "I'm willing to give it a shot."

Amber didn't want to frighten the poor guy, but she was going to have to open the door to get the key. He stepped back as she did and carefully dropped the key when she held out her hand. Then the screen door closed.

"Well, if you need anything, all my information is on a piece of paper on the kitchen counter."

"All right."

She watched him walk down the stairs and out of sight. Mr. Joe circled her ankles, purring out his dissatisfaction.

"I know, I know," she said, picking him up. The tip of his tail softly brushed against her cheek. "He's weird. He's definitely weird."

Mr. Joe meowed in agreement.

"But don't you think there's something kind of . . . interesting about him?"

Mr. Joe leaped out of her arms and went to explore.

Amber had a long day ahead of her, unpacking all her stuff. But for now, she needed a nap. She quickly fell into sleep on the couch and dreamed about screen doors.

CHAPTER 3

"DUDE, YOU OKAY? You don't look so good."

"Headache," Clay grunted, leaning against the arm of Brad's couch and once again mentally cursing his friend for not hiring movers.

"You don't get headaches. You're all Zen in the sawdust, right?" David—the third leg of their friendship stool—raised an eyebrow.

"Funny. Actually I have a new renter in the apartment upstairs."

"So Lisa told me. I'm surprised. That place is tiny. And dull."

"And apparently not very soundproof. Let's just say she likes her music. And likes it loud."

"Wow. I always envisioned a little old lady living there."

Clay grabbed the underside of the couch, his back straining against the weight. "Why are we doing this again?" he asked as he repeated over and over to himself, *Lift with the legs, not with the back.* This kind of thing would've been nothing fifteen years ago. These days he could throw out his back lifting a book.

"Because—" David groaned as they simultaneously stood—"it's the truest test of a male friendship. Most people think it's buying a round of drinks. But it's actually helping the brotherhood move."

"It's the equivalent of slicing our hands with a knife and mixing our blood."

"No, man. This is much worse." Sweat poured off both of them, running into their eyes. "Now start walking before I drop this thing on both our toes."

"What's it made of? Dumbbells?"

David laughed. "Don't even get me started on that one. Brad probably bench-presses this sucker every night."

Clay walked backward and David forward. They managed well until they got to the doorway.

"Lean to the left," Clay said, but by the looks of it, they might have to cut it in two.

"There is no way this is fitting through that door," David grunted.

"It fits!" Brad yelled. He was standing beside the moving truck, about to load a box with a basketball on top. "We got it in there, didn't we?"

"It's so weird how things move in easier than they move out," David said. "With furniture at least. Now, people—that's another matter."

Clay sighed. "Come on. Just tilt it and angle it that way, and I think it'll slide through."

After some maneuvering, they got it.

David nodded toward Clay with that look in his eyes he got when he wanted Clay to spill the beans on something. And this time, they both knew what—his birthday gift. "Speak. I command you."

"Nope."

"Traitor."

"David, I'm sworn to secrecy. I gave Lisa my word. And you can't tell me you don't know how she would torture me if I let it slip. I've already had to hear the word *tee-tee* more times than any man without a kid should."

"Oooh. Yeah. Sorry about that. It's a Cosie phase." David gave a sad-puppy-dog face. "Come on, man. What'd she get me?"

"No way. I'd be dead. You want me dead?"

"Coward. You're a coward and a traitor."

"And alive," Clay said, shooting him a look. They loaded the couch into an already-crowded moving van, pushing it backward, smashing it against the boxes.

"You couldn't spring for something a little bigger?" David gestured toward all the boxes.

"I'm saving for the mansion on the beach." Brad grinned.

"Well, that's it for the big stuff," David said, hopping

off the truck and holding his side. Clay collapsed onto the couch.

Brad climbed in to set the box on the couch next to Clay, then jumped out of the truck too. Clay grabbed the basketball, twirled it on his fingers a time or two. Then he gazed at the signatures. His. Brad's. David's. The rest of the intramural team. He gripped it, feeling the tiny leather bumps under his fingertips. In the hollow spaces of his memory, he heard the squeaks of tennis shoes. The thuds of bodies fighting for space under the basket.

Brad bumped his arm as he climbed in again with another box. "Admit it. You're three seconds away from sniffing that thing, aren't you?"

Clay laughed. "Just about."

He passed the ball to David, who held it up to the sun like it was the Lion King. "Nineteen-one."

"Should've been undefeated," Brad growled. He and David passed the ball back and forth, recounting victories and game-winning plays long past, but Clay found himself sifting through the nearby boxes. Pictures. Trophies. More pictures. One picture in particular. He pulled it out, holding it tight against a building breeze.

Now Brad and David were on the lawn arguing about the game that would never die. "I was wide open!" Brad yelled.

Clay was glad they were momentarily distracted. He wanted to look a little longer. There she was, in his favorite picture of the two of them. Why Brad insisted on keeping pictures like this was beyond him, but it was good to see her face. Her bright eyes. Her wide grin, all teeth, hanging over the most delicate chin he'd ever seen, chiseled perfectly with a dimple right in the middle. And her hair . . .

He decided to dig through another box. He opened one that wasn't labeled and pulled out a postcard, laughing at the absurd picture on it. His and Brad's large cartoon heads atop tiny bodies, with hands both trying to grab for a mike. It was about true. They did have big heads back then. And they were always fighting for the mike. Across the top it read *Neanderthals*, and in the background were five ladies in skimpy bikinis, partying it up. Clay's attention wandered back into the box. Sitting on top was the DVD, Brad's brightest shining moment until his job offer fourteen days ago. He threw the postcard back into the box and quickly closed the lid. But he could still hear the screaming girls, drunk on sunshine, sand, and attention.

His attention.

His thoughts were undone by the long, shrill honk of a car horn, and like they'd manifested themselves from his mind right into the street, he heard screaming and giggling. He glanced at Brad, who looked both excited and mortified— never a good sign.

"This is a nice surprise," Brad said and walked out of view. Clay looked at David, who could only roll his eyes.

"A car full?" Clay whispered. When David nodded, he went on: "Let me guess. Mardi Gras beads, and it's got to be a convertible."

"It's like you're psychic," David said with a smirk.

"Or I've just known Brad for almost fifteen years," Clay said, hopping off the truck. He slid the picture into the front pocket of his shirt and walked to the other side of the truck to find a banana-yellow convertible filled with laughing women, probably none under twenty-five, all wearing bikini tops and flashing smiles like badges and credentials— hangers-on of the worst kind.

The woman behind the wheel got out, her cutoffs so cut-off that the pockets hung past the ends of her shorts. David blew out a breath and Clay looked at the tires. Nice tires. Good tread.

"Hi, baby!" she said, pushing her glasses up to the top of her head.

"This is a nice surprise," Brad said again.

"After last night, I figured I owed you one. It was so good seeing you again."

"It was?"

"Amazing."

Brad smiled smoothly while somehow managing to wink at the other females dangling out of the car.

"What's with the truck?" she said, pitching her thumb toward it.

"I got a new job," Brad said. "Isn't that great?"

David glanced at Clay, who could only shrug. When Brad said, "Isn't that great?" it almost always turned out that it wasn't.

"Where?" she asked.

"Los Angeles. Hollywood."

Like makeup melting in high humidity, the flirty smile that had just seconds ago taken up most of her face slid right off the bottom of her chin and slapped the pavement under her feet. "What? You're going to Los Angeles?"

David smirked and cast Clay the this-oughta-be-fun-to-watch look.

"Isn't that great?" Brad repeated.

Uh-oh. If it had to be said twice, it pretty much meant there was some cataclysmic emotional event about to happen.

"When?" Her lips turned downward and she crossed her arms and her eyebrows.

"Tomorrow." And then Brad opened his hands and looked thoroughly confused. Except Clay knew one thing for sure: Brad was never confused. "I thought you'd be happy for me."

"You told me last night I could move in."

"You can," Brad said, his hands casually slipping into his pockets. "The condo is available, and I already put in a good word for you. Even told the landlord to keep my security deposit for your first month's rent. It's all yours."

David's expression froze in awe. "He did not just do what I think he did," he whispered.

"He really did," Clay whispered back.

For a moment, everything came to a standstill. The wind stalled. The birds stopped chirping. The ladies in the car froze with their mouths open. Even the neighborhood dog quieted.

It was hard to tell if the woman was going to scream. Cry. Explode. Pull a weapon.

But slowly, methodically, she smiled, a cynical edginess oozing into a cool demeanor. "Well then," she said, flipping her glasses back down, "keep in touch."

Brad winked and the convertible drove off. He turned back to David and Clay. "What? Some people are smart. Others are slightly more gifted. Then you have your Rhodes Scholars. And just above that is me." He grabbed them by the shoulders. "Come on, boys. Let me buy you a drink."

The J-N-G, a pub four decades old, was hopping with its usual lively crowd. Bursts of laughter swelled and diminished and then swelled again, almost like an orchestra. Pictures and trophies and other things could be boxed up and stuffed in a moving van, but the memories Clay had in this place . . . there wasn't a big enough box.

The waitress swept in and served their drinks. As always, Brad drew the attention. They swapped smiles as effortlessly as people swapped germs.

Clay stared into his drink, mixing it around and around with the skinny red straw. He couldn't believe Brad was leaving tomorrow. It seemed a little surreal. The three of them hadn't really left each other's sides since college. Their lives had gone dramatically different ways, but it seemed they would have a missing piece of the puzzle.

"Stop judging me," Brad said out of the blue.

Clay looked up just as Brad flashed another smile to yet another female passing by. "Did I say anything?"

"The way you're sitting—it's judgmental."

Clay shook his head. Brad was like one running joke, but underneath the teasing was a simmering disapproval—going both ways, if he were honest.

David, as usual, kept the peace. "A toast," he said, raising his glass. "To going nationwide!"

They all raised their glasses, clinking them the same way they had hundreds of times before. Back in the day, there'd been an endless amount of toasting. They toasted if they won. If they lost. If the wind shifted direction. It was a little harder, the older they'd grown, to find quite that kind of satisfaction, but a big promotion, whatever the nature of it, was worthy.

"Nationwide. Radio syndication, baby." Brad winked at Clay, grinning from ear to ear. "Live from the City of Angels." He was about to go on but got distracted by the blonde at the next table who stood, adjusted her jacket, and sat down again.

Clay kept his glass raised. "My heart weeps for America."

"You'll miss me," Brad said, slamming his drink down with hearty enthusiasm. "So will whatserface in that nice yellow convertible."

Clay knew when Brad was trying to get a rise out of him. And it usually worked. But he'd learned to be more measured in his responses, and he was getting better at it, which was making Brad crazy.

And with a little alcohol in his system . . . crazier. The waitress drifted by, dropped off the check. Brad stared her down, just to make his point even clearer . . . and sharper.

Then his eyes shot up to Clay's. "Why don't you just crawl

back under that antique shop and make up some more . . ." He waved his hand in the air. He also tended to lose common words the more he drank. ". . . theories you never test at the grown-up table anymore."

Clay measured out his smile. He was used to this now. It had become what they always ended up talking about when the day was done and Brad was on the verge of drunkenness.

"Fun times," David said and reached for the check, but Clay slid his fingers across the table and snagged it.

"I've got it this time, buddy," he said. "I'm pretty sure you got the heavier end of the couch."

David laughed but Brad was still rolling. "I didn't do anything unto her, Clay, that I didn't want done unto me."

Clay couldn't even manage a smile now. He took his thumb and wiped condensation off his glass, then off the table, and then he tried to wipe Brad's condescending tone off the radar. They'd been the best of friends when they were taking the same highway. But when their roads split, it got harder. They still managed, mostly relying on fun stories from days past (or Camelot, as Brad liked to refer to them).

Clay pulled out his wallet, riffled through the cash.

Brad was pointing his index finger, slicing the air with it, along with his words. "Remember that summer in Myrtle Beach? You and that cheerleader and her—"

Clay looked up, locked eyes with him.

"Whoa now. Just having some fun, killjoy." Brad put his hands together like a small child. "You know that's my favorite bedtime story. Tell it again, please, Daddy."

Man, he really didn't want their last night to end like this. He had to let it go, not let Brad get him riled. Clay smiled. "'When I was a child, I talked like a child, I thought like a child . . .'"

"Oh, here we go. The hermit has a proclamation. Continue, please."

David, as he always did so well, chuckled through the awkwardness. "Here you two go again."

Clay looked at David's big grin, the way he shook his head; then Clay chuckled a little too. He threw down the cash.

"When do you start, man?" David asked Brad, beautifully redirecting the conversation.

"As soon as I get there. Tomorrow will be my last local show." Brad took a short drink and cast a thoughtful look to the table. "And then I'm off. I can't believe it's really here."

"So, tomorrow . . ." David raised his glass. Clay did too.

Brad hesitated, his face conflicted with more emotion than Clay had seen in a long time. He cast a wary look toward Clay. "It could've been the two of us, you know."

Clay only smiled. "I'm 100 percent certain you are going to do just fine alone, Lucky Chucky."

Brad cracked his famous grin. "Well, thanks to the show, I won't be alone for a very long time." He raised his glass. "To infamy!"

CHAPTER 4

IT WAS HER LUCKY DAY. She always counted her day lucky when she woke up before her alarm. There was almost nothing as soothing and comfortable as opening her eyes to silence, watching the hazy morning light drift across the room, her mind swimming to the surface from whatever dream world she'd just been to.

Amber stroked Mr. Joe as he lay quietly by her side. She was mostly unpacked and settling in fairly well. She'd taken a couple of days to wander the town, get her bearings, find out where the good restaurants were, and try to find a job. It wasn't easy competing against desperate and really broke students. But she kind of blended right in, and nobody so far had asked her if she was or wasn't in college.

College. Ugh. One of her biggest regrets. And now, ironically, she was in a college town.

"No sad feelings," she said, rolling her head to look at Mr. Joe, who blinked slowly in agreement. "Not today. This is my new start. And what's more fun than organizing a new home?"

She stretched her arms lazily over her head and—

The peace of the morning was suddenly shattered by her clock radio. Amber sat straight up in bed to a guitar riff—which wasn't half-bad because she was a huge fan of the instrument. It was much better than the voice that followed.

"Women. Are. Stupid."

Amber stared at the ceiling. Either she'd mistuned her radio when she set the alarm or her ex-boyfriend, Mac, had finally hunted her down. She turned her head, looked around the room. Nope. She was all alone.

"Every single one of them loves to believe in some kind of fairy tale," said the voice.

Amber looked at Mr. Joe, who seemed to sense that whatever was coming out of the radio was nonsense. She smiled. "That part's true. It's in our DNA." She rose and headed for the coffeepot, wondering if this voice was going to correct himself over the statement that women are stupid.

"They like to pretend everything is going to be okay, offer the illusion of security. And abracadabra! Lines are open, folks. Let's see what you got for me today. . . . Oh, come on, let's be real. You want to know what I've got for you, don't you? Nobody really cares what you got."

"This should be interesting," Amber said. She waited a

second for the coffee to finish brewing, then poured a mugful and sipped it as she leaned against the kitchen counter, studying her bulletin board. Last night, she'd finally found the right place for it. It always had to be the perfect wall. And for all the places she'd lived, she always found it. If ever there was a house that didn't have the perfect wall, she would know it wasn't the house for her.

"Tim from Lakeland, you're on the air."

"Live the dream, my brother!" Tim sounded like he needed about a week's worth of sleep.

"Live the dream! That's right! Do you have what it takes?" the host replied.

Tim explained that he did have what it took, for whatever that supposed dream was. Amber had given up on defining dreams. Most of the time they left her a little disappointed and also made her miss a lot of adventure. She decided to just go. Do. Be. Tim from Lakeland sounded like he could use a few pointers.

"Hey, man," Tim continued. *"Just wanted to say congrats on your new gig in Holly*wood!*"*

"Thank you. Looking forward to it. Do you have any idea how many hot, stupid women there are in California?"

Tim replied that he couldn't count that high. Amber pulled out photographs from her box and began tacking them on the bulletin board. Every memory made her smile. And every pinhole through each photograph was a reminder of how many times she'd done this. She couldn't count that high—just like Tim, she guessed.

Mr. Joe was staring her down. She put her hands on her hips. "Really? Now you're my conscience too?"

He let out a soft meow.

"Fine." She stomped over to the ancient rotary phone. "But you know these never go well."

Mr. Joe just blinked.

"I'm going to dial, it's going to be busy, and I'm going to waste my time." She punched in the number that the shock jock kept repeating over and over.

"Name?" a female voice asked.

Amber raised her eyebrow. "Anonymous."

"Chicken."

And then the next thing she knew . . . *"Next caller. Anonymous, you're on the air."*

"You're disgusting." She punctuated it with a strong, disapproving look that only Mr. Joe was presently witnessing.

"Mom, is that you?"

"If I was your mother—"

"Yeah? Keep going." He laughed. *"Would ya punish me?"*

"Men like you—"

"Yes? Men like me . . . ?"

Amber shook her head at Mr. Joe like there was no hope.

"Hey, quick question. How much do you weigh?"

Amber slammed down the phone. "Thug." She walked over to the radio. She'd had enough of this nonsense.

"Fine, so I'm no knight in shining armor," the host continued as she reached for the dial. *"There are no knights in shining armor."*

Amber let her hand drop. She blinked slowly, sat down on the bed, listening to this guy say his thing.

"But you think you're Cinderella, don't you? Don't you? See, I wanna help. I want to help you see the truth. And—news flash—the truth is there are no Cinderellas either. Sure, you say you want the sweet guy, the Prince Charming, but I know you. Guys like that bore you to tears, don't they? Following you around like a lost puppy dog until your mind, not to mention every other part of you, goes numb. Are you sweet? Are you faithful? Huh? Are you honest? *All those things you say you want? No."*

Amber looked at her hands. Mr. Joe hopped onto the bed, but she stood and walked to the window, gazing out over the quiet street.

"On those late and lonely nights, when you can't sleep, when you're in your bed alone, solo, twisting in the sheets, clutching the corner of your pillow . . . you want one thing, and that's a guy like me. And you know it, so you get what you get, girlfriend. Women are just like men. Everyone wants it both ways. So don't come crying to me, Cinderella."

Amber turned and shut the radio off. "That's where you're wrong, buddy. I never, ever believed I was Cinderella."

♥

Clay gently drove the last nail into the custom frame and then propped the poster so he could see it. He wiped dust off the glass and stepped back. There it was, perfectly set up. An original movie poster of Frank Capra's *Meet John Doe*. If he'd watched it once, he'd watched it a thousand times—but the very first time with David, who swore up and down that Clay would love it. Being a film professor, David always had an authoritative opinion—which was usually right.

Maybe Clay was as idealistic as he was sentimental, but either way, it just didn't get better than Gary Cooper and Barbara Stanwyck. It had everything: The pure American with the funny sidekick. The main character exploited by the bad guy, aided by the tough woman reporter, who then falls in love with him. The famous speech by the Colonel on the "heelots." But his favorite line was by the reporter who refers to Jesus as "the first John Doe," who already died for everyone.

If he could get transported into a Frank Capra film, he would. In a heartbeat. And never look back. He was certain he would look good in a fedora, too.

He gazed at the poster, his mind wandering to Brad. To David and Lisa. To . . . the girl upstairs. It was unusually quiet. He'd expected her to wake up to something with a bass beat. But since he'd opened shop today, there'd been nothing but footsteps, the best he could tell. And maybe the TV was on. He thought he heard faint voices, but then that was gone.

Amber.

To keep referring to her as "the girl upstairs" wasn't too respectful.

Amber. It was the color of the dawning light as it passed through the shop windows and seeped into the back room. It was the honey he put on his toast every morning. It was the wheat fields right outside of town.

He'd had a hard time getting her off his mind, and that

wasn't boding well for his theories. In fact, she seemed to be just the opposite of who he'd always imagined might draw his attention. His dream woman, if there was such a thing, certainly didn't play loud music and seem so . . . uprooted.

"Knock, knock."

Clay didn't have to look up; he knew who was there. But he liked to ask because George always had a different answer. "Who's there?"

"I ain't thought that far ahead yet. Let's go. Get the lead out. Come on. I'm a busy man."

George stepped farther into the shop when he saw the poster. "Ooooh. Now there's a woman for you. Oh, my, yes. Wow."

"Only you could sexualize a Frank Capra film."

"You're telling me that when you look at Barbara Stanwyck standing there in the flesh—"

"Or on cardboard at the very least."

"—you wouldn't just want to—"

"No, I wouldn't." Okay, maybe he would. But some things were better left on movie posters.

George sighed, the rattling wheeze in his chest whistling in the air. "You're no fun—you know that, right?"

"Just please don't start talking about all the posters you had hanging in your bunker during the war."

"Sometimes it's the only thing that got me up in the morning, kid." He blew Barbara a kiss. "Come on. I'm a busy man." And they walked out the door at a snail's pace.

The sun was bright in the late morning. Clay shielded

his eyes and blinked, trying to get used to it. Sometimes he worked so long in the back of the shop that he didn't even know what time of day it was. He'd been known to walk out expecting sunlight, only to be met with darkness.

George, smelling strongly of mothballs on this particular day, threw open the back of his delivery truck, which actually had duct tape holding part of the paneling together. Inside, as usual, was a whole mess of antiques. An old traffic light and some street signs were tucked into one corner. Frames. Mirrors. Vanities. Knickknacks. A garden stone in the shape of a squirrel.

Clay sighed. "George. There is no rhyme or reason here. And look at how they're all banged up against one another. Why don't you use some bubble wrap? I've told you a hundred times—wrap them in bubble wrap."

George grumbled, chewed his lip like an unlit cigar. "You're like bubble wrap, to tell you the truth."

"Funny."

"For being an antiques dealer, you sure like things squeaky clean. Maybe you should open an IKEA."

"Hilarious."

"I got a couple of pieces in the back you might like." George hovered next to him. "Like anything? Did you see that squirrel?"

"All right, give me a second to dig around."

"Want me to go get you some hand sanitizer? Because— whoa!" George stopped midsentence, which caused Clay to turn around.

George was stepping away from the back of the truck, his chest bowed out like he was about to take a superhero stance. "Hello there."

Clay ducked out of the truck to see what George was staring—oh.

Amber was standing by the railing, hanging a small rug over it. She waved. Her hair waved too, blown sideways by the breeze, shiny and rippling like a chocolate river.

They both waved back. Only Clay was wearing the sloppy smile, though. George leaned into him and spoke out of the side of his mouth. "I saw that. You've been holding out on me." Then to Amber he yelled, "Where you been?"

She smiled graciously, not understanding. "What?"

"All my life, where you been?"

Clay rolled his eyes, redirecting George's attention to the truck, trying to give an apologetic gesture to his new tenant. "How's the wife, George?"

George deflated right there in front of him. You could almost hear the air seeping out of his body. "Mean as a snake."

"Uh-huh." He looked up at Amber, who was still messing with her rug. "Um, settling in okay up there?"

"So far so good."

"Just call me if you need anything."

"And call me," George added enthusiastically, "if you need anything else."

Amber smiled at them both. "I'll do that."

And she disappeared behind the screen door.

"Behave yourself," Clay said. "She just moved in."

"Lucky you."

"Not my type." It hadn't come out with any conviction, by the way George was eyeing him.

"Really. How do you know that?" George asked. "Wasn't hanging her rug out quite right?" He shook his head. "So help me, man, I worry about you."

"I'll take the wall mirror," Clay said.

George climbed into the truck, and Clay stepped out of its shadow, hoping to get a glimpse of Amber through the open window. But all was still, except the cat, who sat on the windowsill glaring at him.

George took the mirror into the shop and returned, slapping Clay on the back. "Can't believe you didn't take the stoplight. I gotta get going. My high-end clients are waiting for me." He hopped into his truck and started it, then hopped right back out without turning it off. "I gotta go relieve myself. I'm going to have to downgrade my thermos size. Getting old is a killer, man. An absolute killer."

"Yes, you can use the bathroom, George. That's all you've got to say."

"Here's what I'm saying: seize the moment. You're not getting any younger. Not everyone can be this good-looking at sixty," he said, gesturing toward himself.

As George disappeared into the shop, Clay heard that old, familiar voice filtering out from the truck radio.

"So this is it. The time has come, my brothers. It has been a tasty ride so far, but remember, this isn't good-bye to you—the faithful. You'll know where to find me. I'm not going anywhere."

Brad's voice fell silent just as a cloud drifted overhead and a spattering of rain fell. Clay let it wash over him. It felt good. Clean.

"What is wrong with you, boy? Get yourself inside." George ambled back to his truck. "You're just about the only one that I'm worried might really melt in the rain."

"I think I'll be okay. I'll see you tomorrow, George."

Clay lingered in the misty rain for a moment longer, hoping Amber would come out to grab her rug. After a while, he returned inside his quiet shop, his only company the sharp, frozen image of Gary Cooper holding Barbara Stanwyck.

♥

"Well," Amber said, closing the window, "I guess storms don't just pass on by here, Mr. Joe." It had been raining since late morning, but she didn't mind rain. It helped her to stay in one place, not leave all the time. She had a bad habit of wandering off from duties and commitments.

Not the guy downstairs. Clay Walsh. Sunshine or rain, that guy was like clockwork.

That she could tell, he rarely left the shop once he arrived. She'd watched him buy a mirror this morning off the chatty guy's truck. He stood in the rain for a while. But a lunch break? A trip into town? Not that she'd seen.

Mr. Joe jumped into her arms. She gestured around the apartment. "Well? What do you think?" She was fully moved in, just needed to take the boxes out to the trash. They had one too many moves under their belts and were held together by duct tape that had been stretched to its limits. New boxes were in order, but not today.

She placed her empty glass jar right on the kitchen counter so she'd see it every time she came and went. Her lamp was placed by the couch, where she liked to read. Her TV—not the flat-screen kind—sat on a broken table that had to be held up by two books.

She planted a kiss right on Mr. Joe's fur. "Yeah. I agree. Not bad." Sparse. Simple. But not bad.

Mr. Joe jumped from her arms and trotted toward his water dish.

"Good idea. Rainy day. New digs. All I need is a cup of tea."

She filled her teapot, probably the oldest thing she owned. It had been her great-grandmother's. And as the story went, she stole it from Jesse James. But that part had yet to be confirmed. Especially since most of her family was gone. She thought she had a cousin in Tampa, but that had yet to be confirmed too.

Amber set the old tin pot on the stove. It had probably given her some kind of lead poisoning over the years, but she didn't care. She liked it. It was small and fit nicely into a box, about the only thing in her life that really did. She turned the gas on. But nothing clicked. She tried again. No flame.

Then she did what she normally did when stuff didn't work. She shook it.

"What?" she asked Mr. Joe, who sat watching her. "It usually does the trick. At least 50 percent of the time. Of course,

I usually hate my landlord, so . . ." She shrugged as she walked past Mr. Joe. "He did say call if I needed anything."

Amber found his number neatly typed on a piece of paper on the counter. She tapped her fingers against the Formica, looking at the small clock on her wall. It was already after 9 p.m. "It's late. It's raining. That would be kind of mean for me to make him get out and . . ." She laughed as she walked past the cat again. "We both know it. I'm calling him."

Amber picked up the phone, dialed the number.

"Hello?"

"This is Amber."

Silence.

"The one upstairs, stress boy."

"Yes, of course. Yes."

"My stove isn't working."

"I'll be right there."

"Thanks."

Amber hung up the phone and stared at Mr. Joe. "Do you think he's going to be all . . . ?" She waved her hands. "You know, do that rigid thing and act all cold but warm?" There were hardly words to describe it. She started pacing. "And then he does that thing with his hand through his hair, gets all messy. Messier. And just when I think he's not paying attention, he goes smiley on me." She stopped, hands on her hips. "Very confusing signals, I will tell you that. It's like he's speaking four different body languages."

She sighed, plopping down on her couch, thinking out loud. "When he's scratching his face and staring at the ground,

I don't know what he's saying. 'You've got the plague' or 'Ask me out'?"

She glanced toward the window, hoping to see circular truck lights bouncing off the glass. No sign of him yet. Mr. Joe crawled into her lap.

"Tell me the truth, Mr. Joe. Is it me? I mean, I know I bring out the weird in people. And we both know I've got a long and sordid history of bringing out the worst in men."

Light beams.

Then she heard gentle footsteps coming up to the apartment. She took a breath and opened the door.

Clay stood there holding an umbrella, a toolbox, and a blanket. The rain was gentle and cold and was the only noise between them for a moment. Then she opened the screen door and stepped aside.

"Are you coming?" She gestured. Maybe that's what he was waiting for.

But he didn't move.

"You're kidding."

He only smiled, held out the umbrella and the blanket to her. Amber pressed her lips together. This guy was for real. At first she'd thought maybe this "theory" was his idea of some bad pickup lines. But he was actually not coming into the apartment with her alone.

She stepped out onto the stoop and he handed her the umbrella. Then handed her the blanket. She put it around her shoulders, awkwardly juggling the umbrella too. Mr. Joe stared Clay down as he walked in, and he returned the favor.

The screen door swung shut. And there she stood, on the outside stoop of her apartment, in the rain, watching stress boy fix her stove.

He slid out the stove and got to work. The rain continued to pour, but strangely she wasn't cold or damp. She felt . . . safe.

He worked quietly, like he enjoyed the task of trying to figure out what was wrong and how to fix it. Apparently he wasn't a big talker either.

Amber moved a bit closer to the screen, still clutching the umbrella. "No offense," she said, "but I think I could resist you."

"I'm sure you could." She heard a smile in his voice.

"Ah. But you couldn't resist me—is that it?"

He glanced back at her but didn't say anything.

"So," she continued, "this theory of yours. I'm curious."

"You're bored."

Amber scowled. "Don't tell me what I am." The stupid talk-radio dude and his proclamations about bored women came racing back to her mind. She crossed her arms.

Clay looked at her, seemingly genuinely contrite.

She gestured her blessing. "Forgiven."

"You religious?" he asked as he continued to work.

"Spiritual." How to explain this? "I believe in God. But it's not like I believe everything that's in the Bible or anything."

"What parts of it do you believe exactly?"

She didn't want to get into a religious debate. She wanted to get to . . . him. "Your theory. Spill it. I want to know."

He grabbed a wrench and looked suspicious.

"Make me ask again and I'm coming in there, theory or no theory." And to drive home the point, she grabbed the handle.

"Okay, okay." He chuckled.

"Start talking." She turned the handle.

"Open that door and I raise your rent."

Her hand retreated, but she gave him the best stink eye she could muster. "I told you what I did to my last landlord. I will smack you down."

For the first time she heard him give a full laugh. And it was a good, solid, sweet laugh. It made her laugh too.

"So you won't be alone with a woman."

"That's the plan," he said, returning to his work.

"Anywhere?"

"Within reason."

"What does that mean?"

"Out in the open, that's okay. In public. I don't take it too far, like not being alone together in a car or an elevator or places like that." He did that little scratch to his face, that little thing with his hair. "It's only a small part of my theory."

"Which is?"

"I don't believe that dating trains us to be good husbands or wives, you know?"

She didn't really. But it seemed he'd thought long and hard about it.

He continued. "It trains us to be good dates. That's it. Trains us to be skilled in the superficial."

"Who talks like that?"

"I do." He smiled slightly. Confidently.

"Dating is fun. Seeing the smile you bring to another face. Holding hands for the first time. Learning new things—"

"But what do we learn? We learn how to be witty. Charming. Romantic."

"Yes! Yes, yes, yes." Strangely he was making her point for her.

"It's all icing. No cake. It's not enough. Commitment should come first, not the other way around."

"Sounds more like you're training to be a monk."

He set his wrench down and turned a little more toward her. "Do you want to get married?"

She smirked. "Gosh, it's all happening so fast. I don't know. I need—"

"Funny. To someone. Someday."

"Sure."

"Describe your perfect husband. What would he be like?"

"Faithful, honest, good with children. Good with money. Tender. Forgiving. . . . And witty, charming, and romantic."

"What happens when the tough times come? And they will. Most people go into marriage with no clue how to make it last. So most don't last. And I never want to be divorced." Inside those dreamy blue eyes, even from where she stood, she could see something catch the sparkle and swallow it right up. He blinked, then grabbed another wrench. "No one gets good at anything without practice. Everything I do now is preparing me for the kind of husband I'll be one day. God willing."

Amber sighed. This guy certainly knew how to trap and kill a romantic moment.

"Nothing magical happens when you walk down the aisle." He was still talking, almost like the stove might be the only thing listening. "Like it or not, what we do when we're single is what we'll do when we're married."

"What about sex?" She smiled. She kind of wanted to see him flinch at the word.

He didn't. "What about it?"

"That takes practice too."

"No comment."

Amber cracked open the screen door just so he could hear her loud and clear. "Not having sex does not make you a good husband, you know."

"But learning to control myself might. Over half of all marriages experience infidelity."

She closed the door again. She had to admit, she was intrigued. Like a bad accident you can't look away from, but intrigued nevertheless. "So do you mean sex-sex only or any . . . other . . ." What would be an appropriate word for a guy like this? "Stuff?"

"I'm an all-or-nothing guy. Your body is a temple."

"You noticed."

He laughed again but didn't say a word.

"Not even a little kissy-kissy?" This was getting kind of fun.

He tapped his cheek. "Just right there till the wedding bells."

Wow. This guy was no joke. She tried to imagine it. Only

being kissed on the cheek. Never being alone together. It seemed so . . . strange. She'd met a lot of people over the years, but none so . . . *convicted* as this guy.

"How long have you had this theory?" she asked.

"Nine years."

Nine years? "Yikes. That's not normal."

He was reaching behind the stove now, his body stretched out awkwardly like there might be a pulled muscle in his future.

"So let's just have arranged marriages," she protested.

"Couldn't be much worse," he said, though she still couldn't really see his face.

"You don't believe there's a right person out there for each of us? A soul mate?"

Clay finished whatever it was he was doing and shoved the stove back into place. He knelt at his toolbox, starting to put his tools away. "I don't believe our job is the looking. It's the becoming. Once we are the right person, when we're ready—"

"But if you don't ever date, how will you know?"

Clay stood and turned a knob on the stove. A pretty blue flame ignited.

Amber clapped and cheered.

"I make fire," he said in a caveman voice.

"My hero."

Then he sneezed. Three times in a row. He grabbed his toolbox and came to the door. Sneezed.

"You okay?"

Another sneeze. "Yeah."

"Okay."

"Anyway," he said, still on the other side of the screen door, "that's my theory. You asked for it."

He opened the door and they awkwardly tried to swap places, her handing him the umbrella and blanket, their fingers brushing ever so slightly. Other than that, somehow, they made the switch without touching. Now Amber stood inside the screen door and he stood in the cold rain with his umbrella.

"Thanks for the enlightenment."

His expression turned gentle. "I know how weird it sounds. I know making you stand in the cold and the rain seems ridiculous. But a lot of the boundaries that used to be common, that we've thrown away, were there to protect us. We don't have to go around using each other, hurting each other. It doesn't have to be that way."

For half a second, as fast as a lightning flash, what he said made sense. But as soon as she blinked, it was all very confusing again.

"Good night," he said.

"Good night."

And then, as softly as he came, he left, taking the steps one at a time. And right as she shut the door, Amber heard him sneeze again.

CHAPTER 5

"FIRST YOU WANT to strip off the excess foliage. Of course you need to fill the bucket or vase with water to keep the flowers fresh. Next trim the flower stems at an angle, about two inches from the bottom. Take two irises and then two roses. Arrange them in a square. See how the formation is clockwise? Iris, rose, iris, rose. That's the center. Now, Trish, if you'll hold this, I will add more irises around the square. You want to make a dome shape like this. Now bind the stems with the tape, cut the ribbon three times as long as the flower stems, tuck one end into the floral tape, and wind it down the stem. Use the other end to decorate. I'm a fan of bows myself." Amber held up the bouquet. "Beautiful! Like a Greek goddess."

The woman who owned the shop, Carol, said, "We normally just plop them in a vase, so yeah, you're hired."

"Yay! Thank you!" Amber squeaked with excitement. She'd always wanted to work in a floral shop.

"We typically keep the squealing to a minimum. People mistake us for a slaughterhouse. Also, it doesn't jibe well with my hangovers, which I try to keep to Thursdays and Saturdays. But you know, things happen."

"Right. Sorry." Amber smiled at Carol, somewhere north of fifty, her well-worn face wrinkled from too much sun, smoking, and boozing. Her hair, white and brittle, had seen its share of bleaching over the years. But her eyes were youthful and her smile was kind. Amber couldn't help it. She reached out for a hug.

"Okay, okay," Carol said, awkwardly tapping Amber on the back. "Good. Listen, Amber, I need to tell you, I've gone through five girls in six months at this store. I can't afford to lose another. You're planning to stick around for a while, right?"

Amber swallowed. It wasn't her strongest suit, but Carol did look desperate. "I won't leave you hanging. If I have to leave, I'll make sure you have someone to take my place first."

Carol eyed her. "Hmm. So you're one of those."

"One of what?"

But Carol didn't answer. Instead she said, "I'm going out for a smoke. Trish, show Amber what she needs to know, will you?"

Trish, the other girl in the shop, looked to be in her early twenties, with short, dark-honey hair, cut cute and pixie-like. She had the smile to go with it too.

Trish finished tying off a helium balloon, then grinned at Amber as Carol left. "So you don't stick around long from one place to another?"

"Some longer than others."

"Wow. I wish I could do that. I'm one of those unfortunate rooters, you know? I'm anchored so deep that if the town blew away, I'd still be here. It must be fun to pick up and go whenever you want."

"Not always whenever I want. Sometimes when I need to. But certain parameters need to be met, namely enough gas money to even get out of town."

Trish sighed. "Money. It ruins everything. Well, I'm glad you're here, for as long as you are."

"Me too."

"Awesome. Tonight we party then, yes?"

Amber laughed. "Sure. I could use some company."

"Don't know anyone in town?"

"Getting to know a few. Well, one. My landlord. But he's . . ."

"Landlord. That by itself suggests the power distribution isn't in one person's favor."

"He doesn't seem to be like that. He's . . . different."

Trish looked worried. "Jeffrey Dahmer different?"

"No, no. Just . . . gosh, what's the word for it? I don't think there's a word for it."

"Well, I can't wait to show you around town tonight! We will have fun."

"Looking forward to it."

"You in a relationship, some long-distance kind of thing?"

"No. Not now."

"Trust me—there are plenty of boys to be had in our little town," Trish said, wiggling her eyebrows. She nodded toward the cast. "You okay to work with that?"

"Sure. It doesn't get in my way."

"Interesting story behind why it's there?"

Amber looked at it. "No. Not really. I'm just clumsy."

"Nice! We'll get along perfectly. I've dropped like ten vases since working here."

Amber laughed.

"So we'll take you to the Brewhouse tonight. Usually the best place to be on a Thursday. Half-price drinks. Free chicken wings. The men come in droves for the chicken wings. I'm not kidding. I don't know what it is about those little bitty wings, but they're like guy magnets. I'm thinking about getting a dress made out of 'em."

"Sounds spicy."

"Okay, I gotta go sort balloons in the back. We've got a shipment of roses coming in at noon. We usually grab lunch at the deli and eat here in the shop. We got orders stacked ten high, so take one and roll with it. You'll meet Eddie later. He's the one who runs the flowers all over town. Any questions?"

"I'm good."

Trish pointed to the bouquet in her hands. "Yes, you are. And don't you forget it. Any woman that calls down Greek mythology to inspire a flower arrangement has a gift."

Trish disappeared to the back, and Amber twirled the flowers in her hand, touching their soft petals. The smell was outrageous. Just a sniff and she was transported to some dreamy scene with some dreamy guy in some dreamy perfume commercial.

It had been a long time since anybody had sent her flowers.

Beside her lay the order pad. She picked it up and wrote herself a ticket. With lots of irises.

♥

For the first time since Amber had moved in, Clay couldn't hear her footsteps. And her car was gone. His shop had always been a safe haven for him, quiet and peaceful. But now, strangely, it felt lonely for no other reason than his tenant wasn't home.

The front bell rang. He imagined it was Lisa, here to show off Cosie's new Chinese vocabulary, but he braced himself for the toddler's resentment. She had numerous ways to do it, too, including lying on the ground and screaming or giving everyone the silent treatment. She'd also been known to break things, but that hadn't happened in his shop. He and Cosie seemed to have an understanding. If he laughed at her mischief, she promised not to harm any of his things. It was working well so far.

Clay walked to the front. The guest turned out to be the old man who'd dropped off the rocker to repair. He hadn't left his name or anything, had just asked that it be fixed up.

"Hi. It's all finished. Let me get it for you." Clay hurried to the back and returned with the rocker, eager to see his reaction. The work was well worth it. The old man's face lit up when he set eyes on the chair. Clay put it down in the middle of the shop, and the man bent over it, running his fingers around the top and through the slats. He picked it up, turned it over, his eyes searching every part of it. Then he set it down and rocked it gently back and forth.

Clay stood a few feet away, hopeful it was everything he wanted it to be. As the man straightened, he smiled and shook Clay's hand. "Looks great, son."

"Thank you. Clay Walsh."

"Bert Bellman." He gestured to the rocker. "You did a fine job. Wonderful finish, perfect color. Those slats look just right."

"She seemed like she was worth all the hard work."

"My older brother, Raymond, died last year. This is the only . . ." Bert cleared his throat. "Anyways, a couple years before I was born, my dad worked in the fields of West Virginia. Oil. Just outside Morgantown. They lived in a tent."

Clay leaned against the counter, eager to hear the story. It was one of the great delights of doing what he did—knowing the stories behind the treasures.

"Ma and Dad, my brother. In a tent. Most of the families around there did that back then—just the way it was. When Raymond was three, there was a fire. Ma's pregnant with me, and Dad was in the field. It spread so fast . . . Well, the only thing my mother had time to grab besides my brother was this chair. That's it."

"Wow. What a great story," Clay said. "I sensed this little chair was special."

"Possessions don't mean much outside of who they belong to and what they meant to that person. This here rocking chair always stood in our family as a representation of what we were capable of overcoming."

Clay nodded, wondered what that item would be in his life.

"You and your wife—you'll grow old, the kids will be gone, and you'll be able to look at every single thing in your house and have a memory attached to it."

"Oh . . . yeah, I'm not married." Clay looked at the rocker. "But I love hearing the stories behind these pieces I restore. I love the idea of legacy."

"The idea, huh?" Bert chuckled. "Well, if you're going to leave a legacy, you can't be merely an observer, son. You gotta get a little beat up, like this old rocker."

Clay shook his hand. "I will keep that in mind."

Bert left, carrying the rocker like it was a newborn. Clay stood there for another moment, sensing how alone he was, how quiet the shop had become. He'd left one legacy already. Maybe the world didn't need another one left by Clay Walsh.

He decided to go get the mail outside. Maybe he just needed some sunlight.

But the man's words followed him right out the door. The truth was, Clay cherished the idea of legacy. He wanted to leave behind ideas and values that would outlive him. There was comfort in the continuity of life. But there was risk in trying to find a way to preserve it. His best bet was to stay out of the fire.

Back in his workroom, he sorted through the bills, then stopped at the handwritten envelope with his name in fancy, shaky cursive. He ripped it open. Inside was a single tea bag.

He put the tea bag back in the envelope and clutched it. *This. Her!* It was exactly what he needed. At the exact right time, as usual.

"This is the day the Lord has made."

"I will rejoice and be glad in it."

Aunt Zella smiled approvingly, then placed the tea bag in a tiny china teacup. She was pushing eighty, so it was always eventful to see her carry the kettle from the stove to the table and then get the water into the cups. But Clay knew good and well that he should not, under any circumstances, offer to help.

Despite a slight miss, water got into both teacups, and Aunt Zella nodded her satisfaction. She joined him at her small kitchen table, where butter was always kept at room temperature, right next to her pillbox.

Clay let his tea steep. "Good to see you, Aunt Zella."

"So tell me all about it."

"You tell me all about it."

"You bring us any of our canned tamaters?"

Clay cleared his throat. *Us* and *our* were such tiny words, but when she meant herself and her dead husband, they were a little disconcerting.

Aunt Zella turned to the framed picture on the counter. "He forgot, Lloyd. Again."

"It creeps me out when you do that," Clay said.

"Then don't listen."

Clay tried not to. The thing was, it wasn't because she was getting old and senile. She'd been talking to Lloyd for years, ever since he died.

He looked around the room at all the pictures of Lloyd. Birthday parties. Lloyd in his early twenties in his Army uniform. Lloyd's obituary. Every anniversary party they ever threw. Draped over their wedding picture on the kitchen counter was a thin leather-string necklace holding a hand-made pewter Jerusalem cross.

Aunt Zella slapped Clay's hand. "Can't believe you forgot the tamaters again."

"I rented the upstairs, the walk-up."

"No, Lloyd wants to chat about tamaters."

"To a girl."

Suddenly Aunt Zella took a long, gaspy breath. Then she made a choking noise. Her head fell to the table and she went limp.

Clay lifted her arm, but it dropped back to the table. "*Finally.* I thought the old bag would never kick off. I wonder where she keeps her valuables."

Aunt Zella stood and went to get a bag of cookies from the cupboard.

"It's a miracle," Clay said, sipping his tea.

"Is she a pretty girl?"

"Let's chat about tamaters."

Clay watched as she struggled to open the bag. It was everything he could do not to jump up and help her, but he knew how important her independence was. She refused to ask for help.

"How are they?" he asked, watching her flex her fingers. She stood for a long moment staring out her kitchen window, clutching the bag of cookies, then turned to the table and handed it to him, unopened. Her bottom lip trembled.

Clay rose, got her cream off the shelf, and pulled her chair out. As she sat down, frustrated, he squeezed a bit into his palm and took her hand, gently rubbing it in. Right in front of him, she slowly relaxed.

After a while she opened her eyes. They sat quietly, as they did sometimes. She liked to watch the hummingbirds out the window. But today she was watching him.

"That's not your destiny, you know," she said, breaking the quiet.

"What?" Sometimes Aunt Zella was as coherent as a thirty-year-old. Other times she rambled. Sometimes it was hard to tell which was which.

"What happened to your parents," she added.

Clay sighed. He didn't really want to talk about it. "Nothing happened to them. It was their choice."

He didn't think about it much anymore. He was grown now. They all had their separate lives. But at eight, it felt like his whole world had crashed down. And somehow he went from being their son to being their weapon of choice. His mom used him to try to make his dad stop having affairs. His dad used him as an excuse to keep having the affairs. Through it all, he never felt unloved. But he saw what the absence of love could do to a human being, what it could make one human being do to another.

Still, while he was always loved, he was not always looked after. Once the divorce happened, it seemed to usher in a new era of permissiveness. An era that he had trouble finding his way out of.

Aunt Zella took his hands into hers. "There isn't a rule out there that love won't break. For good and for bad."

She had a way of looking right through him, right into his soul.

"It's not love. It's rent."

She sipped her tea again. "That's what they always say."

♥

From the outside, the Brewhouse looked small, almost like a cabin in the woods. Inside was an eclectic mixture of young college kids and some older regulars. Two pool tables sat across the room, the only squares among the circles of people. A jukebox played Maroon 5. The tables by the bar were crowded with a rambunctious birthday party crowd.

Amber, Trish, and Carol sat at a high-top somewhere in the middle, far enough from the music to hear themselves talk, close enough to the bar to hear the tinkling sound of ice on glass. Trish had given her face a double dose of makeup. Her lips, pulpy and red as a stoplight, flashed coy smiles as men passed. Her beautiful doe eyes were lined with black. Amber had made an attempt at it, but she was never really good at makeup. At least the current styles. She could manage a little lipstick. A wink of mascara.

"Hey," she said, nudging Trish. "Sign my cast!"

Trish grinned as Amber handed her a pen. "I thought you'd never ask."

"Carol?"

Carol was flagging down a waitress. "I don't sign anything. Learned a lesson or two about that from my first three marriages."

"I'll sign it."

They all three looked up to find an almost-attractive guy standing there, leaning a bit to the left, his gaze somewhere between intense and asleep. He was blinking a lot and smiling at things like the drink menu and the poster on the wall. Then he managed to focus on Amber. "I'll sign anything you got." The words fell softly off his tongue as if they were barely making it out of his mouth.

Carol grabbed the pen out of Trish's hand and wielded it like a knife. "Back off, Tarzan."

The guy stepped away, beat his chest, and then started coughing.

"Back to your cave," Carol ordered and the guy finally drifted off. She eyed Trish and Amber. "Let me tell you something, girls. Sure, they're fun to play with, those types. But you need to test-drive them in the real world. Do you understand what I'm saying? In here, you got bright lights and loud music and plenty of things to make the vision blurry, you hear me? I'm talking from experience. Too much experience." She regarded the pen in her hand. "Oh, all right. I'll sign it."

"Thank you," Amber said, sliding her arm across the table.

Carol started to sign, then tilted her head and narrowed her eyes, reading something on the cast.

"Sorry," Amber said. "One of my friends can be a little crass."

"That's not what I'm . . . Does that say *Clay Walsh*?"

"Yeah."

"'Old Fashioned' Clay Walsh? That Clay Walsh?"

"I just rented the apartment above his . . ." Amber watched as Trish and Carol exchanged smirks. "What?"

Carol handed back the pen and finished off her beer. "Did he dazzle you with any of his theories yet?"

She knew any expression she mustered wouldn't hide the truth, so she didn't even try to mask it. "Do you know him?"

Trish shook her head but Carol nodded. "Only actually met him once. He's a trip. Used to be quite the player."

"Player?"

"Some girls that worked for me years ago dated him in college. They had some . . . stories. Good stories. Never liked those DVDs though."

"DV—?"

Suddenly a Tarzan yell caused them all to turn. The drunk guy was on the dance floor, waving big.

Amber looked at Trish. "I think that one's for you."

Trish grinned and hopped off the stool, hurrying over.

Carol was waving too, but not at Tarzan. She had yet to flag down a waitress. Finally she gave up. "You have to be under thirty to get anyone's attention around here. I'll be right back. You want anything?"

"No, I'm good."

Clay. A trip, yeah. But a player? Carol apparently didn't know him like Amber did. She sighed and watched the crowd. And then she noticed it. All the young people were grind dancing on the floor. And all the older ones were at the bar. Alone. Carol stood at the end, crowded out by one filled stool after another, still unable to get anyone's attention even as she nearly hung herself over the side of the bar. She smiled at a man nearby. He only looked away.

Was that what Amber could expect in ten years? Sitting at a bar alone, hoping someone might smile at her? Unable to get the bartender's attention? Fending off drunk guys when the young girls were too naive to know what they were doing?

Carol returned with two beers. "Just sayin'. You look like you could use a drink."

"Thanks," Amber said but did nothing more than run her fingers up and down the bottle.

"Something on your mind?"

"You've been married three times?"

"Four. But got one annulled."

"Sometimes I'm afraid of being alone. But sometimes . . . I'm afraid of not."

Carol pulled a cigarette and a lighter from her purse, slid

them in the front pocket of her shirt. "Listen, honey. After a while, you start to realize they're all the same."

"Who?"

"Men. They always got one thing on their mind. It's just that some of them are hiding it better than others. Some of them at least know how to make a good first impression. Jim and Ronny, those two guys—I actually brought them both home to meet my parents. I was love-struck, I'll tell you that."

"What about the third?"

"I dunno. He rode a motorcycle and everyone called him Cupcake." She glanced Amber's way. "I have a thing for sugar and Harleys."

"What about the fourth?"

Carol seemed to fade into the memory and then right back out, with a small smile followed by a tiny frown. "Dimitri."

"Dimitri. Jim, Ronny, Cupcake, and Dimitri."

"Former Russian ballet dancer."

Amber laughed. "No kidding. What's the story behind him?"

Carol leaned forward, closer to Amber, her eyes twinkling and soft against a good memory. "Gorgeous, this one. Jet-black hair. Ice-blue eyes. Features chiseled like he'd just stepped out of a black-and-white movie. And his accent. The way he danced. The way he held me."

"But that one you annulled?"

The hard edge that was Carol came back into full focus. "That, kiddo, was one of those things that happen when you decide you should go for the exact opposite of who you are.

You know? A challenge. A lost cause. Sees the world totally different than you. It's all exciting and different and then . . ."

"Then?"

"Then you realize you can't stand the way the other makes coffee. And then that you can't stand each other." Carol hopped off the barstool. "All this talk about men and cupcakes, I gotta go get some fresh air, and by fresh, I mean smoky." She gave a friendly wink and sauntered off.

Amber wasn't alone for ten seconds before a guy swooped in to fill the barstool. He introduced himself as Mike. Amber smiled and nodded, but it was Carol's words that hung inside her ear, washing away every other sound.

CHAPTER 6

"CLAY, DEARY! Come here!"

"Hi, Mrs. Bronston." Clay pushed his shopping cart down the cereal aisle toward her.

"Did you get yourself a new coupon book?"

Clay held it up. "It holds them all nice and neat, just like you suggested."

She patted his arm with her shaky hand. "Good, good. Did you see the Spam's two for a dollar today? And with the newspaper coupon, you get 'em for a quarter. A quarter!"

"Nice."

Mrs. Bronston leaned heavily on her cane, her hand still on Clay's arm. "Clay, honey, you know how I love seeing you every Saturday morning here at the market."

"I'm just pretending to grocery shop in hopes of running into you."

"But I worry. You're such a nice young man—"

"You bring out my charm."

"Why don't you have some young girls following you around everywhere?"

Clay grinned. "I'm very popular with the ladies. They're just a little older, a tad under one hundred."

"I'll be ninety-four next Tuesday."

"It's like we were made for each other."

"Oh, now," she said, swatting him. "Why don't you try some of those moves on a woman who can bear children?"

"I can be . . . difficult, Mrs. Bronston."

"Honey, you don't know difficult until you know my Louie."

"Lou? He seemed as gentle as flesh-eating bacteria."

She smiled knowingly. "Still miss him. Can't believe he's been gone for five years now."

"What was your secret?"

"To what?"

"Staying married."

Mrs. Bronston shrugged. "I guess in our day and age, nobody thought there was an option to do otherwise." She put her cane in her cart. "Now I better get going before Jerry sells out of pork chops back there." Then she pointed to Clay's head. "Sweetheart, if you'd just brush your hair a little bit, part it all nice and neat, you might get a few looks your way."

Clay smiled. "I'll think about it. Have a good day."

He stood there for a moment, wondering about his hair and whether he should have more fiber in his diet. He was about to reach for a cereal that looked as exciting as algebra when something bumped his cart, which then bumped him.

"Hey there, stress boy."

Her!

"Hey there, pretty girl." Clay blinked. Did he say that *out loud*? He cast a startled gaze toward her. Yes, he did, because she was grinning like a girl who was just called pretty. And she was.

"Did you just flirt with me?"

"No." *Yes. But not on purpose.*

"You did."

"Spam's on sale two for a buck."

"I liked your other pickup line better." Amber eyed his cart. "Are those coupons?"

His heart was pounding now, the way it did when he wanted something he couldn't—shouldn't—have. She was like the middle shelf of the cereal aisle . . . sweet, fun, colorful, and so bad for his health. He clawed his face, then turned his cart around, afraid of what was going to come out next.

But down the pasta and bean aisle, there she was, right by his side, making it impossible for other customers to pass. She didn't even notice. What she was noticing was their baskets. She pointed to his.

"That's quite a system you have going there."

Clay looked down. Everything was nicely divided. His frozen goods, his meat, his fruits and vegetables, soap and shampoo. In hers, everything was piled up. The meat and Kleenex were touching. And everything was name brands.

"I see you like a bargain," she said.

He grabbed some lima beans. "I guess so."

They continued on, her cart next to his.

"Our first date," she said.

"This isn't a date." He looked sideways at her.

"You're so romantic. How'd you find this place?"

"How do you know if I'm romantic or not?" He could definitely do better than a grocery store . . . and for Amber, he would do way better.

"Trust me, you're not. I'm envisioning a date to a restaurant featured on Groupon."

"I might have hidden romantic talents."

"There are a few clues resting in your basket that say otherwise. Lima beans. Not romantic."

Clay grabbed a box of wagon wheel pasta off the shelf. "Eh?"

"No. Candlelight, jazz, sand between your toes—all romantic. Wagon wheel pasta—not romantic."

He put the box back on the shelf, careful to line it up with the rest. He started to move on, but right behind him, Amber reached over and nudged the box out of place.

Keep walking. Breathe.

They rounded the corner, but the truth was that he couldn't take his eyes off her. She grabbed this and that, never checking the price, just throwing it all in a pile. They got to the gum and she grabbed every package of cinnamon gum they had.

"I like cinnamon." She shrugged.

He smiled. The thing was, there didn't seem to be much hiding behind those beautiful brown eyes. What you saw was what you got.

She ripped open one of the bags of gum, pulled out three pieces, and stuck them in her mouth.

"But you haven't paid for—"

"It's okay, stress boy. They don't actually arrest you until you attempt the leave the store without paying." She held out the packet to him. "Gum?"

He took a piece, looked at it for a moment. "Is sugarless cinnamon gum romantic?"

"Depends on who's chewing it."

Then they both heard it at the same time: *Cosie, go tee-tee!*

Laughter erupted between them. "Amazingly, that's not even over the loudspeaker," Clay said.

"Well, come on, stress boy! I don't want to miss the show!"

Amber turned her cart and hurried off toward the bakery. Clay followed. They found Lisa chanting, Cosie posed in defiance, and David melting in humiliation while holding a box of donuts.

"Cosie! Tee-tee! For Uncle Eric."

A small crowd had gathered. Lisa, as always, seemed to be feeling the pressure. She was swiping sweaty hair off her forehead. "She does it at home. Cosie. Listen to Mommy."

A nearby customer hollered, "Can I just get some donuts?"

"In a minute. That's my niece," said Eric, Lisa's brother.

"She can do it," Lisa said to the crowd. "Come on, Cosie.

Tee-tee." Lisa backed up, her arms out. "Just give her some space."

Eric got the crowd going in their own chant. "Tee-tee! Tee-tee!"

Amber nudged Clay. He laughed, the kind of laugh that made everything else in life seem okay and worthwhile. "Tee-tee!" he chanted with her.

Cosie watched the crowd for a moment. Then, emboldened and drunk with attention, she slowly moved toward the potty. The chants intensified with every step. She looked around, urging the crowd to more excitement. She dropped her zoo animals diaper. Her little dress covering her, she sat, in complete modesty, and went into some kind of stellar zone of concentration, staring straight forward, locked on to her mission.

Lisa shushed the chanters, her face bursting like it might be time for her own trip to the potty. The entire crowd quieted. The entire store, for that matter. Even the cash registers at the front seemed to stop.

Then . . . "Tee-tee!" Cosie punched her hands into the air. The crowd erupted with wild applause. Lisa cried, her hand over her mouth as if Cosie had just made the Olympic team. David was eating a donut.

Clay leaned toward Amber. "No one applauds when I go tee-tee." She laughed. He laughed. So far this was better than any date he'd been on.

As the crowd dispersed, they made their way, carts and all, toward Lisa, David, and Cosie.

Lisa gave Clay a self-satisfied smile. "See? Told you.

Shame-free parenting. Bodily functions are totally natural."
This from a mother who encouraged public nose picking.
Thankfully Cosie didn't take to that.

David offered Clay a donut. "Aren't you going to introduce us to your new friend?"

"I'm Amber." She had this confident way about her like
she was sure she'd fit into any crowd.

"I'm David." They shook hands. "Donut?"

"Sure."

"We just ran into each other here. That's it," Clay said. He
was chewing his gum faster than he wanted to.

"That's *the one*," Lisa said and David's eyes widened.

"Oh . . . yeah . . . hi . . ." Now David was inspecting
Amber like she was a steak and he was the FDA.

"And this is Cosie," Lisa said, "whom you've met."

"Hi again." Amber smiled down at her. "Good job doing
your thing."

"So you're the woman upstairs," David said with a wicked
gleam in his eye, directed right at Clay. *This* was why he never
went out in public with these two.

Amber looked at him. Lisa and David did too. "What?
Don't look at me," Clay said, bringing the moment into full-
blown awkwardness.

"Yeah," David said. "Don't look at him. He never men-
tioned you. Then again, why should he? It's not like we're
best friends or anything."

Clay focused his attention on David, defying him to keep
pushing. As usual, he did.

"Amber, Lisa and I are having a big shindig tonight. Two birthdays. One party."

Clay swallowed his gum accidentally. Surely David wasn't going to go *there*.

David slid his arm around Lisa, who added, "Our birthdays are on the same day."

Amber smiled. "Awww. That's sweet."

"I know." Lisa grinned.

David's own grin appeared innocent—Bernie Madoff innocent. "Clay is going to be there—aren't you, Clay?"

Amber clapped her hands. "I'd love to come!"

Several hours later, Clay stood in front of his mirror at home, trying to decide what shirt to wear. The irony was that any woman could tell him instantly, but in order to get a woman, he was going to have to make a statement with a shirt he picked out on his own. Or so the culture told him.

He wanted to pretend he didn't care, but the fact was that in the last nine years, he hadn't once stopped and thought about what shirt to wear. Something was shifting. And today it was David's fault. Maybe tomorrow he would blame someone else.

Luckily for David, his kid was cute and seemed to like Clay a lot. Plus Clay had the surprise, earth-shattering birthday gift that Lisa was depending on. He'd wrapped it in bubble wrap, secured it with wire, and put it in a sturdy box.

Now it was in his backseat. Along with two other shirts he threw back there in case the black sweater didn't work.

As he drove his old truck to David and Lisa's house, he realized how few parties he even went to anymore. As few as possible, truthfully. There was a time—eons ago, it seemed now—that he wouldn't miss a party. He loved people. Loved a crowd. Loved a good time. Loved the challenge of making sure everyone enjoyed themselves. Loved to be the center of attention.

That man had been murdered, thank God. Though Clay suspected, deep down inside, there was always a chance he could rise from the dead. And maybe that's why he didn't get out much. Maybe being around old, dusty, long-forgotten possessions kept him dead enough not to worry about it.

The party was in full swing when Clay walked in. Lisa hurried to take the gift from his hands, rushing it out of sight into another room. He found the drink table, grabbed a soda, then planted himself in a nice doorway to lean against and hold steady.

He saw Amber immediately. She'd already arrived and was chatting with a couple of guys and playing with children all at once. He smiled as he watched her tickle Cosie's tummy. He'd thought about asking her if she needed a ride. But it had remained in his thoughts.

Then, like that, she was looking at him, smiling in that self-assured way that made him feel less and less sure about himself. He looked away right as David bumped his shoulder.

"I saw that. Don't deny it." David gestured with his own drink. "That whole aloof-glance-across-the-room thing. Very nice. Subtle."

"Don't you need to take Cosie to driver's ed or space camp or something?"

"Oooh! Good ideas. Honey?" Lisa said, carrying a tray of drinks past them.

"On it, hon." David smiled. It dropped off his face when she passed. "Thanks a lot, man."

"I do what I can."

They both watched Lisa walk back in with a big Tonka dump truck. She set it in the middle of the floor. Cosie and the other kids flooded around it. And right there with them was Amber, to the disappointment of the guy who had just sat down next to her.

"Make your move, man. Looks like real estate is going fast."

Clay huffed. "Are you my agent?"

"Hey! Everybody!" David suddenly yelled.

A burst of tingling sweat broke over Clay like the shingles. Why, *why* did David always feel the need to—?

"Welcome again to our humble abode," David said, flashing smiles in all directions. "This celebration. Eight years in a row. Lisa and I. Getting older. Still living in sin." Light applause. "To share it with all of you means so much. Has everyone met Amber? Raise your hand, Amber. She's new."

Amber, blushing a bit, gave a gentle wave.

"Also, Clay really likes her. A lot." He lifted his bottle to whispers instead of cheers and walked off.

Clay's whole face itched. He didn't have to look in the mirror to know he was bright red, equal parts embarrassment and fury. He shot David a glare across the room. David only grinned and patted his heart.

His gaze moved to Amber, still sitting on the floor like a little kid. And as she glanced at him and smiled, she seemed to be the only cool air in the room.

But he needed the real thing and stepped outside for a while.

The escape was short-lived. The sun set and out came the birthday cake, glowing with enough candles to be mistaken for nuclear war. To claps and cheers, David and Lisa held hands and blew the candles out together. They served the cake, but Clay had already lost his appetite. As everyone made their way into the kitchen, he made his way to the couch and found a comfortable spot.

Why was he such an idiot? Why did she make him feel this way? Why couldn't he just . . . be normal? Except he believed, truly, that normal wasn't working for anyone anymore.

All these thoughts were racing around in his mind when Amber suddenly plopped down beside him.

"I'm sorry about earlier," Clay said, biting his lip with the kind of force used for gnawing through gristle.

"You or David?"

He looked down. Trapped again.

She patted his leg. "I'm kidding. It's fine. He's ornery. That's what you like about him."

Clay's knee was blushing. "I used to be worse than that," he said, glancing at her.

"I find that hard to believe."

"Good."

The crowd filtered back into the living room, holding cake and watching David and Lisa open gifts. Amber sat quietly beside him, enthralled, as if she'd never been to a birthday party before. He tried not to watch her, but every time one of them opened a gift, her eyes lit as if it were a present for her. How could someone get so happy over someone else's gift?

"Hey," she whispered. "Look at that."

Cosie was walking toward them, right into the room of grown-ups, weaving between their legs unnoticed. Wrapped in a soft pink blanket like a baby was the big yellow dump truck. She rocked it back and forth gently, whispering to it and kissing it, completely oblivious to anything else. She walked past them and into her bedroom, shutting the door.

Amber smiled. "That's the cutest thing I have ever seen."

Clay was pretty sure she was wrong because he was afraid he was looking right at the cutest thing ever. Her knee brushed his and it felt like electricity charging through him. He stayed perfectly still.

"Clay! My man!"

He whipped his attention back to the presents, afraid David was about to announce to everyone exactly what Clay was thinking. But instead he was pointing to the framed movie poster of *Meet John Doe*.

"Classic. Well done." David tilted his head. "Is somebody still pouting?"

Amber pointed to Gary Cooper's fedora. "I like his hat."

Clay couldn't help staring at her now. Could this woman get any more—?

"And for me?" Lisa said. "My present? The usual?"

Clay nodded and Lisa clapped, then mouthed, *Thank you*. She turned to David. "Well, only two left. One from me to you and one from you to me." She handed him the box. "You go first."

David laughed. "All right. Can't imagine what this is." He tore open the top of the package and pulled out the shadow box. It contained a half-smoked cigar, a signed credit card receipt, and a photo of his favorite NBA superstar frozen in a power dunk.

Clay smiled as he watched David's mouth drop open like he was staring at the Holy Grail. He loved this man, who so easily could have walked away from him for more reasons than he could count. David had seen Clay in the two most extreme ways possible. And he was loyal whether Clay was on the north or south pole. Sometimes Clay took him for granted, and he vowed not to do that anymore . . . unless, of course, David was going to continue to needle him. Which he would.

Lisa was giddy. "I saw him at a restaurant last time I was in Chicago. I was too nervous to ask for his autograph in person so I sat and waited three hours for him to finish eating! And then I had to beat the busboy to the table. Not easy."

"You stole a half-smoked cigar and a credit card receipt?"

Lisa let out a silent scream. "I know, right? The cigar was a bonus."

"If that's not love, I don't know what is." David glanced at Clay. "It looks just like you told me."

Clay groaned as Lisa stared him down. "I didn't tell him anything." David loved planting this kind of nonsense. It was like a gift.

"Clay! It was supposed to be a surprise!" Lisa looked racked with disappointment.

David smirked at him, then turned to Lisa. "He didn't ruin it *totally*."

"I didn't say *anything*!" Clay protested, but thankfully Lisa was a sucker for presents and had already cast her attention toward the last one on the table, a tiny box with a big red bow.

David picked it up and placed it in her hands. She ripped off the bow, opened the box, and . . .

Gasps. The loudest from Lisa.

Her mouth gaped open as though a moan might escape. Amber glanced at Clay, excitement in her eyes.

"What's this?" Lisa stammered.

"It's an engagement ring," David said.

"You want to get married?"

"Make an honest woman of ya."

"I am an honest woman."

"It's just an expression."

"I don't like it."

"Is that a yes?"

Lisa stared at the ring. "I thought we didn't need a piece of paper to prove anything."

"We don't."

Everyone watched as Lisa hesitated. Clay would never forget the time he'd been at an NBA game and seen a guy ask a girl to marry him on the Jumbotron. She slapped him and stormed off. David didn't look nervous. But Lisa looked like she was still processing the fact that these weren't earrings.

David tossed another smirk his way. "It's Clay's fault. He's rubbing off on me."

"I hope not," Lisa said, still staring at the ring.

"We're not kids," David said, taking Lisa's hand. "Some things are starting to matter more to me now than they used to. It's not about proof. I know you love me."

"I do. Unfortunately."

"And I love you. I'm not going anywhere, paper or no paper. I'd just like the chance to see you in a wedding dress."

The *yes* was heard four blocks away.

♥

"You're proud of him," Amber said, giving Clay a small wink. Over the past thirty minutes as they sat on the couch together, he'd seemed to loosen up a bit. And by *a bit*, she meant only that his eyebrows had relaxed into a straight line across his forehead. Everything else was stone frozen.

But then Clay smiled at her, and it was the first time she saw relief on the rest his face. "Yeah. He's a good guy."

"Likes to give you a hard time."

"Used to go both ways. But it's how he shows his love."

"It's 'man crush' at its finest." She grinned.

The crowd started to disperse around them. Cranky kids had hit their breaking point.

"So what's this great gift you get Lisa every year?"

"Come on. I'll show you."

They walked to the kitchen, where plates and cups and saucers and serving dishes were piled a mile high. Clay went to the sink, grabbed a towel, and started the water.

"The dishes?"

He smiled, then started scrubbing.

"Want some help?"

"No, I'm fine. I actually kind of find it relaxing."

"And for fun on your days off, you scrub toilets?" She laughed as she took a seat on a barstool. But the guy probably didn't need any more ribbing this evening. "You're happy when you're doing something productive, aren't you?"

"Usually."

David and Lisa came in, entwined in each other's arms.

"Keep your voices down. Cosie fell asleep in her room snuggled up against that Tonka truck. So cute!" Lisa said. "And I love the fact that she doesn't feel the need to carry around a baby like every other little girl. I am raising her to think independently, people. Watch and learn."

Amber laughed as Clay glanced at her with a small smile.

Lisa took a seat on the stool next to Amber's and poured them both a glass of red wine. "Now that's what I call a party."

Amber nodded toward the sink. "Now that's what I call sexy." She didn't have to look—she knew he was blushing.

"Show-off," David called as he slid into a seat at the kitchen table.

"Hey," Lisa said, "are we gonna have a honeymoon?"

"If we must."

"I think I might want to go on a cruise. Any thoughts? Recommendations? The ideal honeymoon?"

David raised an eyebrow. "Amber?"

"Oh, David, leave her be," Lisa said with an apologetic look.

"What?" David shrugged innocently.

"I'll take a pass," Amber said. Clay had had his fill of torture for the night. But it would be the Dominican Republic, if she ever got to choose.

"Okay. Sure. Clay?"

Lisa threw up her hands at him. "David. Now you're just being mean."

Clay dried his hands and turned to face everyone.

"Clay, come on. Ideal honeymoon. Go."

He didn't miss a beat. "A cabin in the woods. A case of bottled water. And not a single distraction from creating a foundation of intimacy with my lifelong bride. Most newlyweds—"

"That's enough."

With a satisfied smile, he turned back and began washing another dish.

David raised his beer in Amber's direction, but Amber found herself watching Clay do his work. The guy could hold his own. Most of the time, it seemed, he chose not to.

He took a lot of heat. Dished very little of it back. Knew what he believed. Stuck to his guns. She tried to think about anyone in her life who felt as strongly about marriage as he did. Certainly not her parents.

With all she knew about him so far, she could pretty much tell that what happened tonight between David and Lisa was Clay's doing in the most indirect way possible. And she kind of liked him for that.

But she was still getting mixed signals from him. Sometimes she could make him laugh. Other times he looked like he wanted to run for his life. Was she just imagining some chemistry there? When she caught him staring across the room at her, was it because he wanted to ask her out or because he was planning an escape route?

Amber listened to David and Lisa decide on their perfect honeymoon destination. She smiled and laughed with them, pretending not to be bothered by the fact that for the rest of the evening, Clay never turned around again.

CHAPTER 7

"YOU WANT HIM! You got him! Lucky Chucky Sexton. Dr. O. The dean of depravity. The vicar of vice."

The guitar riff sizzled through the radio, filtering in from the back room of the floral shop as Amber and Trish worked on a funeral arrangement.

"Live from the City of Angels, in the heart of Hollywood, and far too good-looking for radio. Time to sit down before it's too late. Time to go to school, kiddies. . . ."

"You listen to this?" Amber asked Trish as she clipped a ribbon for her.

Trish shrugged. "Sometimes. He's hilarious."

"He says women are stupid."

Trish shrugged again.

And off he went into the microphone. *"You can't save someone who doesn't want to be saved. How true it is. A friend of mine—we'll call him Moron—has lived with this broad for years. Strike one. Strike two? He knocked her up. Now, no longer content with only partial self-destruction, strike three: they're getting married. What's the point of all this pain?"*

Amber leaned toward Trish. "I saw a couple get engaged Saturday night! It was so romantic."

"Big ring?"

"I don't know. I didn't even notice. But big surprise. It was so cute."

Lucky Chucky hardly took a breath. *"I'm awash in ruin. I know this guy. I love this guy. We were in the same fraternity in college. Yeah, I was a frat boy. I bet you didn't see that one coming."*

Amber rolled her eyes. This guy made her sick to her stomach. The question was, why didn't he affect Trish?

"Now, the only ray of light in this whole apocalyptic meltdown is . . . where there's a wedding, there's a bachelor party."

Carol walked in from the back room, setting some boxes down. "Trish, am I going to have to take that radio and throw it through the front window?"

"Sorry, Carol. Didn't know you were here." Trish rushed to switch the radio off.

Otherwise, Carol seemed to be in a good mood. "How was your weekend, girls? I had me a big date!"

Trish pitched her thumb over her shoulder at Amber. "So did Amber. With Mr. Old Fashioned."

Carol's eyes grew wide and Amber sighed, giving Trish the same look Clay had been giving David at the party.

"Did she now?" Carol's hands slid onto her hips. "Details. And to make sure I'm understanding correctly, you linked *date* and *Clay* in the same sentence?"

"It was a birthday party. Bunch of people. He didn't even invite me himself."

Trish stuck more baby's breath around the tulips. "My theory is he's gay. Any guy who's not trying to play Operation by dessert on the first date has got issues."

"Come on, that's not fair," Amber said.

"What? He owns an antique shop. Hello! Plus, look at that gorgeous hair."

"I don't think so."

"Then he's got a disease. Or some other . . . tiny problem."

Trish and Carol cracked up. Amber managed a smile but then went to the back room for more ribbon.

When she returned, Carol leaned on the counter, caught her attention. "You like the freak show."

Amber looked down at what she was doing. "For now."

"Well, lady, more power to you. Dating Cupcake was the best seven weeks of my life. It was all the mess afterward that practically sent me into a diabetic relational coma." She touched Amber's arm as she walked past her. "Just be careful." Then she hollered from the back room, "And hey, can you wrap that rose bouquet on the shelf in bubble wrap? We're shipping it."

Amber laughed at the irony of Carol's advice. *Just be*

careful. That was the whole problem. Clay was too careful. It was like he wanted to live his life insulated by bubble wrap.

And apparently she was the one who was going to pop all those bubbles and turn his safety net into an ordinary sheet of plastic.

Well, she was addicted to popping bubble wrap.

But chances were, he wasn't even thinking about her this morning.

♥

Right on time, George pulled up in his truck. But Clay didn't hear him. He was absorbed in his thoughts of Amber, trying desperately not to be, but consumed with how beautiful she had looked at the party. The more he tried to think of other things, the more that image of her sitting on the couch drove everything else out.

George honked his horn, causing Clay to race into the sunlight, fleeing his thoughts.

"Come on, I don't got all day," George said.

Clay walked to the back of the truck. "Sorry."

George sighed. "Light load this week. The love seat is solid." He gestured toward it, his hands shakier than usual, Clay noticed. "Vintage too. Needs a bit of work. Hey, by the way . . ." He pulled a picture out of his shirt pocket. "Would you look at that."

He handed the bent photograph to Clay, who unbent one of the edges as he brought it closer for a better look.

"Got it dirt cheap. Auction down in Eustis. Nice, right?"

Clay turned it sideways, trying to figure it out. "Was that a car?"

"Is. Is a car! It's a *Rolls-Royce!*"

Clay turned the photo right-side up again. The car was so beat up and rusted it only looked like a heap of metal.

"It's my new hobby. When I get done with it, watch out. My brother-in-law's got this body shop. Scrap yard. Just what I need."

Clay patted him on the back. "If anyone can do wonders on it, it's you, George."

George slipped the photo into the front pocket of his flannel shirt again and patted it twice. "Okay, now. That love seat is calling your name, right?"

"George, how long have you been married?"

"Thirty-six years."

"How did you . . . know?"

"Know what?"

"Know."

"Know?" George seemed genuinely confused. He stared into the back of the truck, fixated on the love seat. Then, "Oh. Know. *Know.* Good question. Let me think."

Clay smiled, ready for a good story.

"Well, we grew up together. Same grammar school. Junior high. High school. Never thought much of her, to be honest. Sophomore year she asks me to the Sadie Hawkins Day dance. That's where the girls ask the boys—not sure if they still do that or not. Do they?"

"Not sure."

"I don't want to go but I don't want to hurt her feelings either, so I say yes. It's only one night. After the dance she decides to kiss me and, well, I kiss her back. Not so good. She still can't do it right. Point is, now I had to date her for at least a month or so because I felt guilty for kissing her and, you know, didn't want to make her feel cheap."

Clay shifted. This was way more information than he thought he might get.

"After a month, right before I'm going to dump her, her mom gets diagnosed with tuberculosis and she starts freaking out, man. Crying all the time. Calling me. It just didn't seem fair to break up with her then—I mean, my people knew her people. So almost a year goes by and things calm down and I figure it's time. But I realize junior prom is only two months away and you only get one junior prom. I figure, take her to the dance. That's it. So I take her. After the dance, we, uh . . . Well, now I absolutely felt guilty. But I didn't care. It was over. That's no reason to stay with somebody. Know what I mean?"

Clay couldn't even nod, but he did something with his expression that kept George going.

"Then. *Then* she thinks she's pregnant. So now we got to date at least a few more weeks to wait and see, right? She ain't, so I'm scot-free. But when I show up to swing the ax, the first thing she does is blurt out that her dad just lost his job and how grateful she is to me for being the only security she has in her life. That's two or three more months automatically. Then Valentine's. Senior prom.

Graduation. Then I'm nineteen and getting drafted into the Army, and . . ."

His words trailed off and the horror of thirty-six years washed over George's face. The bright-pink flush of his cheeks dimmed, right in front of Clay. Clay felt a lump grow in his throat as the two men stood in silence for a moment.

Then George pointed into the truck. "You want the love seat?"

The sun had set a good hour ago, and Clay would normally have left the shop by now. But instead, with a single light on in the back, he sat on the right side of the love seat that George had managed to talk him into.

And he thought about George.

Wasn't it better to just be alone? He couldn't stop picturing the hopeless look in George's eyes—that sickening realization that thirty-six years had passed. That he was sixty now. That his life was almost over.

But as Clay looked into the emptiness of the quiet antique shop, it seemed its own hollow grave. Four clocks ticked, each on its own rhythm and time, reminding him that they were not on his side. One was a grandfather clock that had lost its ability to chime out the hours. But it ticked, nevertheless, authoritatively.

The single lightbulb above him drew his attention. The room was quiet enough that he could hear it buzzing, its light waning ever so slightly. It'd been threatening to end its life for three years.

Within the light, he could see sawdust all over the place, a fine haze dusting every surface. He loved the smell of it. The soft feel of it in the palm of his hand.

But . . . what if that's all he ended up having in life? Someone else got the perfectly carved piece of wood and he was left standing in the sawdust.

He continued to sit on the love seat, wondering whose it had been. Where it had come from. Did it ever host two lovers?

Clay looked at the ceiling again, hoping to hear above the ticking clocks the gentle padding of her feet. It was quiet, but she was up there. From the shop door he could see the square light cast onto the ground from the window. She was right there. So close.

Why . . . why didn't he just go ask her out? Why couldn't he stop watching her at the party?

Why was she getting to him like this?

Girls had come and gone throughout the last nine years. Many of them nice young ladies. Most ended up thinking his theories were outrageous and outdated. Or often, boring. They at the very least lost interest. Some read the signals wrong, and friendships became complicated and burned up against the hot sizzle of misunderstanding.

Clay rose and went to the old phonograph sitting near the front door of the shop. It was the first thing Amber had looked at when he noticed her there. He turned the crank, lowered the needle, and that same piano solo played.

There was nothing to do but watch it spin.

Then, above him, he heard her walking.

♥

"Well, that was a good movie," Amber said, turning off the DVD. "Honestly, I'm not sure I could resist a man in a fedora. Especially Gary Cooper. Wow." She took money out of her pocket and placed it in her money jar. It wasn't close to being filled yet.

But it wasn't money or her jar that was on her mind tonight. She paced her apartment, biting her fingernails. Why was she so caught up in this quirky guy? Clay was starting to make Cupcake look normal. Why did he seem so drawn to her and then terrified to sit on a couch with her?

"It makes no sense, Mr. Joe," she said. She got her teapot, filled it with water, turned on the gas.

Darn. It works.

"Why am I so intrigued by him? He seems like a bad idea, right? Right? I mean, typically at this point, I'm telling the guy that we're moving too fast. And then we move too fast. And then somehow I justify it. Then the fights start. Then we decide we're in love. Then we realize we're not. It's a general pattern. This is like breaking the mold. Shattering it. Turning it into sawdust."

She leaned against the counter, trying to get a grip. She had to find a way to get this guy off her mind.

But as she stared into her sink, an idea struck, which was usually when she got herself into trouble.

Against her better judgment, she went to the fridge. "Don't say a word," she said, pointing a sharp finger Mr.

Joe's direction. His tail twitched. "And don't give me that tail. I know what you're thinking." She started grabbing food out of the fridge, tossing it on the counter. "You know what *I'm* thinking? I'm thinking I'm alone. No offense. But you can't tell me I'm pretty. And by the way, he did say that. Did I tell you? Yep. Right there by the Cocoa Puffs. So I don't think I'm chasing after the wind here."

Mr. Joe got interested in all the food that was being pulled out of the fridge and jumped on the counter.

"It's just that we're going to have to go about this in an unconventional way. Typically I smile a lot and find something in common. The problem is, I don't have anything in common with him. At least not that I know of. Maybe we do. He's so uptight about personal space that the only real conversation we've had has been at the grocery store. But hey. I'm not above a challenge." She glanced at Mr. Joe. "Now. Keep your mouth shut at what you're about to witness."

♥

Clay climbed the steps to the apartment. It was cold tonight, so he'd brought an extra blanket. But as he looked up, Amber was already standing out on the stoop, bundled in her coat, smiling. She held the door open for him and he walked in. The screen door closed behind him.

"So, um, you say that you just threw the switch and it ground to a stop?"

"Yeah. It might be time for some new kitchen appliances."

Clay stooped down to unplug the disposal. Amber peeked her head in and watched him for a moment, then said, "So why antiques?"

"My great-aunt Zella—my mother's mother's sister—she used to own this place. I worked for her part-time while I went to college."

"I drove by the university when I first got to town. It was stunning. All those fall leaves. That stonework."

"Yeah. Bolivar University. It's where David teaches. Zella, too, before she retired. She taught mathematics."

"So you and David both went there?"

"Same fraternity. Same major."

Amber looked genuinely perplexed. "You were in a frat?"

"I was."

"Wow. *Wow.*" She laughed. "What happened?"

He was about to answer when a massive glop of food dropped out of the disposal under the sink. "What . . . ? How did all this food . . . ?"

"I never finished college," she continued.

Clay reached for a dustpan, paper towels, anything to try to clean up the mess.

"Seven years, off and on. I could never seem to—watch out for that mousetrap under there. Anyway, to focus. Got everything but my language requirement. I'm only three credits in Spanish away from a BA in like six different degrees."

Clay glanced at her, trying to both listen and figure out what was going on with the disposal. Mr. Joe walked by, eyeing the food. All ground together, it did look an awful lot like cat food. The smell was kind of . . . fishy.

"So you bought this place from your great-aunt when she retired."

"She gave it to me. For graduation."

"That's some present."

"Yeah. You could say I owe her."

"She's still alive? That's why you keep it?"

"She is. But I keep it for me."

Clay stood, wiped off his hands, put them on his hips. He studied his shoes for a moment, trying to find a way to make her understand. "I know I'm a punch line. But when I was in college, I wasn't like this."

She looked at him with a gentle tilt of her head. "I'm sure you weren't that bad."

Clay tried to keep his expression steady. "My senior year, everything changed. My goals. What I wanted out of life."

Amber studied him as if she were staring straight into his soul. "What do you want out of life?"

"To be a decent person. That's it. A good person."

She shook her head. "Are you for real? That's it? A good person?"

"I needed to believe my life could be different than it was. That I could be different."

She didn't appear totally convinced. But at the same time, she seemed genuinely interested. He guessed he could understand her skepticism.

"Don't even tell me you found Jesus or something."

The swallow reflex kicked in. His Adam's apple sank down his throat. But there was no other way to say it. "More like He found me."

She cast him a doubtful look.

"I know, I know. But it's the truth. And that's why I took my aunt up on her offer, why I keep the shop. It's a safe place for me. Not very ambitious. Nothing heroic. I guess I wasn't destined for greatness."

She looked at him for a long time, and Clay got the feeling she was about to bolt. But then she said, "You know what? I think the world has enough greatness. Not enough goodness. That's my theory."

And then they were smiling at each other. And he realized it was the first time anybody had ever smiled after all that explanation.

Then he sneezed.

"You're doing it again," she said.

Another sneeze. *Great.*

"You're allergic to me, aren't you?"

"Not you." Clay bent down to put the disposal back together, sneezing all the way through. He stood, wiping his eyes, trying not to sneeze again.

"You're allergic to *cats*," she said.

Clay reached for the disposal switch. It roared to life. "You're all fixed."

"I am? That was fast. Are you sure? My therapist said it would take years."

She was fun. Clay grabbed his toolbox. Amber opened the

door for him and stepped aside. He went down one step and turned to find that she'd already slipped into the apartment, standing at the screen door, watching him.

"Good night," she said. "And thanks for coming at this late hour to fix my . . . my . . ."

"Disposal."

"Yeah. That. Thanks."

"You're welcome."

He walked down the rest of the steps. He heard her close the door. At the bottom, he looked up, hoping she might open it again. But all was quiet.

Except the clamoring of his heart. And the ticking sound that never went away.

CHAPTER 8

AS THEY ALWAYS DID after a good game of one-on-one at the college after work, they finished with a game of horse. There were very few people Clay would confide in, but David was one of them, mostly because he was a straight shooter, on and off the court.

Still, Amber wasn't easy to talk about. Of course, he knew there was no use hiding what he felt from David. He'd probably seen it before Clay had.

"I think," David said, "you think too much. Now, shoot that ball. We've only got fifteen minutes left."

Clay shot and missed. The ball thumped to the ground and bounced to the fence. David laughed.

"See what happens when you hurry things?" Clay said, watching David retrieve the ball. "Fact: most people know more about someone after a job interview for delivering pizzas than they—"

David stalked back to the court. "Hurry things. *Hurry* things?" He shot Clay a look. "Whatcha got?"

"H-O-R."

David found a spot at the top of the key. "Mama called it 'paralysis by analysis.'"

He shot the ball and it swished through the net. Clay grabbed it and headed toward the spot where David stood.

"I'm not sure if . . . I mean, I don't have to have someone. You shouldn't . . ." Clay sighed. "I'm trying to say that I do fine on my own."

"Oh yeah. You got it going on." David shook his head. "Just shoot."

Clay missed again. He walked to retrieve the ball. "What do I really know about her? I just want to be smart."

"You're so smart you're an idiot. *S*, by the way. Throw me the ball."

Clay tossed it to him.

"Quit looking for a formula."

Clay wiped his face with his shirt. "She's just not . . . what I expected."

"Good."

"So you think I should . . . ?"

David slapped him on the shoulder. "I'm done talking about this. You're either going to go for it or not. Either do it or don't." He shot and missed. "See that? I knew you were rubbing off on me!"

Clay sat on the concrete bench off to the side of the court.

"Come on, man. Aren't we gonna finish the game?" David asked from under the basket.

"Lisa's really happy, isn't she?"

David walked over and sat next to him. "Seems to be."

"What should I do?"

David gave him a tired glance. "Clay, why are you asking me what you should do? Ask your theory what you should do. That's what drives you every morning when you get out of bed. That's what sleeps next to you every night. It doesn't matter what I think." He ruffled Clay's hair and stood, grabbing his bag.

Clay's phone, which sat on the other side of the bench, dinged.

David raised an eyebrow. "Did you just get a *text* message?"

"What? I text."

"No, I text. You. And I'm standing right here. So . . . ?"

Clay picked up the phone, laughed, and glanced at David. "It's nothing. It's . . . Her refrigerator broke."

David threw his hands up. "You smile over a fridge breaking? Dude, I will never be able to understand you. I will, however, beat you tomorrow. Same time."

David walked toward the university building that housed his office. Clay grabbed his bag and hurried off. He was in desperate need of a shower.

Thirty minutes later, he was climbing the steps, toolbox in hand. The sun was setting and the orange hues of the last light encircled Amber as she sat at the top of the stairs. She'd pulled out a chair and had a blanket around her shoulders. When Clay got to the top, he could see that she was drinking hot chocolate with mini marshmallows on top.

"Here," she said and dropped a tiny hot-pink pill into his hand.

"What's this?"

"Allergy medicine."

Clay glanced at Mr. Joe, who was pawing at the screen. "So the fridge . . ."

"Yeah, I don't know. I mean, it's out. Luckily I didn't have much food in there."

Clay walked inside, gently shutting the screen door. He set his toolbox down and for the first time noticed a large glass jar sitting on the counter. It had a few dollars in it, only about a quarter full. He went to the sink and took the pill, cupping his hand for water.

"Saving up for something?" he asked as he tried to scoot the fridge out from the wall.

"Gas money."

"That's it?"

"Just a jar."

He glanced at her as he got the fridge pulled out. "That's not much of a story."

She only shrugged, sipped her hot chocolate, watched him.

He started grabbing the tools he thought he might need. "You know, the stories are my favorite part of what I do.

Folks rarely drop off dusty lamps or family heirlooms without telling a story, the 'why' under the surface that gives those things meaning. No matter how faded or everyday they appear, everything has a story."

She smiled, a playful grin that seemed to say she knew more than she was saying. "I agree."

"You do?"

"That's why I have that." She pointed to the other side of the kitchen—to a large, cork bulletin board on the wall. Clay walked over to see it better. It was covered with pictures, mementos. Quotes.

"I've lived in fourteen states so far," she said. "And I try to keep in touch with at least one person from every place I've been."

"'Love is the only gold,'" he read from one of the quotes at the top.

"Tennyson. Alfred, Lord Tennyson."

"Oh yeah. Al. He's great."

"I collect famous quotes, in case you didn't notice."

Clay read another. "'We make a living by what we get. We make a life by what we give.'"

She smiled. "Winston Churchill."

"What's this under the quote? This list?"

"It's all the things I've done to try to live that way."

Clay leaned closer, reading.

1. Let cars merge onto the highway.
2. Carry someone's groceries.

3. Pay for a soldier's meal.
4. Pay someone's toll behind me.
5. Give up the parking space.
6. Give away my coupons.
7. Forgive.
8. Tell someone they're pretty.

The list went on. His eyes roamed the rest of the bulletin board. It was delightful and disorganized, worthy but messy. It was like he was staring right into what made her tick.

He nudged a drawing of a rainbow so it was straight.

"Hands off the rainbow," she said.

He returned to the fridge.

"The first time I read that quote by Tennyson, I was at a high school football game. Home game. Our team was the Fighting Quakers."

Clay laughed. "Fighting Quakers. You're serious."

"We had a Quaker for a mascot and everything. Red and black were the school colors. I played French horn in the marching band. Stood right behind Jeff Furbay, who, for the record, I had a major crush on. The game was boring. Not even close. So I read. Did homework. It was third quarter. Two minutes left. Snow was starting to fall. I was sipping hot chocolate with tiny marshmallows." She paused and lifted her mug in a *cheers* motion. "And then I read that."

Clay paused, turned to look at her. "And?"

"And what?"

"That's it?"

"Yeah. That's the story behind the quote. You said you liked stories." She grinned; then her eyes drifted to the jar on the counter. "When the jar is full, I know I have enough."

"For what?"

"To get far enough away if I need to. Make a fresh start. Go where the wind takes me. Follow the warm fuzzies."

Clay returned to studying the back of the fridge. "Life isn't just warm fuzzies."

"It isn't just rules either, religioso."

Clay peeked out from behind the fridge. That was funny.

"And besides, it's how I ended up here. I hit empty on County Line Road."

Was this girl for real? "You're kidding me. You just packed your car full of everything you owned and started driving until you ran out of gas?"

At that moment the breeze rippled her blouse, then caught her hair, lifting it up and out. It seemed like she could float away right there in front of him, tail to the wind. The whole image flew in the face of the measured preciseness to which he clung so tightly. So . . . religiously.

She was watching him as he climbed out of his thoughts. "Now that's a story," he said.

"Since we're into stories . . . ," Amber said, waving her cast. "My last boyfriend didn't want me to wear nail polish. I did."

"So he broke your hand?"

"He didn't mean to. But he did." For the first time, she

wasn't looking into the apartment but staring away, out into the darkening sky. "Once was enough for me."

"No nail polish." Clay tried to wrap his mind around it.

"Yeah," she said, her playful tone back. "Sounds like something you'd come up with."

"Depends on the color."

"It was clear."

He laughed. They both did. Then they slowly settled, the laughter dying, but it seemed neither wanted it to.

"Anyway, he was nothing like you." She shadowboxed the air with her free hand. "My one and only fight. I lost."

"No. He did. He lost."

Her hand dropped to her side. She looked like she was about to cry, the kind of cry that comes from a deep compliment.

Clay cleared his throat. He didn't want her to cry. "Well, I better get to this." He squatted behind the fridge and for the first time noticed the wires. They were dangling from the back like they'd been yanked out. He moved his head a little to look at Amber again. She blinked innocently. He returned to behind the fridge, where he couldn't suppress a smile for a good five minutes.

Over the next week, the faucet handle on her bathtub mysteriously lost a screw. Then she blew a fuse, twice. A panel from the wood floor inexplicably popped up. Her window got jammed. And then, on Saturday, the screen door fell off.

Though he'd climbed the stairs a dozen times, this time

his feet felt heavy as he looked at the screen door leaning against the doorframe. He knew she was just inside. Waiting for him.

Clay got to the top and there she was, smiling as iridescently as sunlight bouncing off ocean water.

He set his toolbox on the stoop. "You're wearing me down, woman."

Amber lifted her hand. The cast was gone.

"Hey!"

"All better."

He looked at the screen, surveyed the situation, then returned his attention to her. "How did the door get off its hinges?"

"Why haven't you asked me out yet?"

He kept his gaze on her. "Doors don't just fall off their hinges."

She stepped closer to him. And he stepped closer too—there wasn't a door in the world he wouldn't open for this girl at this moment.

Clay looked down at their feet. They stood on either side of the threshold, the toes of their shoes just inches apart.

"Hint, hint," she whispered.

He could feel her breath—cinnamon. His chest rose and fell and there was no stopping it. He didn't even try. He didn't want to try to stop any of it.

He nudged his feet one inch closer to hers. She did the same. She was so close, looking up into his eyes, her brown hair falling away from her face, her arms clasped behind her back, her eyes reflecting more light than the sun was providing.

"If I do ask you out, will you stop breaking things?"

Amber nodded vaguely, not completely admitting to her evil deeds.

It all felt so right. And so out of control. The words of those who loved him rushed to his thoughts. He could hear them practically chanting in the air. But crashing into the enthusiasm were all the hateful words he'd heard his parents scream at each other. On an October night, two days before Halloween, they'd wished each other dead.

It wouldn't be until years later, but a woman would one day say those exact words to him.

And right in front of him was this beautiful girl, wavy hair trickling down her back like a waterfall. He nudged his shoe once more. She came closer too. When was the last time he felt so breathless?

"My rules," he said quietly. "My way."

She nodded sincerely. "Okay, stress boy. Okay."

CHAPTER 9

IT WAS A LONG DEBATE with Mr. Joe, but after several attempts at dressing safe *and* sexy, Amber decided to just go with safe. Stress boy had enough on his mind without having to deal with her thighs. Which, she thought, were a nice blend of strength and tone. But that was neither here nor there.

The weird thing about it all was that she didn't have to worry. She was pretty sure she could show up in a T-shirt and sweats and he'd be fine with it. In the end, she threw on a simple cotton dress and a jacket—an old standby that had gotten her through lots of different circumstances: job interviews, car breakdowns, slow dances . . .

Clay came to the door and got her, as she suspected he

would. This wasn't the kind of guy who was going to honk his horn and wait at the bottom of the stairs. He opened the door to his old pickup, which had a lot of charm to it, she had to admit. It rumbled and purred like Mr. Joe when he was hungry.

But what happened next, she never saw coming. How could *anyone* see it coming? Sure, she'd tried not to get her hopes up about this being an overly romantic date. The guy seemed to have aversion to romance. She thought he might choose something really docile, like a petting zoo. Or a G-rated movie. Possibly kayaking—that way he could keep a good paddle's distance away from her. But *this*?

He did have a nice sense of humor. Maybe it was a joke. Amber gazed up at the sign. "You're kidding, right?"

Clay checked his watch. "We're right on time."

"You're not joking, are you?"

He only smiled and opened the door of the Agape Counseling Center for her.

Agape? She didn't know how to pronounce it, much less what it meant.

Inside, there was a small waiting room with nobody waiting. And then they were directed to Dr. Stuart's office.

"Come in, please. Sit down." He gestured broadly to the two chairs in front of his stately, methodically organized desk. Amber noticed Clay admiring it. Several framed diplomas lined the walls. Bookshelves squeezed to specification sat behind him. A leathery, spotted scalp divided two white tufts of hair, one above each of his temples. His round body was stuffed into a maroon sweater vest and dark slacks. His expensive leather chair squeaked with the tiniest movement, so he folded his hands on his desk, made a steeple with his fingers, and stretched a joyless smile across his paunchy face. She'd been wrong before about people, but the way he blinked at them made her feel like he had a superiority complex. Or a tic.

On his desk sat a pile of books. Amber picked one up because it was offered there like a bowl of chocolate candy. *Red, Yellow, Green—Your Guide to Marriage Compatibility.* Unbelievably, it had a traffic light on the cover. And it looked like a workbook.

"Clay, Amber, this is truly such a wise choice," Dr. Stuart began. "Very mature. Discerning. So first, let me simply affirm your prudent decision to take solemnly the idea of holy matrimony." He looked at them both. "Have you set a date yet?"

Amber kept staring straight forward, focused on the little ceramic church sitting on the corner of the desk, wishing she could crawl right inside it.

"Hm?" Dr. Stuart nudged. "How long have you been engaged?"

"We're not," Clay said. "We just met."

Amber shifted her eyes to the counselor, who, not surprisingly, looked surprised. But he proceeded to the workbook and all the steps they were going to need to take in order to assure themselves a solid, functioning, long-term marriage.

"And happy?" Amber asked.

"What?" Dr. Stuart said, looking up from the book.

"Is happiness guaranteed? You know, if we pass the traffic-light test here."

Dr. Stuart chuckled. "Well, of course, Amber. What could be unhappy about everyone getting along?"

Amber took her book and stood. "Well, thank you. Truly. Clay has never met a bullet point he didn't like, so I'm sure one of us will be fantastically intrigued by this process." She shook the counselor's hand way more fiercely than she intended. "Also, congratulations on being such a vital part of our first date."

Dr. Stuart's eyes shifted to Clay's. "First date?"

"It seemed safe," Clay replied.

And just like that, the rage that was building slid right out of Amber's heart. He wasn't a jerk. Quite the opposite, in fact. He was . . . scared.

"Yes, well," the counselor said, a bit flustered as he eyed Clay. "Maybe end it with a stroll in the park? Hm?"

Nearby was Tuscora Park. They walked together a little while. It seemed absurd, counseling plus a walk. But soon enough, to Amber's surprise, an easiness set in between them. The wind was getting cooler as each autumn day passed, but the leaves were still vibrant and gorgeous. She'd always been intrigued by the seasons, what they meant, all the symbolism they carried and the hope of each one arriving year after year. But autumn . . . There was nothing like the burst of color the leaves displayed, right before they died on the cold ground below them. It was such a true look at life. Bright colors. Then death. Over and over again.

"Come on," Clay said gently. "Let's go sit on the swings."

She'd almost forgotten he was there, he was so quiet. They each sat on a thick leather strap. His swing kept perfectly still. Hers rocked back and forth.

"So," he said, "let's get started." He opened his book to page 1. She did too, mostly out of politeness and curiosity. But she kept getting distracted by the delighted squeals of children on the playground, running and playing, laughing at the simple fun of being chased.

The simple fun of being chased. She glanced at Clay, busy studying the book, his finger tracing the words as he read. It didn't seem like she was being chased. It seemed like she was being . . . test-driven.

Amber sighed, turning to the second page. What had she expected to happen today? It was stress boy, after all. How could she have had any fantasies that this was going to go at all normally? She'd had her hopes set on spicy marinara. He was stewed tomatoes. She wanted artichokes. He was canned peas. Was she really that surprised?

Amber watched him concentrate and her heart melted a little. This was important to him.

So she should give it a try anyway. She wasn't a fan of canned peas, but maybe she was missing something she didn't know about.

She flipped to page 14. "Do you regularly use or abuse drugs or alcohol?"

Clay looked up. "Not since college. But I think we're supposed to go in order."

"Just so you know, this is what some might call rushing it."
He was back to reading again. "Do you have any pet peeves?"

But Amber was back to looking at the leaves. The wind had kicked up, and burgundy, orange, and yellow leaves rose into the air. The sky looked large and deep today, and she watched the leaves drift against the wind, floating slowly down like they were being cradled by invisible hands.

"Do you have any pet peeves?"

"Just one." A particularly beautiful leaf landed at her feet and she bent over to pick it up, twirling it between her fingers. "Leaves are cool. They start out as little buds. And then, like literally overnight, there they are." She rubbed the leaf against her cheek. "You know, I think that's like us. We come out of the womb, green as all get-out. Clinging to the branch that holds us. Perched in a high and safe place. We watch the world, and then we become useful in some way, like providing shade. But that's not good enough. We want to kind of get down there, you know? Be with all that's there, below us. But it's scary. I mean, we've clung high and safe for a long time. But we know . . . we know if we just let go, we're going to get to see the most amazing things. Then our time comes. And we can feel ourselves changing. At the moment we let go, we're at our most drop-dead gorgeous. We're bursts of color that make people stop and stare. So we take a magical flight down, caught by the wind—at its mercy, really. We don't know where we'll land. And sometimes we don't get to land where we want. But sometimes, if we're lucky," she said, looking at the leaf in her hand, "we get to be cherished."

"Would you pay over four dollars for a cup of coffee?" Clay had a pencil out now, checking off boxes.

"Once you hit the ground, you dry up and die, but that's not the most interesting part of the story."

Clay glanced at her as though he'd just noticed she was talking. "Four bucks for a cup of coffee?"

"No way."

He smiled in relief, not noticing that she wasn't in any way smiling back.

Her eyes narrowed and she folded her arms. "But I'd pay eight dollars for anything with chocolate in it."

Well, that remark landed them at the financial planner's office the next day. Same tidy desk. Different fellow. This guy was more uptight than Clay, which was saying a lot. His name was Fred. His personality was as heavily starched as his shirt.

Fred was looking over a binder that Clay brought in and Clay was leaning forward, hanging on his every word. Amber was desperately needing a four-dollar cup of coffee.

"Hmm," Fred said, finally closing the binder. "You'll need more than that. Much more."

Clay nodded thoughtfully.

Fred continued. "That's why the current loophole in the tax liability law makes our new multigenerational mutual fund package so attractive. In twenty years, the cost of a college education is expected to be as much as eight times its existing rate. If you care about . . ."

She didn't, and somewhere between 401(k)s and life

insurance adjustments, she slipped into a coma. An hour later, loaded down with pamphlets and flowcharts, they took a walk downtown. It was a good thing. She needed the air.

Clay had his free hand stuffed in his pocket. Quiet settled between them once again, but it didn't seem uncomfortable. And that was the mystery of Clay Walsh.

"What's wrong with planning ahead?" he asked her finally.

It deserved a snarky reply, but it was a genuine question and he had a genuine heart and all this absurdity somehow made sense to him. So instead she said, "Next question."

"Um, okay." He took his workbook and opened it to where he'd bookmarked it. "How many children would you like to have?"

She could've answered, but a beautiful green dress—the color of pine trees in the Northwest—caught her attention in the window of a quaint dress shop. It looked silky and had gorgeous detail. A thick band crossed over one shoulder. She didn't know where she'd wear such a dress, but it would be fun to have it in her closet. Just in case things transpired from financial planning to the grand ball at the palace. Of course, if not, she wasn't opposed to wearing it to dance around her apartment. Mr. Joe would appreciate it.

"What's wrong?" Clay asked, looking up.

"Isn't that gorgeous?"

Clay's gaze shifted to the dress, his eyes bloodshot from reading. He regarded it for a moment, then shrugged. "Overpriced. Okay, what experience do you have raising children?"

"What are children?"

Well, that landed her at David and Lisa's house, where she was watched meticulously by the three of them as she diced steamed carrots into squares tiny enough to feed a snail.

Lisa asked the obvious question. "Is this necessary?"

"Smaller pieces," David said. "Her molars aren't all the way in yet."

"No coaching," Clay said.

Lisa shook her head and came to sit by Amber. "I am so sorry."

"It's fine. This is good practice for when I'm old and decrepit and can't put my dentures in anymore."

Lisa laughed and hugged her.

"He's trying to scare me off," Amber whispered.

"He's so good at that," Lisa said.

"So," Clay said, "do the two of you think Amber and I are a good match?"

Amber kept feeding Cosie.

Lisa groaned. "Clay. Please. You understand that this is the kind of conversation you have in the corner of a room when the said individual is not listening."

"We have nothing to hide from each other."

"We've got the workbooks to prove it," Amber said.

"Laugh it up. But the fact is, we're learning things about each other. Important things."

"He now knows," Amber said, "that I'm allergic to wool. So he'd never buy me a wool coat. Just for an example."

Lisa sighed. "Yes, because nothing decimates a marriage like wool."

Clay frowned. "I'm being serious. Do you think we're a good match?"

Suddenly Cosie's hands shot up in the air and she clapped excitedly. Everyone laughed. Amber could only smile at Clay's shocked look, but as his gaze drifted to her, he smiled back.

David grabbed his arm. "I'm taking Clay outside."

♥

"Here," David said, handing him an iced tea. "I'm afraid to give you anything stronger at this point. You're already talking too much."

Clay shrugged and took the glass, looking out at the small yard they had set up, everything revolving around Cosie. Playhouse. Play garden tools. Balls. Scooters. It seemed like Happy Land. "I know. You think I'm crazy."

David stepped up next to him, looking out at the yard too. "Clay, there's nothing wrong with getting to know one another. But there's kind of a flow to it, you know? You find out what she likes to eat. Then you find out she's a night owl. Then you find out she has a weird addiction to Stevie Nicks music. It progresses from there. I mean, this book and these questions . . . what is that?"

Clay didn't look at him. "What's your question?"

"Why are you pushing her like that?"

Clay stared at his drink. The truth was, maybe he had no idea how to get to know a woman in a safe way. He had a wretched history to prove that point. These talks always came way later. Usually too late.

David softened his tone. "You really do like her, man. I've seen a lot of women around you. We've been friends for a long time. There's pre- and there's post-, and we won't go into pre-, but you've never had trouble getting a woman's attention in any era of your life." He held up his hands as Clay started to protest. "I know, I know. Some have claimed you've strung them along, when all you were trying to do was preserve your theory. They never really got you, anyway."

"I never meant to hurt anybody."

"I get it, man. And over the last nine years, I haven't really seen anyone who was good for you anyway."

"I'm better off on my own."

"But you like her."

"She's . . ."

"Tempting?"

"Yeah."

David laughed. "Glad to hear it."

Laughter spilled out from inside the house. Through the glass door, they watched Lisa and Amber in the living room, playing with Cosie.

"What's holding you back, bro?"

Clay didn't have an answer really. At least not one that anybody wanted to hear. David turned toward the yard, but Clay couldn't keep from watching Amber.

"We set a date," David said, taking a sip of his tea.

Clay smiled, toasted him.

"Next month."

"That was fast."

"Nothing fancy. Lisa wants to keep it small. Have it here in the backyard. Just a few friends coming in . . ."

"Nice."

". . . like Kelly."

The air caught in Clay's throat as if it'd grown a hook and pierced his tonsil. "*Like* Kelly? Or Kelly?"

David studied the ice in his glass. "Flying in from Phoenix. By herself. She just got separated from her husband." He gestured as he tried to explain. "He had a thing. Some girl from his office. They're trying to work it out."

Clay let out a steady breath. He'd thought she was happy. Maybe that was just hopefulness.

"I'm sorry, man. Lisa had to invite her. You know that." He clinked his tea glass against Clay's. "Still my best man?"

Clay smiled and nodded even as a sickening chill ran down his body.

♥

"You're a natural," Lisa said as Amber held Cosie in her lap. She flipped another flash card. "She always gets hung up on one times two."

"So I passed?" Amber grinned.

Lisa set the flash cards aside, then put her elbow on her knee and her chin in her hand. "Are you honestly this desperate?"

"How long have you known him?"

"Since college. He dated one of my friends for a while, the two of them set me and David up, and here we are."

"What was Clay like . . . back then?"

"A *lot* more fun." She leaned over and brushed the hair out of Cosie's eyes. "Everybody loved him. He had this wild kind of energy, out of control but not over the top. I know— you wouldn't know it now."

Amber glanced out the window. Clay and David were still talking.

"He used to cohost this stupid—and I do mean stupid— campus cable show with another friend of ours. It really started out as a joke our sophomore year, but it got bigger and bigger. It was crazy. They actually traveled with that thing. Then hosting spring break parties, producing DVDs . . . He didn't tell you?"

"No."

"Well, they raked it in. Built this . . . What would you call it? It was like a machine. Everything was about to take off and explode. Clay had all kinds of offers. New York. Chicago. Advertising dollars were almost beyond comprehension. And then . . ."

Amber waited. Lisa was lost in a memory, her eyes distant.

"Then what?" Amber asked finally.

Lisa blew out a hard breath. "He said no. To it all. To everything. Shut down the whole business. Made a bunch of bizarre apologies. Gave away what was left of his money." She looked out the window at the two men. "And he's not been the same since."

They both looked down and saw that Cosie had fallen

asleep, breathing the deep breaths of a child who had nothing to worry about. Amber kissed her forehead and handed her to Lisa, who whispered, "I'll be right back."

Amber leaned into the couch, wondering who Clay had been. Wondering who he had become. And wondering what happened in between. Even when he smiled, there was a certain sadness in his eyes. It never seemed to leave. No matter how blue they glowed against the daylight, there was a hovering darkness right behind them, dimming the sparkle that surely would've been there otherwise.

An hour later, he walked her up to the stoop of her apartment.

At the top of the stairs, she tapped her workbook. "You got awful quiet. Aren't you going to ask me any more questions?"

"Nothing good happens after eleven."

She laughed, shaking her head. "Most people at least give it till midnight."

He stepped back, didn't say anything.

"Okay. Well, thanks for the . . . adventure." She unlocked the door and started to step inside.

"Hey, Amber?"

She turned, startled to find him so close. They were almost touching. She held her breath, hoping they might.

"What?" She looked up at him, into his eyes. He blinked slowly like he was taking every part of her in.

"Would you please do us both a favor and decide what we do next time?"

She smiled. "Next time?"

And then he stepped away, that beautiful, lost, soulful gaze finding his shoes again.

"Good night, stress boy."

"Good night, pretty girl."

♥

Clay sat alone in the diner, reading his book, making notes. It was the only twenty-four-hour diner in town. Tonight, at almost 1 a.m., it was mostly empty. A couple of truckers hovered over their chicken-fried steaks at the counter and a small table of college kids huddled in the corner. He'd been here a time or ten, in his younger days.

Through the front door came a guy, his arms laced around a girl's midriff. Clay sighed, wishing he could erase the memories that seemed to be triggered by the smallest of things. But they were always right on his doorstep.

"Clay Walsh? Is that you?"

Clay looked up. "Betty?"

She grinned widely, revealing that she'd gotten her teeth fixed. Last time he saw her, she'd been missing two. It was hard to believe she still worked here. When this was his old haunt, she'd seemed like she was a hundred years old, always with a bend in her back and a stain on her shirt.

She wiped her hands on the white apron that hung off her like a surrender flag. Her hair was sprayed and combed back, as stable as concrete if a strong wind hit.

"My, my! Look at you! What's missing here?" She gave

him a wink. "I know. A table full of girls smothering you like a glob of gravy."

Betty always had a way of saying things. He smiled at her. "Funny."

"How long has it been?"

"At least nine years."

"Whatcha doing here sitting all by yourself at this time of night?"

"Thinking."

"More people should try that out."

"Betty, can I ask you something?"

"Sure. Let me just . . ." She slid into the booth, grabbing the table with two unsteady hands. "Oh, wow. It feels good to get off my feet. How's your aunt Zella doing?"

"Still kicking my butt."

"Nice to hear. Heard you were holding down the fort at the antique shop. Just a rumor?"

"No, it's true."

"Maybe it's just me, but the Clay I knew didn't seem like the antique-shop kind of guy." She shrugged. "I need to bring some things by. I got a lot of clutter that sits around, not being useful for anything except a place for dust to settle. I probably shoulda downsized years ago." Her eyes held a wistful peace, as if selling her belongings was the beginning of untethering herself from the earth. "So what'd you wanna ask me? Whether or not the Buckeyes are going to embarrass themselves again this year?"

"O-h . . ."

"... i-o."

Clay played with the edges of his workbook. "It's kind of personal."

"Honey, when you get to the place where you can't laugh without peeing yourself, there's not too much that's off the board anymore. Know what I mean?"

"Not yet, but okay," Clay laughed. "I wondered ... why you're not married."

Betty blinked. The question took her by surprise, he could tell.

"I mean, isn't it okay to be alone? What's wrong with that? People think you're crazy, but there's some benefit to it, isn't there?"

"I suppose there is. I can go do what I want. Go buy what I want. Don't have to answer to nobody but myself."

"Do you get lonely?"

"Sure. But heck, trust me when I say I seen plenty of loneliness in the eyes of people who aren't alone, sittin' right by each other, close enough to touch, but might as well be the Grand Canyon between 'em. You can eat every meal of every day together and be lonely."

"My thoughts exactly. Is that why you never married?"

Her old, rugged face turned plaintive for a moment. Her thoughts drifted between them like silent sailboats through dark waters.

"What makes you think I never got married?"

"I ... I just assumed. I mean, you're here every single day. You never wore a wedding ring."

"I was married."

"Really?"

"Yep. His name was Earl."

"Tell me," Clay said, leaning forward.

"Well, we got married when we was seventeen years old. He died at twenty-five in the war."

Clay leaned back. That wasn't what he expected. "Gosh, Betty. I'm sorry."

"Don't be sorry. It was the best eight years of my life."

"But . . . you've lived all this time, never remarried?"

"Why would I do that? He was the one and only for me. There would never be nobody else." Betty looked at her hand. "Never even had a wedding band. Couldn't afford it when we got married. Planned on getting one, when we had some money." She chuckled at a memory. "Our first anniversary we was so poor that we could only buy us a candy bar. We split it right in half and ate it by the fire. Every January 20, I go get me a candy bar in honor of Earl. Eat half of it." She grinned and patted her belly. "Then I eat the other half for good measure. No need lettin' a candy bar go to waste."

Clay touched her hand. "It sounds like an amazing love story."

"The question is, why don't you got yourself a pretty lady by your side? Heaven knows you had enough of them linin' up to get your attention."

Clay's face warmed. "Well, I'm working on it."

Betty glanced down at his workbook. "Like homework or something?"

"Something like that."

"You're gonna need a bigger book than that to understand a woman, Clay Walsh."

"Maybe I'm trying to figure out me."

"What's there to figure out? Earl and I knew each other three weeks when we got hitched."

Clay laughed. "I'm going to need more than three weeks. She kind of . . . terrifies me."

Betty gave a knowing smile. "I see. It's that kind of thing."

"Yeah. Guess it is."

"You know, marriage is kind of like a tea bag. You don't know how strong it really is till you get it in some boiling water."

"A tea bag, huh?" He thought of all the tea Aunt Zella had sent him over the years.

"And the water don't boil till you're over the heat, and the heat don't come till you say, 'I do.'"

"I just want to make sure she's right for me, and . . . well, maybe I want to make more sure I'm right for her."

Betty nodded gently. "You know, Clay, I always knew it about you."

"Knew what?"

"Knew you were a better man than the one that came to this diner at all hours of the night. I said a prayer for you once."

"You prayed for me?" Clay was deeply touched. He only thought of Betty as the lady who kept the food coming. He was astonished that she would do such a thing for him.

Astonished that she would see something in him other than the jerk he was. "What did you pray?"

"That you'd see you were worth more than you thought." She slid out of the booth and stood up again with as much effort as when she sat down. "What can I get ya? Piece of pie? We got peach tonight."

"No thanks, Betty. Coffee's fine."

"Coffee it is. I'll bring it black because it looks like you're going to need something strong enough to slap some sense into ya."

"I can always use a good slapping."

"Tease. All right, I'll get you your fries and gravy too."

Betty walked off and Clay watched her go behind the counter. He smiled at the thought of her husband, that kind of love, the kind that carried on even after death. Then he took his paper place mat and flipped it over, pulled his pencil out of his book, and started writing.

CHAPTER 10

"'WHAT PERCENTAGE of your annual income is appropriate to spend on a pet?'" Trish looked up and fanned herself. "I can see how he's got you all worked up."

Amber only shrugged, assembling a floral arrangement for a woman's eightieth birthday party. She thought it should be bright.

"Let me see that," Carol said, grabbing the workbook and flipping through it.

"Not all the questions are like that," Amber said.

Carol slipped on her glasses to read. "'Do you believe in the death penalty?'"

Trish slipped into a low, sultry voice and moved her shoulders like a bad Marilyn Monroe impersonator. "Oh . . . yes . . . mmmm . . . death penalty."

Amber shot her a look.

"Fine. I'll stop. But no thanks. Truly. I gotta have a real man," Trish said.

"Clay is a real man."

"I've been around the block, ladies. I haven't found one yet that does more for me than a good piece of chocolate." Carol slid the workbook back to Amber. "But I'm still looking."

"He's reliable. Handy." Even as the words came out of her mouth, Amber winced.

Trish nodded, unimpressed. "My vacuum is also very reliable."

"And I can give you the name of my handyman, Ronald," Carol added, "if that's what you're looking for."

There was a pause and Amber just looked down. She hated the things they were saying about Clay, how they mocked him. How much of this had he endured over the last nine years?

Carol said, "Trish, go get me another package of pins, would you?" Trish disappeared to the back and Carol scooted toward her. "Amber, sweetie. Don't you think this might be a ploy? Like a 'hard-to-get' deal? This isn't for real, is it?" She pointed to the workbook. "I mean, on a first date? A marriage counselor?"

Amber sighed, looking away. "I know. He's quirky."

"There's quirky, and then above that there's peculiar, then odd, then Clay."

"You don't know him like I do."

"What do you really know about him, huh? He can fix

things. So could Ted Bundy." Carol looked at her, sighed. "You really like this guy?"

"I . . . I don't know yet. I'm getting there. I mean, so far what I've been looking for in men hasn't worked out so well. It's kind of refreshing to know a well-mannered guy."

Carol pushed her playfully. "What do I know, right? Shoot, I married Cupcake, so don't listen to me!"

"We've got another date this Saturday," Amber said.

Trish came back in. "Let me guess. To the DMV to test how well you parallel park?"

Amber smiled. No . . . something a little more romantic than that.

The week crawled by, but Saturday finally arrived. Clay was right on time at noon, as she expected him to be. She stood behind the screen door and watched him look down at the shoe box sitting on the stoop.

He picked it up and read what she had written on top. "'Choose.'" He glanced at her. "Ultimatums already?"

She laughed. "Inside the box, silly."

He lifted the lid and peeked inside. "Scraps of paper, folded in half. Mysterious. Or we're doing crafts. I'm terrible with glitter."

"Pick just one."

"Okay."

He reached in, pulled one out, opened it, and raised his eyebrows. "The hardware store?"

"Come on! No time to waste!"

The hardware store was just around the corner from the antique store. It took them more time to park than it did to drive there. Clay kept glancing at her like he was dying to know what was going on.

"Aisle three," Amber said as they walked in.

He obeyed, then stood with his hands in his pockets, surveying the aisle. "Axes?"

"Well, you're awfully hard to seduce, so I'm having to take extreme measures."

He gave her a smirk. She liked his smirks.

"I knew you'd be the death of me," he said.

"Come on, pick something. Anything sharp." She posed in front of them like Vanna White.

"You're truly scaring me," he laughed.

"I know. It's kind of fun to watch."

An hour later, after a quick and mysterious stop at the grocery store, they were at Atwood Lake. She'd discovered this beautiful place the day after she arrived, when she was looking for interesting places and things to do. Clay carried two large logs from the truck. Amber pretended to search for twigs, but she wanted to watch him. He was a curious soul, but she thought if she could just observe for a while, in a different environment, maybe she'd find what made him tick.

He dumped the logs by the rustic fire pit, grabbed his brand-spanking-new splitting maul, and started chopping. Amber forgot she was supposed to be pretending to get twigs.

He caught her watching but she couldn't even get herself to look away.

Clay struck a mountain man pose, making her giggle.

She started picking up twigs again, somehow making her way right next to him. "Why don't you let me give that a try," she said.

He stopped midswing. "Seriously?"

"What? You don't think a girl can swing an ax?"

"I don't think a girl who has a cat and a penny jar and antihistamines on hand can swing an ax."

"Cash jar. And I bought those antihistamines just for you. Now, watch and learn." She held the ax high overhead, for effect, and wobbled it a little, just to see what he would do. He looked on edge, braced himself. She laughed and decided she better cool it. He was already a bundle of nerves most of the time. She brought the ax down and split the log right in half.

"Whoa!" Clay looked at her, wide-eyed.

"Come with me," she said. "I also make fire."

With a single piece of flint sparked against the steel rim of the fire pit, the flame caught.

"Sparks are flying." She smiled.

"What's in the bag?" he asked, pointing to the supersecret grocery sack she'd been teasing him with.

She pulled out—with great flair and drama—a bag of marshmallows.

"Perfect," he said.

Amber took a stick and stuck a marshmallow on the end,

handing it to him. She did the same for her stick. Then held it to her mouth like a microphone. "Mr. Walsh, the world wants to know: when are you going to kiss her?"

Like an eager reporter, she pushed the marshmallow into his face. He looked at the ground.

She dipped the marshmallow into the pit and caught it on fire, glowing as orange as a pumpkin.

"No comment?" she asked, the marshmallow now ablaze in front of his face.

"You're incorrigible."

"I know. And thank you. How do you like your marshmallows?"

"Burned to a crisp. You?"

"Melty and warm, smooshed together and enveloped in the arms of the chocolate, all under the safe covering of a graham cracker." She grinned. "Yum."

He laughed, shook his head, and scorched the daylights out of his marshmallow.

Two hours drifted by like fifteen minutes. They did less talking than she expected. But he was more playful than she thought. They swung on the monkey bars at the nearby playground. They walked along the lake, throwing stones. He pointed out all the native trees. They watched the kayakers.

And he never once touched her.

What she wouldn't give for a . . . what? What exactly did she want from him?

"Well," she said after they'd returned to the fire pit and had their share of marshmallows, "we should go."

"Oh?" He looked surprised.

"I've got plans for later. But first we have to go parking. No lake is without the perfect spot for making out in a car." She pointed her finger at him. "And don't tell me for a second you don't know where it is."

He smiled but lost a bit of color in his cheeks.

"I'm kidding. I'm actually taking you to an emotional self-defense class. I believe you'll qualify right away as a black belt." Amber winked and he chuckled, shaking his head at her, his messy hair falling over one eyebrow.

Once in the truck, with the windows rolled down, he drove them north, around the east side of the lake. It was quiet once again. He wasn't much for small talk, which she appreciated. She wasn't either. But even with all the fun they'd managed to have, there was still this massive wall between them. It was like he was untouchable. Or she was. One of them definitely was. Communicable-disease untouchable.

"May I?" She reached for the radio. He nodded.

Amber scanned through the stations. Country? No. Hip-hop? No. A radio preacher?

"'. . . because by one sacrifice he has made perfect forever those who are being made holy.'" Loud and punctuated by a nice Southern accent.

"What about this one? Huh?"

Clay laughed. "Keep going."

She hit heavy metal, Latin, opera, classical, and then . . .

"There is only one thing—and I'm talking only one

thing—*that, without fail, no red-blooded woman alive on this planet or any other can resist. Are you listening?* Indifference."

Amber growled. "Lucky Chucky. Spare me."

Clay looked sideways at her. "I'm sorry. Did you say something?"

She laughed. His sense of humor always caught her by surprise.

"Who are you again?" he continued, eyes on the road once more but a hint of a smile breaking through.

"Oh, you are so hot." She playfully punched him in the arm.

"Yes, I am." He pointed to the radio. "By the way, that man knows what he's talking about."

She groaned again. "Please."

"Zach from Collegedale, what can I do for you?"

"Oh, Zach, please, for the love of all things good, hang up," Amber begged.

"Yeah, um, I'm turning twenty-one next week, and me and all my buds are going to be embarking upon a major bar crawl, so—"

"Get to the point, Zach."

"Yeah, Zach," Amber said, sticking her elbow out the window.

"So if I walk up to some female standing in a group of other females at a club, what's the most effective way to pick up the first female?"

"Hit on her friends. Next caller."

Clay reached for the dial and shut the radio off. "Come on. It's workbook time."

♥

"You really like this book, don't you?" Amber asked. They sat on the bottom stair, right below her apartment window.

Clay didn't know. Maybe he did; maybe he didn't. But he knew that he liked to ask her questions. And he liked to watch her answer them. And maybe, when it came down to it, he could use help in learning how to talk to a woman in a real way. In the old days, he spoke the secret language with little effort—but he did not know the language now.

This was . . . different. And admittedly, he was really bad at it. But he knew if this was going to turn out to be even close to what he hoped for, they were going to have to have some real conversation. He was going to have to broach some tough subjects.

She was busy filling out her workbook when he blurted out, "I know him."

"Who?"

"Lucky Chucky."

Amber laughed like it was a punch line. Clay bit his lip, hoping she would figure out it wasn't. She did. Pretty fast too.

"David does too."

She closed her workbook. "You and David are friends with Lucky Chucky?"

"Brad is his real name."

"Not sure he deserves a real name, but okay." She shook her head. "I'm honestly not making the connection."

"When I didn't want to play frat boy anymore, he and

David were the only ones that stuck around. Everybody else walked."

"I see. Loyalty is big to you."

"He's a victim."

"Please." Amber rolled her eyes.

"Hear me out."

"All right," she said, propping her chin up with her hand.

Clay tried to think how to explain it. "It's like this. He's the kind of guy that has always gotten away with everything, but only because people let him. Is that his fault? He's a product of the system."

"That's ridiculous."

"Just like I used to be."

"Before you 'saw the light'?"

"Became a 'religioso.'"

She laughed like it was all too absurd to imagine. "But you were never like that."

He could do nothing but try not to let the regret spill onto his lap.

She looked him over. "No. You were never . . . Anyway. Lucky Chucky. If I have to say his name one more time, I'm going to gag."

"You're the one that turned the radio on, not me."

She picked up her workbook and flipped the page. "'Do you like each other's friends?' Definitely yellow light. And I'm being kind because I want to say red light."

Clay flipped to the page, trying to find where she was reading. She was always jumping all over the place.

"Speaking of friends, you're meeting my family tonight."

"What?"

"I know. It's all moving very fast. Page 19 has the questions to prepare you."

"Your family? Here?"

She nudged him. "Don't worry. Only one of them bites, and I'm almost certain she's had her rabies shot." She stood and walked up the stairs to the apartment, then called back, "You need to change into something more . . . less . . . Think date."

Clay looked down at his sweatshirt. "But I—"

"You'll figure it out. I'll see you at seven."

Amber closed the door and Clay closed his workbook. He trotted to his truck, wondering about whom he would meet tonight, wondering what shirt qualified, wondering how in the world he was ever going to tell her what he used to be.

At home, in front of the mirror, as he buttoned up his shirt and his resolve, he knew he would have to tell her soon. But how? And how could he explain Brad? Everyone wanted to hate him. Blame him. But Brad was a product of a culture that revered him. He'd been swallowed up by it just like everyone else.

Of course, Brad would never agree to this theory. Clay knew that for certain. He'd talked to him about it on several occasions. There was one night in particular, out on the back deck of a restaurant, when Clay thought he might've had a breakthrough. Brad had fallen hard for a girl. He thought it might be true love. But Clay just couldn't get through to him.

He still couldn't. But he wouldn't stop trying. The guilt of taking Brad with him down his own dark spiral, back in the day when Brad would've followed Clay off a cliff, kept Brad on speed dial in Clay's heart.

It was in the basement of a wild house party that Clay had first suggested to Brad the idea of making DVDs. And this idea had come to him while he was licking his own wounds, knee-deep in the disintegration of a relationship that had ended by his own hands, by his own sin. The soaring success of their show planted the first seeds of a harvest that would reap nothing but destruction.

Clay picked up the phone and dialed.

"Hello?"

"Hey, Brad, it's me."

"Clay? Hey, man! What are you doing?"

"Just wanted to see how things are going out there for you."

"I've only made it halfway through the hot blondes, but by next Saturday I think I'm going to be able to start on the brunettes. Of course, there are always the half-hot blondes, which I'm not opposed to if they've got good bodies."

Clay clutched the phone, listened to himself breathe.

"Look, man," Brad said, "it's not the same without you guys. Not at all. Who am I going to beat in basketball?"

Clay laughed. "Trust me. My game is slipping by the hour."

"It's because you don't have sex, Clay. Sex makes even the smallest man leap tall buildings in a single bound."

Clay blew out a tense sigh. He wondered if he had anything left with Brad. Anything in common anymore. But he couldn't give up. He'd try to sow better seeds every chance he got. Maybe one day, as they had for him, they'd take root. It just didn't seem like it was going to be today.

"Well, listen, I better—"

"Wait, man. Sorry," Brad said. "I just like seeing you sweat, but I can't even see you, so it's lost its fun. What are you doing? What are you up to?"

Clay looked down at himself. "Currently, I'm trying to pick out a shirt."

"Man, things are really falling apart there. First you can't pick out a woman. Now you can't pick out a shirt."

"I can't pick out a shirt . . . for a woman."

Silence. Clay grinned. It wasn't often he could make Brad speechless.

"You have a . . . ?"

"Date."

Clay tensed, expecting Brad's crass advice to roll out. But instead, there was more silence, then, "Go with white."

"White?"

"Yeah. White button-up. Jeans. Irresistible to women. White does something to women. That whole purity thing. And in your case, also signals they're dealing with the priesthood."

"Okay then. White."

In the background, two giggly girls were shouting Brad's name.

"I gotta—"

"I know. I just wanted to check up on you. Make sure you were staying in trouble. Listened to you today on the radio."

"You . . . did?"

"I'll see you soon. David's wedding, right?"

"Funeral. But yes, I'll see you then. The bachelor party should be fun."

Clay hung up and turned toward his closet. He reached for a white shirt, but just as quickly his hand retreated. White . . .

Amber touched his shoulder as they took seats around a high-top table at the Brewhouse. "Nice job on the shirt. I like it. Black looks good on you."

"Brings out the dark cloud hanging over his head," Carol whispered to Trish.

Apparently they all worked together. Carol was the owner. Trish was the freeloader. Amber had introduced them ten minutes ago and already this was starting. He knew one thing about himself these days: he rarely made a good first impression.

Amber shot Carol a look.

Trish's lips were in a tight smile. "Amber tells us you're reliable."

Amber lifted her hands innocently. "You are. I said more things too."

"And handy," Carol added.

Amber sighed, her eyes all of a sudden kind of sorrowful.

"Your family is awesome." He winked at her but at the

same time felt a twinge of sadness, realizing what a gypsy kind of life she must've lived, bouncing from place to place, finding family in floral shops or wherever she could. At least he had Aunt Zella.

"So, Clay," Trish said, "what do you do for fun?"

"Workbooks." Carol flashed the shortest smile in recorded history.

Then they looked at him like they were waiting for a serious answer. "Well, I really enjoy woodworking and restoring antiques. This guy the other day brought in an old children's rocker. It was his brother's, and they were in this tent and . . ." Their eyes were glazing over. He really *was* boring. "I also like fixing appliances that mysteriously break."

Amber laughed.

"You two are soooo weird," Trish said. She grabbed Amber's arm. "Come on. Let's get a refill on drinks."

Clay's heart swelled with apprehension as they left, because Carol looked like she might lean over and eat him alive.

"What?" he finally asked.

"I know who you are," she said, her eyes narrowing.

Clay looked down. How could she possibly know that?

"What are your intentions here?" she asked.

"I don't have any."

"Wrong answer."

"Who I was," Clay said, but he barely heard himself say it, "it's not who I am."

The crowd noise filled the pause between them, but it still felt like a heavy silence.

"She is one sweet girl, and you better have intentions."

"My intentions are good."

"Yeah? Well, your good intentions might end up shattering her heart." She took a long drink, then continued. "You're as quirky as a veggie burger, I'll give you that. I've been married three times plus an annulment. I married a guy named Cupcake. So I get quirky. I get the appeal. I really do. It's fun for a while. Something different. You think to yourself, *This guy isn't like the rest.* But the truth is, they're all alike. You're all alike."

Clay shook his head.

"She likes you. You get that, right?"

He glanced over to Amber at the bar, laughing with Trish.

"So help me, if you break her heart, I am coming after you and bringing Cupcake with me. That girl has had enough in her life. She doesn't need another disappointment."

Clay met Carol's eyes. "I'm doing right by her."

"Sometimes doing right is more than not doing wrong."

Amber and Trish returned. Amber slid next to him and Trish got Carol engaged in a conversation about two guys in the corner, one of whom was apparently asking about Carol.

Amber tapped his arm. "Everything okay?"

"Fine." Clay glanced at Trish and Carol. "But definitely yellow."

CHAPTER 11

AFTER DRINKS, he didn't want to say good night. It was a little chilly for a walk, but Clay liked walks. He'd learned how much he liked them after his life had taken such a dramatic turn. With few friends left and a lot of questions to answer for himself, he'd started walking. Sometimes for two or three hours, with nowhere to go, really. He'd follow train tracks and running tracks. Bike paths. Wilderness. Lakeshores. And the more he walked, with no music and nothing but air and space, the more he began feeling that tug on his heart, the inexplicable whisper that said so much without uttering a single word. It was most often, aside from his workroom in the back of the antique shop, where he found peace.

And now, with Amber beside him, as darkness settled over

their town, it was exactly where he wanted to be. And who he wanted with him. She was such a marvel to watch, dancing to no music, singing off-key, struck by the way a star twinkled. Over the past nine years, he'd been looking into himself so much that he'd rarely looked up and out. He didn't notice the trees changing or the blazing spray of color at dusk.

Or in this case, how the streetlamps cast a warm aura over the cold concrete sidewalk in the town square. She was kind of like his own personal streetlamp.

She'd wrapped her arms around herself as the wind picked up. He took his coat off and helped her slip into it. He noticed the way her body curved as she pulled her arms through the sleeves. He noticed how he kept his hands on her shoulders longer than necessary.

"Thank you, kind sir."

"My pleasure." They continued to walk.

He watched as she stuck her hands in the pockets of the coat, scavenging like a little mouse. She pulled out a small plastic shopping bag. "What's this?"

"I got you something, my lady."

Amber stopped, looking genuinely shocked. "You did?" She held up the bag. "Wrap it yourself?"

"No, I paid extra for that."

He watched her dig into the sack. First she pulled out the magnifying glass. She peered through it, her eye enlarging as she tilted it up to him. "I'm completely blown away by how hot your pores look." He laughed as she examined the magnifier with a questioning expression. "Um . . . thank you?"

"There's more."

She reached in and pulled out the CD. "*Mastering the Spanish Language.*"

"To help you focus. *Comprende?*"

"*Comprende.* And *gracias.* Very thoughtful."

"It's a start."

She stepped closer to him, the way she always wanted to test the boundaries—the way she always melted his heart, even with a cold wind beating against his back.

"It is," she said. "Keep trying."

Another step closer. He stared into her eyes and it took everything in him to turn and start walking again.

Within a step or two, she was right by his side, so close he could smell her perfume. "Where are we going, anyway?" she asked.

"I wanted you to meet someone." He pointed ahead. "There it is."

Her face lit. "Oooh! A diner! I love diners!"

He shook his head, chuckling. "Only you could get excited about a diner."

"You meet some of the most interesting people at diners. It's always late. And you're drinking coffee. And you're talking. Come on!" She started running and he tried to keep up. He managed to beat her to at least open the door.

Inside, he guided her to his favorite booth. Betty looked up, noticed Amber, and gave a kind wave and a knowing smile. "Be right there. French fries and gravy?"

"Sound good?" he asked Amber.

"Right on," she said.

"Want me to take the coat?"

She shook her head. "I kind of like it. It's warm. And it smells like you."

"Sawdust with a hint of varnish and top notes of paint stripper?"

She smiled coyly at him as Betty arrived with two baskets of fries and one bowl of gravy. "It's fresh from the skillet. Doesn't get any better than that."

"Betty, this is Amber."

"Hi, sweetheart. You kids holler if you need anything. I'll bring you some coffee as soon as it's brewed." Betty gave an affectionate wink as she walked away.

Clay started to reach for his workbook and realized they hadn't brought them. He wasn't sure what to do with his hands.

"I guess we're going to have to explore each other without them," Amber said, an eyebrow raised.

"You know me well," he laughed.

"Let's see how well." She grabbed three fries and dunked them straight into the gravy. He realized at that point that it might be true love. "How old were you when they split up?"

Clay leaned back, not expecting that question. Had not even known he could possibly be that transparent. How *did* she know him this well?

"Eight." Then he realized it. Of course she knew. It was her story too. "You?"

"Thirteen. Bad time for a girl to lose her daddy."

"Where is he now?"

Thoughts surfaced, clouding her eyes. "I don't really know. My mom died years ago. And someone told me Dad did too, somewhere in Mexico on an oil rig, but I don't know. He was dead to me way before that."

"I'm sorry."

"It's weird, but still, sometimes . . . I miss our old house. My room. My place at the dinner table."

Yeah. Clay could still see his. *Star Trek* sheets. LEGO boxes in his closet. He never got rid of those. He wondered what became of them. The light above his bed flickered every third night for no apparent reason. Out his second-story window, there was a field that he watched sometimes, imagining a lion lived there, its tail blending into the golden wheat just like in *The Ghost and the Darkness*.

At dinner, he sat next to his mom. Dad was at the head of the table. Neither seemed to be in charge, though. The ice in the dinner glasses was always almost melted, thin like a wafer, hardly cold to the touch.

The first time he heard them fight, he'd been jolted awake in the dead middle of the night by a bloodcurdling scream. He hid under the covers, suffocating in the heat of his own panting breath. He trembled so hard that the bed shook, knocking against the wall but barely audible compared to the noise in the next room.

And then, like debris from a ship smashed against a rock, the pieces of their family slowly drifted apart. The divorce was quick. His dad got remarried six months later, started a new family, moved to Washington State. The birthday cards were sporadic for years, then stopped when Clay turned eighteen. Somewhere, so he'd been told, he had four half siblings.

His mom had some sort of nervous breakdown, lost her job, started drinking, recovered, started drinking again, and never recovered. Not really. Last he'd heard she was living with a guy on a boat somewhere off the coast of the Florida Keys. But that was four years ago.

"This coat sure has a lot of pockets to explore." Amber grinned at him. "Like someone else I know." She fished around. "Hmmm. What else you got in here? Anything interesting?"

"Doubtful."

"A pen and . . ." She pulled something out. "What's this?"

Clay tensed. The place mat. He tried to reach for it. "I forgot about that."

"Can I see?"

"No."

As usual, she didn't listen and opened it anyway. Clay sighed and slouched in his seat.

"Seems to be a checklist." She eyed him. "Nothing gets romance flowing like a checklist."

"Just . . . please, just—"

"'Magnifying glass.' Check. 'Spanish CD.' Check. Check. Check. Check."

Clay looked away, trying to hide his embarrassment. Here it was, right out in front of her, everything that made him the dullest guy to ever walk the earth.

She paused, then read, "'Respect her emotions as well as her body.'"

A thin layer of sweat began to coat his face. He was about to attempt some sort of profuse apology when she smiled gently and folded the paper, slipping it back into the pocket.

"Check." She leaned into the table, her hands tucked in her lap. "How is it that you're not already married?"

Sometimes she was truly baffling. The checklist had not turned her off in the least bit. "I could ask you the same question."

Betty arrived with the coffee and two mugs. "You two look like you just stepped outta that movie *Sleepless in Seattle* with all the lovey-dovey looks passing back and forth here. You make a cute couple, I'll give you that." She poured as she glanced between them. "What else can I do for ya?"

Clay smiled tensely. "We're fine, Betty. And also, thanks for creating a perfectly awkward moment. *Awkward in Ohio.*"

Amber cracked up laughing.

"You're welcome. It's a gift of mine."

Amber watched Betty walk away. "Well, it's true. We are pretty cute together."

"I think you're the cute part," Clay said, "and I'm there by proxy."

"Stop. You're adorable. And I love *Sleepless in Seattle.*"

"Figures."

"You don't?"

"I'm allergic to cats."

"So?"

"Bill Pullman was the nice guy. Kind. Reliable. But because he happens to itch and get puffy red eyes and sneeze all over the place, it's okay for Meg Ryan to run off with Tom Hanks. The boring guy with the allergies always gets dumped in the movies, and it's not right. It must be stopped." He cocked his head to the side. "Am I boring?"

She paused, looking thoughtfully at him. "The Bill Pullmans of the world don't always get dumped. Case in point: *While You Were Sleeping*. Sandra Bullock falls for the smoking-hot brother who ends up in the coma. But isn't it the boring, stiff, idiosyncratic younger brother, the one who searches for the most truth, who gets the girl in the end?"

"Okay. Good point."

"And for the record, I always thought Bill Pullman was hot."

"Now I'm starting to think Bill may be my toughest competition."

"When he's the president of the United States, battling aliens and flying an F-16, yes. Otherwise you're fine." She grabbed his wrist, checked the time. "It's almost eleven. If we don't get home soon, one of us turns into a pumpkin, and I'm betting it's not me."

She made him laugh. A lot. He pulled out some money and put it on the table. "If you don't mind, I gotta go to the little boys' room. Stay out of my pockets."

Clay went to the bathroom, splashed his face with water, stared into his reflection, unattractively highlighted by bright fluorescent lights. "You *are* boring. You are. She's bored out of her mind, Walsh. You used to be so . . ." He looked down. What he used to be was dangerous. Sure, he'd been fun. But it came with a lot of destruction.

He looked himself in the eye again. "She does laugh at your jokes. When you manage to get one out. Just be a little more . . . less brooding. Don't think so hard. Just go with it." His hand gestures to himself were suggesting it was going to take more than a pep talk. He sucked in a deep breath. "No. Don't go with it. That's what got you in trouble. Pace yourself. Be . . . careful." He straightened, grabbed some paper towels, wiped his face off. "In other words, be boring."

Clay opened the bathroom door, rounded the corner, and was stopped dead in his tracks by the crowd in the restaurant. Everyone was looking at him and cheering and clapping and chanting, *"Tee-tee! Tee-tee! Tee-tee!"*

Instinctively he wanted to crawl under a table, but he found Amber in the crowd. She was chanting the loudest, wildly clapping, grinning from ear to ear. So he decided to do the exact opposite of what his gut was telling him.

He bowed. Then raised his arms in victory.

The crowd went nuts.

CHAPTER 12

RIGHT ON TIME. And they weren't waiting for the weekend anymore either. It was Wednesday, the day Amber got off work at four. At four thirty, Clay was at her door, knocking.

Her new Spanish CD was playing as she greeted him. "*Buenos días*, stress boy. I'm thoroughly enjoying my presents."

"*Bueno.*"

"You're sure you can take off work this early?"

"Well, I am the boss."

"Very well." She picked up the shoe box she'd made for them. "Shall we?"

"I can't let you get all the kicks." He held up his own shoe box, which had been tucked under his arm. It read *Amber* on top. He shook it and opened the lid. "Pick one."

That landed them at the library. They sat at a cozy table near the window as late-afternoon sunbeams majestically anointed the stacks of books they had opened all around them.

"'Tis easier to keep holidays than commandments,'" Clay said. "That's Benjamin Franklin."

"Ha. That's true. I definitely prefer holidays." Amber looked down at the book she was holding. "'Our lives begin to end the day we become silent about things that matter.'"

"Nice. Who said that?"

"Martin Luther King Jr. How about this one? 'When you're attracted to someone, it just means that your subconscious is attracted to their subconscious, subconsciously. So what we think of as fate is just two neuroses knowing that they are a perfect match.'"

"And who said *that*?"

"Nora Ephron, *Sleepless in Seattle*."

"Would you like to come over to my house tomorrow?" He blurted it out, shattering the silent code at the library. He didn't seem to mean for it to come out that loud. And then he looked as if he wasn't even sure he'd meant it to come out at all.

Amber gazed at him, waiting for a punch line. But he was serious. "See where you live? Yes. That I would like."

"Make some dinner together?" The slightest pink blush colored his cheeks.

Amber couldn't resist the grin that was emerging. "Alone? Just the two of us?"

Turned out, no. They had a third wheel. Clay picked Amber up in his truck, then went to get Aunt Zella, who sat between them on the upholstered bench that was the front seat of his truck. She should've known better, but if it was going to be anyone, she might as well get to know some of his family.

They pulled into the driveway of Clay's house. Amber peered out the window, unabashedly curious as to what kind of home Clay Walsh would live in. It wasn't too surprising, all things considered. Redbrick, older but well maintained. And unbelievably, there was a white picket fence around the yard.

Clay smiled at her. "You love it."

She nodded.

Amber helped Aunt Zella out of the car, and Clay unlocked the front door. Inside was clean, full of light, minimally decorated with lots of neutral colors. Definitely could use a woman's touch, like a rug or a lamp or some kind of a paint splash. On a wall just inside the front door was a small, framed scroll with what she guessed were the Ten Commandments, apparently written in Hebrew. For how much he heeded those rules, she'd kind of expected them to be painted across his ceiling or something. She gave the frame one more sideways glance. It felt like the commandments were staring her down. Probably because she'd never been good at keeping them.

She kept following him. No TV. Lots of books, piled everywhere. A basketball sat in the corner.

"Come look at our garden," Aunt Zella said.

As Amber followed her to the back door, she peeked into the bathroom. Toilet seat down. Bed made in his room.

Neat and tidy. Just like his life. Anything else, she supposed, would be too shocking to get over.

Outside, there was no back porch. A couple of deck chairs, sans deck, were all that made up the backyard. A grill sat near the door on the grass. Aunt Zella pointed to the garden. It was the tiniest square piece of land, three or four feet wide, right along the side of the house, bumping into the brick. A few empty tomato vines limply clung to the soil.

"Clay grows tamaters for us. Right there. Cans them too. He's well trained."

Clay walked out and turned the grill on.

"I'm showing Miss Amber here our garden."

Clay gestured at it. "Aunt Zella, it's just that little square. All the plants are dead anyway."

"You mind your own beeswax. She looks impressed."

Amber smiled, trying her best "impressed" look. Clay shook his head. Aunt Zella took her hand and walked around the house with her, pointing out the garden box with a few tools visible under the almost-closed lid. She stopped there, grabbing a hoe and a packet of seeds. Then she shuffled back to the garden.

"Hold these, will ya?" she asked, handing Amber the seeds. With shaky hands, she began turning the soil at their feet. Amber watched the dirt turn over and over, gently and methodically.

Clay called from the back door, "Aunt Zella, it's too close to frost. Won't make it."

Aunt Zella dismissed his input, waving an aggravated arm at him. She took the seeds from Amber and started sprinkling them on the ground. Amber watched quietly.

Then, in a soft voice, Aunt Zella said, "Sometimes, even when the soil isn't perfectly fertile and the season isn't well-timed and the seeds might sprout during the coldest of days, it doesn't mean a nice tamater plant won't make it. Sometimes you gotta throw all your seeds into the soil and see what happens." She started tossing the seeds everywhere.

Clay threw his hands up. "Really? I just bought those seeds for next season. On clearance."

Aunt Zella gave Amber a knowing wink. "And sometimes I just do stuff like this to make him think I got the dementia."

Forty-five minutes later, Clay had produced a beautiful meal. Steak. Steamed green beans. Potatoes au gratin, for goodness' sake! Apparently it was a recipe passed down from Aunt Zella's side of the family.

Clay pulled out chairs for Amber and for Aunt Zella, who was seated at the head of the table.

Aunt Zella gestured toward the table and Clay simultaneously. "No candles? No flowers? I'm ashamed of you. Ashamed. Let's pray." She held out a hand to Amber. Then the other to Clay.

Amber reverently bowed her head. She'd never been around a table where people held hands and prayed. She breathed quietly, shallowly, waiting to see what would happen. It was the kind of nervous quiet where you can hear your chair squeak with every small movement. She tried hard not to move.

After a stretch of silence, Aunt Zella said, "Thank You."

And like that, it was over. Amber looked up, and both Clay and Aunt Zella had already opened their eyes and started eating. It was sincere and reverent and so . . . simple.

The meal passed with Aunt Zella sharing childhood stories of Clay—a wild, rambunctious, delightful little boy who could engage a crowd of strangers on the street as easily as he could a room full of adults or a playground full of kids.

"Oh, boy, he always had me laughing. Had everyone laughing. I'll never forget seeing him on the playground one day at South Elementary School. There was Clay—couldn't have been more than six or seven—with a toy guitar, pretending to be Elvis. All the girls were chasing him around and screaming."

"Aunt Zella . . ."

"I'm just saying. You used to be a chick maggot—"

"Magnet."

"—to borrow a term from your decade."

"Okay, okay. Enough about me. Aunt Zella, isn't it about time for you to nap or something?"

Amber helped him clear the plates. By the time they'd started washing the dishes, Aunt Zella was in the living room in the recliner, fast asleep, clutching her jar of canned tomatoes.

"That is so precious," Amber said as Clay handed her another plate to dry. "You're blessed."

"We have this ritual—tradition—which she's very fond of. Whenever too much time goes by without a visit, she mails me a single bag of tea as a reminder."

As he scrubbed a pan, Amber noticed the sleeve he had rolled up. It rose when he reached for the soap. And there on his forearm was a barbed wire tattoo. It startled her and she tried to look away but she couldn't. Then he noticed her and quickly pushed his sleeve down. She cleared her throat and kept drying.

"Then you and Aunt Zella, you drink the tea together?"
"Yes."

She dried her last dish and turned toward Aunt Zella again. "She looks so peaceful."

"She's faking."

"Oh, she is not."

Clay stepped closer. Reached across Amber for a towel, brushing her arm and then her hand.

Amber turned from him, happy to be pursued. Two could play at this game. She stepped away, gazing at the bookshelves. "You read all those?"

Clay followed her to the living room—she could hear his footsteps behind her. "Most of them."

She glided her fingers across the spines. *The Rule of St. Benedict. The Confessions of St. Augustine.* Then she pulled out a hardbound copy of *Flowers for Algernon.* "I read this in tenth grade. So sad. 'Anyone who has common sense will remember that the bewilderments of the eyes are of two kinds, and arise from two causes, either from coming out of the light or from going into the light, which is true of the mind's eye, quite as much as of the bodily eye.' That hung on my bulletin board for a while. It was actually first said by Plato." She was putting the book back on the shelf when her attention was caught by another book. "Is that a Bible?"

"It is."

"May I?" She pulled it out carefully, reverently. It was heavy, the leather soft, worn. "What parts of it do you believe exactly?"

He only smiled like that was a conversation for another day.

"Okay. Well, any favorites, then?"

"'Old things are passed away; behold, all things are become new.'"

Amber looked down at the pages. "That's in here?" She thumbed through, feeling the paper. It was so thin but strangely strong and durable. Some of the pages were crinkled. This book had been read many times.

She came to the front. A dedication page.

For Clay, from Kelly.

"Who's Kelly?"

"She gave him the Bible," Aunt Zella said from the recliner, eyes still closed. "Changed his life."

"Told you," Clay said, nodding to Aunt Zella.

He reached for the Bible but Amber turned. There was a photograph sticking out that had been tucked between the pages. She slipped it out and studied it. College days for sure. Clay's bright-blue eyes drew all the attention, but there were others in the photograph. David. Lisa. A girl hanging across Clay's shoulder. She was tall and thin, with silky white-blonde hair. Hollow, defined cheeks. Beautiful lips. Her eyes were doe-like, more innocent than the other three.

She looked up at Clay. "Don't want to talk about it?"

"It's complicated."

"Amber is a bright girl," Aunt Zella spoke up again from the recliner. "Give it a shot."

Clay took Amber's arm and guided her away from the living room. They walked to the front porch, where he leaned against the brick, staring out into the neighborhood. His expression drifted in and out of sadness.

"Kelly was my last real girlfriend."

"Before all your theories."

"She was the first girl I ever actually cared for. She gave that Bible to me just before we broke up. I used to make fun of her. . . . I don't even . . . I can't understand why she ever liked me. What she saw in me." Clay lowered his head, as though the words would hardly come out. Amber touched his shoulder and waited patiently. "She wanted to . . . she wanted to wait. And of course, I didn't wait. I never waited. Nobody ever made me wait. So I hooked up." The muscles of his jaw protruded. A dog barked next door. "With one of her friends."

"Oh . . ."

"It gets even messier." A long sigh escaped his lips. "On the rebound, she started dating some other guy. He got her pregnant. And they got married. I hurt her. . . ."

She watched him mindlessly rub his forearm, right where the tattoo was hidden underneath his shirtsleeve, then looked down to the Bible she was holding. "Is that what made you change?"

"It wasn't one big thing. It was more like a lot of small things that added up. And that book didn't help much. Sometimes I wish I'd never opened it at all."

"Why?"

"Once I read it for myself, I couldn't make fun of it anymore. Maybe someone else could, but I couldn't. I felt accountable for the first time in my life."

It was quiet for a moment. Amber let him think, made herself process all he was telling her. This was more than he had ever opened up about.

The mood lightened a bit as he glanced at her, smiling, like some weight had been lifted off him. "There was . . . something. A sense. Like a voice but—"

"You hear voices?"

"No, not like real . . . Wait."

"What?"

"Shhhh. There it is again. A whisper. It's telling me . . . it's telling me something about you!"

She hit his arm. "I'm serious. Tell me more about all of this."

"I can't explain it. Still. Even now. It's not easy to put into words without sounding like a crazy person."

"I already think you're a crazy person."

"Ask her to go to church with ya sometime."

They turned to find Aunt Zella standing behind the screen door, still clutching the tomatoes.

"Thank you, Aunt Zella."

"You go to church?" Amber asked.

"Not much anymore. I did."

"The people there weren't perfect, so he felt out of place," Aunt Zella said.

"I believe that," Amber said with a small smile.

Clay looked at her. "I just drifted away from it. Had my fill of the hypocrite show."

"Well, I've never been to church, so I think you and I should go sometime. I would like to experience that with you."

"Why?"

"Because."

"Good Lord, you two! Both of ya. Take me home already. This is getting painful."

CHAPTER 13

"GOD LOVES EVERY boy and girl. Everywhere around the great big world. Every color and every size. Some are silly and some are wise. But God loves every one the same. He knows your giggle and he knows your name!"

And then all the little kids at the front of the church shouted their own names at the top of their lungs. The congregation laughed and applauded.

Clay glanced at Amber, who was enthralled, clapping and laughing too.

That was the squeaky, shiny kind of show everyone liked to see. Clay's gaze drifted to an older couple, three rows up, one seat over. Dressed in their Sunday best. Then another man, sitting alone, arms crossed.

When he first started attending church, it was all he'd hoped it would be. He went through a whole repentance process with the help of others in the church. Then the head deacon had an affair with the secretary. And the music minister ran off with another man. And the walls all started crumbling. He could trust nothing coming from the pulpit. No handshake. No pat on the back. It struck him one day, as he was trying to make his life right, that in many ways, the people inside the church were just as broken as the ones on the outside.

Then came the Sunday when he just didn't get out of bed. And then another. And another.

Pretty soon he didn't step inside the church again. But sometimes he would take his Bible to a bench nearby, where he could see the steeple rising into the sky and all the beautiful stained glass. Inside, it was too messy. But outside, he liked the strength of the stones and the stately invulnerability of its walls.

A boy, six or so, dressed in a miniature suit, walked up to the stage, holding a small Bible. The teacher nodded and he began to read. "'Mercy and truth are met together. Righteousness and peace have kissed each other.'" His face twisted into a question mark. "'*Kissed* each other'?"

The crowd chuckled, and as the laughter died down, Clay did the only thing that felt right at the moment. He slid his hand over Amber's, his fingers slipping between hers, like vines entwining. They both pretended to watch the front of the church, but every single movement she made registered right in his heart.

He imagined the two of them as husband and wife. Cooking and fighting over how much salt to add. Hiking on a Sunday after they'd finished cleaning out the garage. Going to look for a good vehicle—a better, more reliable one.

He saw himself standing next to a black minivan, last year's model. And there she was, eyeing the red convertible.

And then, awash in morning sunlight, waking up in his bed.

He swallowed and chased the thoughts away.

♥

"Come on." Amber looked at Trish, then at Carol. Trish was blowing up balloons. Carol tied ribbon. "I want your real thoughts. Be honest."

Carol looked as if she was trying to carefully consider it. "The two of you seem so different, that's all." She paused, the kind of pause that is less comma, more exclamation point. "He's different." She cast Amber a look that said, *Please tell me you know that.*

"I know."

"You could do so much better, Amber. Truly," Trish said.

Amber thought about church the day before. She'd never felt more comfortable in her life. More safe. "He held my hand in church yesterday." She glanced between the two of them. "It felt like home."

Trish let out an exasperated sigh so loud that it sounded like she'd let go of a balloon. "Amber. People get that kind of feeling from holding hands when they're in fifth grade behind the gym. You know?"

"Home, Trish. What's better than that?"

Carol kept snipping ribbon, but the snips got louder. And faster.

Amber decided there was no use trying to persuade them. She knew what she knew. There was something special about this man, something that resonated beyond the typical chemistry she'd measured so many relationships by.

"I've been debating," Carol said. Her face was tight with concern. And she'd picked up a DVD case.

"What?"

She handed the DVD to Amber like a doctor might hand over bad test results.

Trish peeked over Amber's shoulder to look. "Cool! I've always wanted to be in one of those!"

College Coeds X-Posed. On the cover of the DVD were scantily clad women in bikinis, holding up beer bottles and screaming at the camera. In stark contrast to that chaos was the background, a beautiful beach everyone seemed to be ignoring.

"Why are you giving this to me?" Amber asked.

"Check out the name of the producer," Carol said somberly.

Amber turned the case over. Her attention was instantly drawn to his name. *Clay Walsh.*

"You should watch that sometime," Carol said flatly, then started snipping ribbon again.

Amber set it down on the counter. She didn't even want to touch it. "I don't need to. It doesn't matter. The man who made this? He's gone. Never even met him. And I never—"

Suddenly the door chimed and Trish, gaping at whoever had come in, let go of the balloon she was blowing up. It shot up and around the room, forcing everyone to dodge it. Carol and Amber turned to see who Trish was gawking at.

She stepped in front of both of them to get to the cash register. "What can we do to you? For you?"

A man, casually dressed, his hair slicked back a little heavily with gel, walked to the counter. He flashed an appreciative smile at Trish.

"She's on medication," Carol growled, heading into the back room. "She doesn't know what she's saying."

"I know *exactly* what I'm saying," Trish purred.

Amber watched the guy. Good-looking. Cocky. You could tell by the way he walked that he was a player. Within a couple of seconds, she knew, he had everything and everyone in the room sized up.

"I just need to get some flowers."

Trish had seemingly lost her words. She just stood there grinning like a hyena.

Amber cleared her throat. "Sure. What would you like?"

"They're for . . . an old friend."

Trish elbowed back in and Amber stepped out of her way. "We have a new selection of *passion*flowers. In the back. I could show you." She leaned on the counter, squeezed her elbows in to create the ever-so-popular cleavage pose.

Amber was about to turn away. She didn't want to see this train wreck. But the guy looked at her and said, "I was thinking roses?"

Trish was still gushing, so Amber nodded. "Sure. What color?"

"Um . . . not sure."

She thought for a second. "White roses are always safe."

"Perfect."

"Give me five minutes."

Trish started the small talk, but Amber could feel the man watching her.

"Take your time," he called. She smiled politely, gathered what she needed, listened to Trish introduce herself.

"Looks like you almost know what you're doing," he said, once again to Amber.

"Thanks." He was still watching her. "What?"

Then the casual lean on the counter. The wide smile. The total disregard for Trish, inches away from him.

Amber snipped the end of one of the roses. "I'm taken."

At that exact moment Trish popped a balloon, startling everyone. She tilted her head, running a finger along the edge of her bangs. "I'm not."

"Trish, can you get me that box of note cards?" Amber wondered if the girl could make any more of a fool out of herself, except maybe by jumping straight over the counter and into his arms. Someone had to save her from herself.

"Sure." Trish trudged out.

Amber wrapped the bouquet and tied it carefully. "Trish is just getting the cards so you can write something—"

"Doesn't this say it all?" the guy asked.

Amber offered a tight smile, looking him directly in the

eye. "Guess it depends on the girl." She handed him the flowers.

He plunked two twenties on the counter. "Go buy yourself something special." And out he walked.

Trish rushed back in, looking for him, suddenly as deflated as the balloon resting on the counter. "What happened? Where'd he go?"

"Trish, that's not the kind of guy you want to mess around with."

"You've got Stiff as a Board. I've got Fluid as Water."

"He's smooth—you're right about that. Too smooth."

"There's no such thing."

"He's a player. Can't you see that?"

Trish turned to her. "You don't think I see?"

"I don't know. You're kind of throwing yourself all over this guy."

"I'm just trying to find some fun in life. Enjoy it."

Amber relented, let the argument go. If Trish wanted to live out a beer commercial, that was her decision. She pushed one of the twenties toward her and put the other in the cash register.

"What's this?"

"He said to go buy yourself something special."

Trish squealed all the way to the back room.

Carol returned, rolling her eyes at the absurdity. "I'll give you this: you're a bit more of a straight thinker than Betty Boop back there."

Amber smiled. "I understand her. The attention—it's sometimes . . . intoxicating."

"Just remember. There's always the hangover." Carol started counting the money in the cash register. "You seeing Straight Laced tonight?"

"No. He's got a bachelor party to go to."

Carol raised an eyebrow. "Straight Laced just got crooked?"

"He has to go. It's one of his best friends."

Carol bit her lip, closed the register, and walked over to where Amber was cleaning up stems. "Honey, you know that . . . um, bachelor parties are . . ."

"I know what you're going to say. Nothing good happens after eleven."

"Well, no, I would never say that. But generally, yes, that's true—except it's more like 1 a.m."

"I know him, Carol. Nothing's going to happen. He's a good guy."

"He's still a man. Just remember that."

"They're still out there, you know—the good ones."

"If you say so."

Clay would be fine. He always was.

♥

David checked his watch. "Where *is* he?"

Clay was observing the architecture of the hotel. "We probably don't want to know."

"Dude. It's my bachelor party. I mean, if there is one thing the guy is not going to be late to, surely it's a bachelor party."

Just then they heard the squeal of tires, high and piercing

like a pig being slaughtered. Racing around the corner was the familiar-looking yellow Mustang, a white, smoky curtain hanging behind it. Multiple Mardi Gras beads swung from the rearview mirror, but only one girl this time. Brad was in the passenger seat, throwing peace signs up as the car screeched to a halt. On the dashboard a bouquet of white roses slid to the right as the car stopped.

David and Clay exchanged glances and David groaned. "White roses. Really. That's an insult to white," he whispered.

Brad jumped out, dressed like the West Coaster he'd recently become.

"About time," Clay said. "We've got dinner reservations at 8:30."

"Clay," Brad said, putting his arms around both guys' shoulders as they walked into the hotel, "this is not that kind of night. This is the kind of night where you relax."

"Let's not ask the impossible," David laughed, winking at him. "Come on, the party's started upstairs and I'm not even at it!"

Brad had booked a suite at what he called the "hotel of many memories," and it was already crowded with ten guys, some of whom Clay knew. Five of them had been good college buddies who had walked away, trashing his name as they went. But it had been nine years, and he supposed time healed some things.

He managed his way through a few conversations, idle chatter mostly. Brad, thankfully, took up most of the attention. He was still the life of the party. Still knew how to get everyone going. Fifteen minutes in, it was loud and rowdy and everything a bachelor party usually was.

Clay checked his watch. Ten more minutes and they could leave for the restaurant. That had been his job: to find a good restaurant. He already knew David's favorite steakhouse. It wasn't hard—red meat, beer, and some good-looking bartenders.

Mostly, Clay thought about Amber. He couldn't get her sweet smile out of his mind. He couldn't shake the idea of her at his house . . . all the time. Reading. Drinking tea on the porch. Going crazy and trying for some cucumbers in the garden.

Clay stood at the large window that overlooked the city, staring past his own reflection in the glass, when Brad passed by to the bathroom area.

He leaned into the mirror, adjusting his vest, primping his hair. "So . . . when do I get to meet her?" he asked, watching Clay from the mirror.

"You don't."

"She have a name?"

"Yeah. It's whatserface."

Brad laughed, raised his beer to Clay. "She coming to the wedding?"

"You about ready, pretty boy? Dinner's at 8:30."

"Yeah, you already said that."

David stepped to the window. "Look, the limos are here." He turned to Brad. "Aren't you gorgeous enough yet? We're hungry. Who wants some red meat?"

The rest of the guys hollered in agreement and the rowdiness picked back up, until there was a loud knock at the door. Everyone quieted.

"Hotel security. We're getting complaints about the noise. Open the door."

Brad settled everyone down. "Just play it cool, okay?" He cracked open the door.

A large, burly security guard walked in, eyeing everyone, followed by the hotel manager, who looked equally perturbed.

"Which one of you is the registered guest?" she asked.

Brad pointed to David. "He is."

"Oh no you don't," David said. "It's under his name."

But the security guard walked up to David. "Sir. I need you to take a seat please."

David looked genuinely confused. They all did. Until suddenly the hotel manager took off her scarf. Then unbuttoned the sleeve on her white blouse.

"David," she purred, "sit down."

The security guard pulled a chair to the center of the room. An alarmed look passed over David's face and right into Clay's heart. Brad smiled and shrugged, and then the guys started chanting for David to sit down. Reluctantly he did.

Clay caught David's attention. "David, please. Don't do this."

The woman circled the chair in five-inch heels. Clay looked at Brad, pointed at him. "Open that door."

The woman's long red nails fingered the top button of her blouse.

With a smirk and a glint of anger in his eyes, Brad deadbolted the door. Then flipped the safety lock.

The woman was untucking her shirt. Clay moved into David's line of sight. "Think about Lisa. About Cosie. *Cosie*."

David swallowed hard, one minute glancing at all his cheering buddies, the next looking at Clay with a bead of sweat on his brow.

Brad made his way into the center of the room, his face blistering. "This doesn't hurt them. Grow up, Clay. What's the big deal? This is what men do. What a *man* does. You're pathetic, you know that?" He looked around the room and in a louder-than-necessary voice said, "Does anyone else have a problem with this?"

Adamant *no*s. The woman had frozen, half her blouse undone, one leg hiked up on the corner of the chair, her eyes darting back and forth.

Brad stomped to the door and unlocked it. He yanked it open, but his tone had cooled, just like his glare. "You want to go, Clay? You go. The rest of us are going to stay and enjoy the interrogation."

The room closed in on him. Everyone stared. Hard. David looked at the floor.

Clay took a deep breath, steadied himself, and walked out the door. It slammed behind him.

But he could still hear the boos.

♥

Amber tried music, but she wasn't feeling it tonight. She finished unpacking the groceries and for a moment thought about breaking something. What was left? The thermostat maybe?

On the counter rested the new Bible she'd picked up for herself. The translucent pages still fascinated her. She flipped through it. *Where does one begin?* she wondered.

She wandered over to the bulletin board and stared for a long time at the rainbow tacked to the bottom. It had been a source of comfort to her for so long. A symbol of hope that there was some kind of treasure at the end of it for her, someday, somewhere.

But she knew the truth—behind the rainbow was a lot of fantasy, a lot of myth that she'd bought into. She slowly untacked the drawing from the board, and the photograph that hid behind it fell to the ground, sliding across the floor with a hissing sound, coming to rest at the corner of the couch. She didn't touch it but stood over it. Though she didn't even need to see it because she knew it by heart.

She'd never felt prettier before or since that photograph was taken.

The wedding dress had been the find of the century, eighty dollars at a Goodwill store. The very idea of how she found her dress was like a sign that she should marry him. They had little money but were inseparable.

The strapless gown had hand-beaded floral lace details, a break-front skirt, and a long train. She could still hear the sounds of the day: his little nieces and nephews running around and laughing at the reception, the helicopter that disrupted the ceremony briefly, the way he whispered in her ear that he loved her.

She swiped the tears from her face before they dripped off

her chin. Where her parents had failed, she'd always vowed to succeed. She believed in true love. She believed that love triumphed over all.

Amber stooped to the ground, right over the photograph, tilting her head to look at it more clearly. With delicate fingers, she picked it up. Within a second, she'd ripped the photograph in two, right down the middle. She remained in the left half, still dazzling in that dress. She brushed the hair out of her face, pinned herself back on the board, and put the rainbow over the photo. She tacked the leaf she'd saved from her "date" with Clay next to the rainbow, next to the bride who might never be again.

The other half of the photograph went down the well-working garbage disposal.

Then Amber went to her bed, lay down, clutched the edge of her pillow, and let the tears come.

♥

Clay stood in the street, clawing through his hair, his heart primitive and wild inside his chest. He heard footsteps behind him.

He'd known Brad would come after him. He always did after they had a falling-out. But it was never pretty. And it was never to set things straight.

"You owe me two hundred bucks!" Brad yelled.

Clay stepped back to get better footing. He knew Brad well enough to know there was probably a fight coming.

"What?" Brad said, anger dulling the flashy grin he wore

like an accessory. "I didn't realize I needed your permission, O holy one."

The two of them stood there on the darkened pavement, chests heaving. Then Clay turned. Started walking.

"Taking your toys and going home, right on cue," Brad yelled after him.

Clay stopped. That old feeling—like a foot on his chest, like fire up his neck—returned instantly, as if it hadn't been gone for nearly a decade. He swallowed, breathed, tried not to listen.

"So noble," Brad sneered. His tone dripped with the resentment of dozens and dozens of unspoken words. "So . . . superior. We bow before thee."

Clay finally turned, struggling to keep the emotion, both the anger and the hurt, from boiling over.

Brad threw his hands up. "You're an inspiration to us all. *As always.*" He laughed, the kind of laugh that Clay had heard a thousand times, usually reserved for the women left in Brad's trail of indifference.

He wanted to punch him. Just swing right into his face, right into that stupid mouth of his. But even as he balled up his fist, he realized he couldn't.

Brad really thought that what happened in that hotel room was harmless.

He didn't understand anything Clay believed in. To Brad, it probably seemed as if an alien had one day come down and abducted his friend and returned with an unknown being.

Clay slowly released his fist and stuck his hands in his pockets. "When did it happen? How did we . . . ?"

"What?" Brad asked.

"When did treating women with respect become the joke?"

"Oh, come on."

"You want to laugh at believing love can be something sacred? Go ahead. Laugh."

Brad gave a Roman soldier salute. Behind him, Clay saw the men streaming out of the hotel lobby, heading toward the limos that idled at the curb. Apparently the party upstairs had broken up even without him.

"Brad! Let's go!" one of the guys yelled. Three hung out of two of the sunroofs, chanting something incoherent.

"Catch you later, Spartacus."

Clay stepped out of the glow of the streetlight and headed into the darkness. He just needed to walk. The rowdy sounds of drunk men followed him.

"Hey. Clay."

He turned to find David walking toward him, his shoulders slumped with a night not gone as planned. David glanced back once at the limos waiting for him. "I didn't know he was going to do that. I swear."

"I know."

"All I wanted was a steak."

Clay nodded toward the limos. "Looks like you're getting your wish."

A horn honked.

David gestured to the dark street ahead of them. "Going for a walk?"

"Yeah."

David took Clay's hand and shook it hard, looking him straight in the eye, the wordless thanks of a close friend. "See you tomorrow."

"Okay."

David headed back toward the hotel, disappearing into his limo.

Yes, he had to walk. Walk long. Walk in the dark. Walk through his emotions. Just walk. Maybe never stop. He stuffed his hands deep into the pockets of his jeans, wishing he had a coat. The cold air stung his cheeks and rippled up the inside of his shirt.

He was barely a hundred feet down the street when he heard, "You." A large hand grabbed his arm and whipped him around, throwing him off-balance. The "security guard." Standing behind the dude was the woman, buttoning up her blouse while looking right at him.

Clay yanked away from the man's grip.

"You know how much you cost her in tips tonight?" He poked Clay hard in the chest. "Don't you think you should do something about that?"

It rushed back to Clay like it was yesterday—like he was in a bar, in a brawl, angry at whatever or whoever had cast him a dirty look. With one fluid motion, he shoved the guy, who stumbled backward, caught off guard, his eyes flashing with rage.

Clay wasn't about to back down, either. In those days, he'd never backed down even when common sense told him he should. Clay started for the guy, but the stripper stepped between them like she'd probably done a hundred times in her life. She held her hands out and cast the guard a back-off look.

When she turned to Clay, she was plaintive. "Hey, if you weren't feeling it, that's cool. But why didn't you just leave, then?"

Clay saw the hard lines of a woman who'd never been treated right, the overly done makeup of a girl who couldn't bear to look at herself in the mirror anymore. It was hard to even tell how old she was. He gazed at the road behind her.

"Look at me," she said, her voice gruff. "Somebody ask for your help in there?"

There were no right answers here. Clay knew it.

She stepped closer to him, wobbly on her heels, her voice getting meaner. "All you did was guarantee my kid won't get much of a birthday present."

Clay could only picture Cosie with her dump truck wrapped in a pink blanket. He wondered how many times this woman had dressed up as a princess when she was a little girl, spun in front of the mirror, dreamed of Prince Charming. What could he say to her? He wanted to tell her there was hope, that there was good, solid love. Life-changing love.

"You think you're better than me?" She looked him up and down. And then she took the guard by the hand and took off in the other direction, her strides shortened by five-inch heels.

Clay stood there for a long time, hollowed out by what was supposed to be an ordinary night of fun with friends. He looked up, but the stars were hidden by an inky black sky. So he started walking.

He didn't have any friends. Not really. Not any who got him, got what he was trying to do, understood the path he'd chosen, understood *why*. There was really only one who clearly saw the path of destruction he'd left in so many lives. And he'd vowed every single day to try to make it up to Him.

No, he didn't think he was better than her. The truth was, he was certain he was worse.

He walked. And walked more. His heart and his legs trembled with exhaustion, but he couldn't stop. He thought of that money jar Amber kept, how it freed her to go when she wanted. To run.

Clay stopped in the park, sat on an empty swing, too tired and emotional to go home. Above him, the chains creaked with each sway of the swing. He wrapped his fingers around them, reminding himself that he'd yet to really be free of his chains and probably never would be.

CHAPTER 14

LIKE A WIND BURST, Amber flew out the door, banging the screen, hurrying down the steps toward him, clutching the shoe box, her eyes wild with excitement. She yanked open the truck door and slid in, hauling what could only be described as a massive purse. Popping off the top of the box, she said, "It's my turn! Choose."

Clay reached in, pulled out a piece of paper.

"What's it say?"

"'Get lost.'" He was pretty sure he already was. It was a new day, but he hadn't been able to shake last night. Any of it. Here was a ray of sunshine sitting right beside him. He was the black hole sucking up all the light. He tried a smile.

"Start driving."

They drove awhile, up into the hills, with Amber giving specific instructions to turn here and turn there. An hour later, they were driving by a dilapidated old barn, crushed by invisible weight, collapsing into itself.

"Don't you wonder," she said, gazing at it as if it were some field of wildflowers, "what its story is? What passed by it over the years?"

"Where are we going?"

"This is it." She leaned out the window, letting the wind tear through her hair. "Look at the color on those leaves." She slid back in. "Something wrong?"

"I'm fine."

"Make another turn."

Clay looked ahead. There was nowhere to turn. "Where?"

"Just turn. Any old road you find."

After fifteen more minutes of turning this way and that, they were thoroughly embedded in the rural outskirts of town.

"Do you have any idea where we are?" she asked.

"None."

"Perfect. Then pull over."

Clay pulled to the side of the road, though they hadn't seen a car in miles. A red barn, sturdier than the last, sat in the middle of a still-green field, near an old silver maple, its roots struggling out of the earth, causing a dry and dusty circle around it. The remnants of an old fence disappeared behind the barn and out of sight.

"Get out."

"What?" His attention snapped back to Amber.

"You heard me." A playful half smile belied her serious tone.

"Just me?"

"Just you."

Clay got out, walked toward the barn. When he turned back, she'd cranked up the radio in the truck and opened the doors so the music spilled out like sunlight through a rain cloud. With a single finger, she beckoned him.

He was so . . . empty of the joy he'd had only days ago. He wanted her in his arms. It was what he wanted most. More than anything. But the fact of the matter was, she was too good for him. She needed more than what he had, which was a vacuous set of goals that didn't matter to anyone but him.

But at the same time, he couldn't resist her, and before he knew how he got there, he was standing right in her midst. She took his hand, which he found to be trembling, into hers. And she slid his other hand around her waist. And then she danced with him.

Clay wanted to be swallowed up by the moment. He couldn't even hear the music anymore. All he could feel and think about was her.

He moved closer, trying not to clutch her, trying to be all that he promised he would be. He kept his hands in place, pressing his cheek against her soft hair. At some point the music ended and a commercial came on, but they kept dancing. He didn't want to stop. And that's why he had to.

He stepped away, looked at Amber with regret. Let go of her hands.

Her eyes searched him for some answer, but there was nothing he could do or say. Like always, she seemed to sense when it was too much for him. She put on a cheery smile. "I brought a blanket!" She ran back to the truck.

Clay could only watch her go.

Soon they were lying on their backs, sprawled out like kids, staring at the sky. Clay stared beyond the sky. And he assumed God was staring back at him.

"You haven't said a word about the bachelor party."

Clay rolled to his side and opened his workbook, which she had dutifully packed alongside tuna sandwiches. Right to page 27. Amber seemed caught up in watching a bird perched on the barn.

"How many sexual partners have you had in the past ten years?"

Amber's eyes widened. She put her hands over her face and screamed like she'd just witnessed a murder.

"We're almost done," he tried.

"And this was almost a normal date," she said, peeking between her fingers.

"What do you mean?"

"What do I mean? A normal date, Clay. Normal." Her nostrils flared with frustration.

"A *normal* date. You mean where two strangers hop in bed first and then try to figure out later if they have anything in common? Is that what you mean by *normal*?"

She sat up, took his book, tossed it to the side. "What is with you today?"

He looked away. It was something he couldn't even put words to. Beside them the barn creaked in the wind.

"Why are you so hard on everybody?" She curled her knees into herself. "Most of us are just doing our best to . . . to not feel lonely. And it isn't easy." She scraped her hair out of her eyes and shot him a sharp look. "Do you like living by yourself, Clay? Without anybody to . . . ?" She started to drift away from him. Not physically. But her eyes were losing that intense shine he loved so much. "Buy me flowers. Make me a card. I don't need you to make me your community service project."

"I'm not . . . That's not—"

"I need you to dance with me." Her expression softened. "That was okay, wasn't it?"

"Yes."

"Clay, I know it's in you. I know it." She gestured dramatically. "Flatter me. Excite me. Sweep me off my feet. Tell me I'm the most attractive woman you've ever seen even if you don't really mean it. I don't care."

"Lie to you?"

"Exactly. A normal date."

"I've wasted a lot of words. I don't want to waste any more."

"On me." Her eyes brimmed with tears. "Oh, you're scoring all kinds of points."

"It's not about scoring points."

"I'm sorry. That's right. It's about red-yellow-green." She grabbed his book again and threw it over his head. "Fine. I've been with five. I've had sex with five men. Heavy petted with about four more. Give or take."

Clay swallowed. He didn't want it like this. He didn't want to hear this. Not like this. Not with tears running down her face.

She swiped them off, her eyes furious. "And I've been married."

Clay froze. "What?"

"Yep. Once, if we're counting. That's not even a question in the book, by the way. What else do you want to know?"

He was breathless.

"It was like I was living by myself anyway. Well, you know what I mean by that, don't you? So one day when he was actually home for a change, I walked up and set the divorce papers down in front of him and made myself some oatmeal. We never even discussed it."

A thousand questions raced to his mouth, held back only by the fact that he couldn't get that many words out at once. "Did he—?"

"I'm not going to live back there anymore, Clay. And I'm not going to tell you a bunch of bad things about him to try to make myself feel less responsible. I can't blame him for my decision. And you can't either." She swung both arms wide. "But this is who I am."

She got up, shooed him off the blanket, and started packing things up. He sat there in the grass watching her, terrified. He was losing her.

And then it just burst out, like someone else said it. "I

can't even remember how many girls I've been with." It was the most repulsive thing to say out loud. Clay could barely look at her, but when he did, she didn't seem repulsed. Why wasn't she running for the hills?

She dropped the blanket and knelt next to him, reaching for his arm. He didn't mean to flinch, but he did anyway.

"Can we start over?" Amber said. "Get in the truck and get lost again?"

"It's too late."

She stayed there beside him, but she should be running. Long. Hard. Far.

The wind whistled through the missing slats of the barn. The smell of hay came and went. Clay stared at the wide-open sky, wishing somewhere there was a cave to hide from himself.

Amber turned to him, her emotions settled down. "Why haven't you invited me to David and Lisa's wedding? It's the day after tomorrow, isn't it?"

It was the oddest question, so far from what they'd just been through, so random.

"You want to go?"

"Do you want me to?"

He nodded.

She leaned into him, her hand on his chest. "I don't want to crowd you. Or change you. Or change what you believe." She moved into his line of sight. "Do you hear me on that, Clay? You're good, through and through. I believe that with all my heart. All I want is for you to say how I make you *feel*." Her hand moved toward his face. "Can you?"

Why weren't there any words coming? The backs of her fingers brushed against his cheek.

"How do I make you feel, Clay?" Her hair fell over her shoulders. "Do you feel?"

Her face was a few inches from his. He had nowhere to look but into her eyes.

"Do you think about me before you go to sleep?" Her fingers traced the top of his shoulder. "Don't you wish you could just turn your head on your pillow and see me looking back at you?"

Now her hand stroked his arm. He closed his eyes, afraid of what she might see if she looked deep enough.

"I need to know that you want me," she whispered. "I need to know that. It's important to me. *Me . . .*"

Clay finally opened his eyes. It felt like his soul was splayed open. What more could he hide from her?

Gently, like warm water, she leaned in to kiss him.

And he turned his head.

Her hands fell off him. She sat up, pushed away. Her eyes looked . . . frightened. Then angry. She left the blanket, kicked the workbook as she went, and got into the truck, slamming the door so hard that the cluster of swallows perched on the barn instantly took flight.

He lay down again and stared up into the sky. He was what he had always suspected and for nine years had tried to deny.

An emotional wasteland.

CHAPTER 15

THEY'D RUN OUT OF KLEENEX and were now handing Amber the tissue they wrapped flowers in.

"This hurts."

"Of course it does," Carol said, patting her back.

"This," Amber said, holding up the wadded tissue paper.

"Oh." Carol glanced at Trish. "See if you can find something a little softer."

"But the other thing too," Amber admitted.

While Trish went to the back, Carol pulled Amber into a tight hug. "Honey, I had no idea you were married before. If I'd known that, I would've told you to be careful."

Amber lifted her head. "You already told me to be careful."

"Every time a woman has a significant relationship end, it steals a corner of her heart and she never gets it back."

"It hasn't ended. . . . We're just taking a break."

"*Up.*" Carol sighed. "Honey, one of the first signs it's over is when you don't get invited to a wedding."

Amber burst into tears again.

Trish returned. "I was going to use this sweater for after work, but here." She handed it to Amber. "It's washable."

"Thanks."

"Tell me what happened with your ex-husband," Carol said gently.

Amber closed her eyes, trying not to think about him, but there he was.

He wandered the house, drifting by her like fog, never reaching out for her. Flinching when she tried to reach for him. She began waking in the middle of the night to find him out of bed, holed up in the other bedroom with the door locked. In the coldest, darkest night she sat up and waited for him to come out of that room, hopeful he would just sit and talk to her, tell her what it was she was doing so wrong—why she wasn't good enough for him.

"You were right," she said, looking at Carol. "Clay and I, we're too different." She was beginning, though, to think she was the one who was too different. She was the one who caused hot-blooded men to freeze like the tundra. She'd never gone more than a few weeks without a man in her life, but she could also count on one hand the days that she hadn't been lonely. Fresh tears flowed and Amber blotted her face with the sweater.

"What? What is it, honey?"

"I'm a cliché."

Carol reached for a box of chocolates. "Trust me. Trish is a cliché. You're nothing close."

"It's true. I am." Trish nodded.

"Here. Take a piece," Carol said.

"Where'd you get these?"

"It's fine. They're a customer's. He's not due to pick his order up until later. Trish can run down to Walgreens. In the meantime, we need to make sure you're okay." She grabbed both of Amber's shoulders. "You can't quit on me."

"I wish I were dead." She stuffed chocolate into her mouth. "No, I wish *he* were dead."

"Make up your mind."

"I quit."

"You can give up on love. That's fine. You just can't quit this job. I need you."

Amber looked at Carol through streaming tears. "I move on. That's what I do. That's what I'm good at."

Carol put another piece of chocolate in her hand. "What happens, sweetie, when you run out of places to move on to?"

"The world is pretty big."

Carol took Amber's hands into hers. "The world is pretty messy too. Everywhere." She sighed, pulling her lighter from the pocket of her pants. "Get some roots, baby girl. Then when those big windbags huff and puff and try to blow your house down, you stand your ground and you don't even sway." She looked to the door. "Speaking of puff, I need to step outside for a moment. You okay?"

Amber stretched out the smile she knew Carol needed to see. "I'm fine. I promise. He wasn't the first man and he won't be the last."

"Thata girl."

Carol went outside. Amber could see her through the window, lighting her cigarette, facing the wind so her hair would blow out of her face. Maybe Carol needed her as much as she needed Carol right now.

She handed Trish her sweater back. "Thanks for sacrificing this."

"Anytime." Trish rubbed her shoulder. "Listen, I know a thousand guys. Literally a thousand guys. I mean, with the university, they outnumber the ants. You're such a sweet, attractive girl. I could get you a date by tomorrow night. I promise. You just say the word and I'll hook you up with a twenty-year-old."

"Thanks. But I think I better put the brakes on for a bit."

Trish shrugged. "Your choice. You okay to hold down the fort? I gotta go get more chocolate from Walgreens."

"Yeah, I'm fine." Though her eyes felt kind of swollen.

Trish grabbed her purse and was gone, leaving Amber alone with the fragrance of all the roses around her. Right now, it kind of smelled toxic.

Yeah, the world was one big messy place. But maybe she was the messiest of all.

♥

Right in the middle of the shop, where he had more room, Clay started tearing off the upholstery. There was no use saving it. It was disgusting. Beyond repair. Maybe on the surface it looked okay, but underneath it was soiled. In fact, it was soiled so badly that it reached the wood, where it had begun to mold.

What was the use of a love seat, anyway? It wasn't even long enough to sprawl out for a good nap. He kept ripping at the upholstery. The problem was, it was stapled to the wood so securely and randomly that he was having to use a lot of muscle to get it off. He stood, catching his breath, wondering why anybody would staple the fabric like this. It was as if they thought it might stand up and walk away. He squatted, looked at the wood. It was cracking anyway. Split right down the middle at the back.

This was going to require an ax.

Just as he raised it, the door swung open and George walked in, humming and grinning. "Olly olly oxen free!" He stopped at the sight of Clay. "You look terrible." George didn't expand on what he thought looked terrible—Clay in general or the fact that he had an ax frozen over his head. George's gaze slowly moved from the immediate scene to the love seat, now more appropriately called the hate seat. "What are you doing to that poor piece of furniture?"

"I'm fixing it."

"Obviously. Love your work." George opened the front door with a gentlemanly flair and grinned widely. "Why don't you step away from murdering innocent love seats and come look at some other priceless antiquities you could fix? Got a two-for-one special on nightstands. I'd throw in the sledgehammer for free, but I see you have a mighty fine ax already."

Clay just stared at the love seat. It looked filleted.

"Come on, I got some good stuff out here. Let's go."

He followed George outside, where the sunlight felt blinding. He shaded his eyes as they walked to the back of the truck. George was whistling and his steps were bouncy.

"What are you so happy about?" Clay asked.

"Almost done with the Rolls-Royce," George said. "She's a beaut! Just needs a bit more engine work."

"Good for you." Clay patted him on the shoulder.

"Also, my wife had a heart attack a couple of days ago."

"What?"

"She's dead. Found her facedown in her breakfast." Sadness washed over George's expression but left as soon as he gestured toward the truck. "Now get on with it. Look at those nightstands! As long as you keep the ax out of the picture, I think you could do something nice with them."

"George, I'm so—"

"Come on now, hurry it up. Got things to do. I'm picking up a bumper for the Rolls-Royce in an hour."

Clay stared vacantly into the truck, regarding all the used and damaged goods that were piled and squeezed together, one on top of the other as high as the truck would hold them. He wanted to believe that anything could be fixed with enough elbow grease and a vision for what it had once been and could be again.

He stepped back. "Not today, George."

"Clay! You're breaking my heart! Not even that bookcase with the little hearts carved into it? You're such a sucker for that kind of thing."

Clay looked at George, his aging eyes desperately waiting for a reply. Fifteen minutes later, ten pieces of furniture and antiques sat next to the truck. George was beyond delighted, which on any other day might be normal. But what was there to delight in when his wife had just died? Clay kept his baffled thoughts to himself. Plus, he figured with how things were going with Amber, he was going to have a lot of time on his hands.

"Well, I gotta get going." George hopped into his truck, hung his elbow out the window.

Clay stepped up next to him. "You won't miss her?"

George diverted his eyes and pitched a thumb toward Amber's apartment. "Hey, what about you? Huh? Do you love this girl? If you do, life's too short. That's all I got for you. But . . ."

"What?"

"If it doesn't work out, can you give me her number?"

"Hilarious."

George started the truck with a roar; then it settled into a low, sputtering rumble. "Mind stopping by the funeral this afternoon? Helen always liked a crowd."

"Sure, George. Of course."

George started to say thanks, but his bottom lip quivered and he just nodded his reply.

The truck pulled away, a cloud of dust in its wake.

♥

Amber peeked out the window. All was quiet. Walking over to her new Bible, she reached under it and slid the DVD out. No matter how hard she tried, she couldn't imagine it. It seemed even on Clay Walsh's worst day, he was still some kind of saint.

She needed to accept that behind all of this . . . What term could she even use? What would she call it? *Relational austerity?* Yeah, behind the relational austerity, he was probably just being polite. Probably trying to find some way to break it off because he didn't find her . . . whatever. Attractive, interesting, fun. Maybe she didn't follow the rules right. The truth was, she didn't know all the rules. She'd never cracked open a Bible to find out. Above all else, she knew she was just a complication to what he'd been working so hard to achieve. He'd set out his theories and here she came, like a whirlwind, blowing everything to bits.

The DVD glided into the player like it was on air. Amber knelt in front of the TV, blinking slowly as the images and sounds began to stream from the box. Her hand slipped over her mouth. She wanted to close her eyes, but she couldn't look away.

♥

In a cemetery high on Park Hill, with a breathtaking view of the town below, Clay stood next to George, the only two people there besides the pastor. George, in his ill-fitting suit, stood with his hands clasped, looking at the wooden box of a coffin, all that he could afford. Some purple wildflowers, the only ones Clay knew of that grew in the fall around here, lay clustered on top.

The pastor and his black book stood near the head of the coffin. He quoted all the usuals: "dust to dust," "love is patient and kind," etc. After five minutes, he was done. "Is there anything you would like to say about your wife, Helen, Mr. Franks?"

"Yes, sir." George stepped forward, eyes on the coffin. "She made the best fried chicken I have ever tasted, and that included when I had to work for three months down in the South. It had this crunch to it that I can't hardly describe. And she'd fry up the whole chicken, too, just for the two of us." He respectfully stepped back in line with Clay.

"All right," the pastor said. He led them in a prayer, then walked to George and held out his hand to shake. "Good meeting you, George."

"Thank you, Pastor. Thank you for coming on the short notice." George fumbled in his reach for the pastor's handshake—his hands trembled, so he used both of them to cup the other man's.

The pastor walked down the hill. Clay and George stayed for a long time, George just blinking slowly at the coffin, like there was so much to take in, more than one person could possibly take in.

Clay didn't know what to do. Maybe George needed some time alone. "Well, I should probably—"

And then George dropped to his knees, covered his face. His wail was picked up and carried into the wind, dispersing the sound into a soft cry.

Clay knelt beside him, putting a hand on his shoulder. Below them, the faint sounds of traffic came and went.

"She's all I got," George cried. "She's all I got." Tears gushed down his face as he looked at the coffin. "We ain't had it perfect, that's the truth. Most of the time it didn't even feel like love. But I always been difficult and she never left me. Never even threatened to. She threatened to hit me with a frying pan, but I probably deserved it."

Clay watched a lifetime of memories flood George's face as he kept trying to stop tears that wouldn't.

"I called her Hel a lot—always got under her skin, but sometimes made her laugh. She kept tellin' me to get her a different nickname and I said I would as soon as I found one that fit her better." He chuckled, but his chin trembled.

Clay didn't leave George's side. The sun had nearly set when the gravedigger approached, said they were going to have to put her in the ground now. George stood and draped himself over the coffin, giving it one long kiss and a hug, his arms barely reaching halfway around the box. He stepped back and they watched the man crank the coffin slowly into the ground, four inches at a time.

George turned to Clay. "You get on now. You got more important things to do."

"George, I—"

"*I* nothin'. Get on now. I'm fine. You go. Don't you have a love seat to repair? All that damage you caused?" Through misty eyes, George gave Clay a knowing look.

"Okay." Clay shook his hand, squeezed his shoulder, then moved down the hill, wrapping himself with his arms, chilled by wind that was no longer warmed by the sun and by the lonely man on the top of the hill, saying his long good-bye. As he walked, he noticed the sky was dim and purple. It was the first time he'd noticed such a thing apart from when he was with Amber. He looked back once.

George held the shovel and was lifting the dirt, dumping it little by little into Helen's grave, all by himself.

He'd tried to call, but no answer. Now he stood on the stoop, where she used to keep the shoe box for him, where he'd made her stand in the rain under an umbrella. He knocked. All the lights were off. The curtains were drawn, but not all the way, and when he peeked in the windows, he could see a little bit, mostly just the kitchen counter.

The money jar she always kept there was gone.

Mr. Joe stared at him from the floor, his ears flat, his eyes narrow.

Hurrying, Clay jumped into his truck and drove to the floral shop. Things were locked up, but a single light glowed from what looked to be a back room. The sign clearly said Closed, but he pounded on the door anyway. Again. And again.

Then the woman who owned the shop, the one he'd met the other night, came out. She opened the door.

Carol—that was her name. Less memorable than the glare she'd fixed on him all night.

"We're closed. And at this point, I'm not sure flowers are going to do you any good."

"I'm not here to buy—"

Carol shot him a look like maybe he should reconsider that option.

"Do you know where she is?"

Carol stepped outside, closed the door, drew a cigarette out of her pocket and then a lighter. It was dark enough that when she lit up, the end of the cigarette glowed bright orange like a mini sun. She puffed on it for a second, indifferent to the cold. "I gave her one of your old DVDs."

Clay searched her eyes, her expression, her words. What was she saying? *The* DVD?

"You know the one."

Clay put his hand over his mouth, but it didn't matter—he was speechless. He turned away, trying not to imagine what Amber might think or feel when she saw it. What she would *see*. He wanted to yell at Carol. Why would she do such a thing?

He leaned against the shop wall, staring into the empty street, smoke drifting by him, but that wasn't what was suffocating him. He knew the answer to his question—Amber had to see him, fully.

The cigarette dangled between Carol's fingers. Ash floated to the ground. "And you know what? She didn't even flinch.

I told her to look at the name on it. And she didn't care. She believes you're a good man."

Clay looked at her.

"Are you a good man?" She puffed the cigarette again. It choked out the cool air, hanging like a veil between them.

He didn't know how to answer that question.

"Because she's good. Yeah, maybe she's impulsive and a wild horse and has a past like all the rest of us. But in her heart, she believes in love. And for the life of me, I don't know why, but she believes in you."

"Where is she? Just tell me where she is."

Carol threw her cigarette to the ground and stomped on it. "You're going to have to work harder than that."

♥

She'd intended to stop at three. She was on five.

Amber slammed the shot glass down on the table. Her head swirled.

Trish was giggling. "Now we can do this *every* night!" She tilted her head at Amber like she needed to be thoroughly examined. "Okay, I can tell this is going to take extreme measures. Wait here. Don't leave. I'm going to get something to cheer you up."

Trish disappeared but Amber hardly noticed. All she could see were those images. The girls. The words. The way Clay egged it all on, not a care in the world about who those girls were or what they needed. Of course, they didn't seem to care either. They seemed to relish the attention.

Was she so different from them? She'd relished attention too in her life, but never like she did from her husband. They'd been married six weeks when she'd decided she
needed to be more seductive. Sexy. Sensual. More like the
girls on the magazines in the supermarket. Maybe that was
the problem. Maybe he wanted more of that.

She bought new clothes. Thought about plastic surgery.
Wore more makeup. Had her hair highlighted. She wore her
skirts shorter. Did crunches and leg lifts and tried to wear
the kind of shoes that accentuated her calves. She plucked
her eyebrows and tried false eyelashes. They couldn't afford
it, but she snuck the credit card and bought the expensive
kind of skin cream, the one that claimed to be miraculous.
She switched perfumes. She tried to giggle more. Let her shirt
hang off her shoulder. Stopped wearing ponytails.

She left him little cards. Bought him tickets to the game.
Started drinking his favorite kind of beer.

But he grew more and more distant until one day he
stopped touching her at all.

It had been a Tuesday, February 14, when she sprinkled a
trail of rose petals leading to the bed and lit candles all over
the house. She cooked his favorite meal and bought some
beautiful lingerie. He was late coming home from work, but
she waited and waited anyway, trying to keep the dinner hot
and the candles from dying in their own wax.

Two hours later, he came in. She opened the door for him,
gestured to the table, set with good dishes she'd borrowed
from a neighbor. She'd put a tablecloth down and made a

beautiful bouquet of flowers from some she'd picked up at Walmart.

When he looked at her, she posed playfully, like a model. He looked at the dinner.

"Your mom's meat loaf recipe," she said.

His gaze roamed the room. He noticed the candles, then the rose petals leading into the bedroom.

And then he looked back at her. "The thing is, I'm really tired. It's been a long day, and I was hoping to just take a shower and go to bed. Wrap that all up," he said, nodding to the kitchen, "and I'll nuke it tomorrow, I promise."

He disappeared into the bedroom. She heard the shower turn on and the door to the bathroom lock.

"Look who I found playing darts!" Trish's excited squeal popped Amber back into reality. Hanging from Trish's arm was the guy from the other day, who had come into the shop for the white roses.

Trish took both his shoulders and pushed him toward the table. He slid into the seat next to Amber, looking crazy handsome under the darkness of the underlit bar. His hair was more spiked this time, less slick. He looked more genuine, but maybe that was the alcohol talking.

"Hi," he said.

"Did your friend like the roses?" She hoped the words came out right. She was starting to feel like they were sliding back and forth inside her mouth, tumbling out in the wrong order, if they came out at all.

"Loved them."

The guy grinned at her and Amber ran her fingers through her hair. "You want me?"

He blinked like he wasn't sure he'd heard her correctly.

"Am I the most attractive woman you've ever seen?" Well, the words were coming out just fine now. And fast, too.

"Sure."

"Are you allergic to cats?"

"Never."

He took her hand, helped her out of her seat, guided her by the small of her back through the crowd to the dance floor. A slow song played. She didn't recognize it, which was unusual. But she wasn't focused on the music.

He pulled her close without hesitation, as if he assumed that was exactly what she wanted, and he was exactly who she wanted, and this was exactly where she wanted to be. They chatted lightly, their faces close. He seemed transfixed by her, like nothing was going to get in his way. His voice was low and soothing. He complimented her. He loved her hair. Her eyes. Her smile. "You're lovely," he said at one point, pressing her close to him, putting his cheek next to hers. His hand caressed her shoulder. His cologne was barely there, just a hint, as if he knew how close a woman would have to be to smell it. He brushed her hair away from her face, smiled at her like she was all that mattered in the moment.

Two or three songs later—she wasn't counting—he asked if she wanted to go someplace more private. Amber wasn't even sure if she said yes, but by then he'd taken her hand in his and was guiding her out the door.

From the bar, Trish waved and grinned like Amber's wild-est dreams might be coming true.

Outside, it was cold. The guy wrapped his arms around her, held her tight against the wind. In the parking lot, he opened the door to a red sports car—a rental, he told her—and she got in. It smelled like his cologne.

He slid into his seat and started the engine, which roared to life and then purred. He grinned at her, touched her arm, noticed her calves as she crossed her legs. Without another word, he drove off.

Amber stared out the window, numb, as his car raced around curves on a street she wasn't familiar with. She didn't know where they were going. And whatever beauty the al-cohol had painted moments ago, it was leaving her system quickly. It was just a starless night, empty of moonlight.

But she didn't care.

Within minutes, they'd arrived at a hotel. A valet took his keys and he helped her out, his hand at her elbow, then at her hip. They walked across the hotel together like some ordinary couple.

"I've got a suite," he said as they got into the elevator. He moved close to her, brushed her hair off her shoulder, kissed her neck. "What's your name?" he whispered.

"Does it matter?"

"I'm—"

"I don't want to know."

His fingers glided down her arm, the back of his hand sliding along her hip.

On the eighth floor, the doors opened. He wrapped an arm around her waist and led her down the hall, swiped his card to unlock a door, stepped in.

Then he turned and noticed she hadn't moved.

"You coming?"

Amber looked down at her feet, resting at the threshold.

CHAPTER 16

"I'M A DINOSAUR." Clay ripped open the package of sugarless cinnamon gum he'd grabbed from the candy rack beneath the counter. "I mean, look at me." He took another packet and threw it on the counter, just for good measure. "Are you even over twenty-one?" he asked the clerk.

The kid's eyes were wide as he watched Clay shove two more pieces in his mouth. "It's a liquor store, so yeah."

"But see, you're not even asking me my age."

"You said *dinosaur*, so I was thinking north of twenty."

"Can you be sure? Maybe I look old for my age."

"Well, you're buying gum. You have to be at least three to purchase it, so—okay, what are you doing now?"

Clay took the cardboard box that held all the packets

221

of cellophane-wrapped cinnamon gum and dumped it on the counter. "What's the point? Am I right?" He gestured at himself, at the gum, at the ceiling.

The clerk's eyes went even wider. "Are you going to rob me?"

Clay pulled out his wallet, causing the clerk to flinch. He shoved the pile of gum forward. "What's this stuff cost, anyway?"

"A buck fifty a packet."

"For gum?"

"They sell it cheaper over at the 7-Eleven. Across the street. Where most people buy their gum."

Clay glanced over his shoulder and out the front window, for the first time noticing a man behind him, holding whiskey, waiting patiently but swaying ever so slightly.

The man smiled, closed his eyes like he might just doze off, then said, "Cold as Ice."

"I'm not cold!"

"It's the flavor of the—"

"Is that what she thinks? I'm cold? Is that what everyone thinks? I'm trying to do the right thing here. I'm trying to—"

"The mint gum. Called Cold as Ice. Hides the evidence." The man grinned, pointing to his bottle. "Will burn the taste buds right off your tongue, though."

Clay turned back to the clerk, who was staring at the gum.

"So . . . you want all these?" the clerk asked.

Back at home, Clay sat on the living room floor, chewing four pieces of cinnamon gum at a time until the flavor wore off. She was right. Cinnamon was really good. Underneath his hand, he spun his basketball against the floor. With his other hand, he scanned stations on his old radio, but everything sounded so . . . useless. It was that far into the night, when even the radio stations went to sleep.

He closed his eyes, wanting to pray, wanting the God of the universe to come down and tell him what to do. But even the loudest attempt at a prayer didn't seem to leave the room. It didn't even make it high enough to bounce off the ceiling. It just hung there like dust in the air.

"God . . . God . . ." He squeezed his eyes shut, unable to believe his life could ever get this complicated again. Years ago, after he read the Bible for the first time, it seemed he had to wade through months of sorrow, seeing the full effect, the full horror, of his sin. But coupled with that was a settled, sturdy, strong hope like a roaring tide that washed over his iniquities, then quietly retreated, leaving the sand smooth and beautiful.

He rose, grabbed another piece of gum, and walked to his front door, where the Ten Commandments hung on the wall. Even through the darkness he could see it clearly. It had been a gift from Aunt Zella when his life had taken such a dramatic turn. The scroll had been Uncle Lloyd's, whom he didn't even know that well. He had met him only a couple times over the years. Lloyd had died when Clay was a teenager but was kept alive through Aunt Zella's vivid and sometimes-hallucinatory memories of him.

The story went that it was Lloyd's father, who'd been

to Egypt and Israel on an archaeological expedition, who brought the scroll back for Lloyd, just a child then, as a gift. When it was passed to Clay, he framed it himself.

The words were in Hebrew, but Clay didn't need them in English. He knew them by heart. All of them.

I am the Lord thy God. . . .
Thou shalt have no other gods before me.
Thou shalt not make unto thee any graven image. . . .
Thou shalt not take the name of the Lord thy God in
　　vain. . . .
Remember the sabbath day, to keep it holy. . . .
Honour thy father and thy mother. . . .
Thou shalt not kill.
Thou shalt not commit adultery.
Thou shalt not steal.
Thou shalt not bear false witness against thy neighbor.
Thou shalt not covet. . . .

It had been the last one, the one about not coveting, that brought him to his knees so many years ago, bleeding him out from each wrist. The selfish desires of his heart had created in him a monster of lust. He realized that this commandment especially revealed his heart's innermost intentions. God made Clay understand that He saw all his secrets. He saw every night with every woman. He knew each of their names, even when Clay didn't. There was nothing hidden from Him.

It was the strangest feeling, to be convicted but not condemned.

God had torn him down but then had slowly built him back up. He had crushed him and then restored him. The more honest Clay became, the more God revealed to him the condition of his heart—a heart born into darkness, a heart that had trusted in the ways of the world.

From there, God marked out Clay's need for deliverance from the power of sin.

It was then that he saw the beauty of the law. Fell in love with it. Understood why it was like honey on King David's lips.

But now as he stood in front of it, Clay could see his own reflection, even in the darkness. In fact, better in the darkness than when the lights were on. He stared into himself. Disgust stared back.

No matter what he did, he had an amazing talent for hurting people.

It was, apparently, what he did best.

He took the frame off the wall, his gaze tracing the eloquent markings of the Hebrew language, his thumbs resting on the ornate trim.

And then he let it go.

It slipped from his fingers, tumbled downward in a way that made it seem weightless, then smashed into the ground as if it weighed a ton. The glass cracked with a quick snap, like a spine breaking in two.

Then he heard a knock.

Clay gasped, looking up at the front door right beside him. He'd not heard anyone come up the steps or seen any car lights. *Amber. Thank You, God. Thank You.* He stepped over the broken frame, grabbed the door handle, and yanked it open.

She stood in the darkness, the porch light glowing over her head like a halo, her face streaked with tears. In her hand, she held a bottle of wine. In her eyes, she held a measure of desperation.

"Kelly . . ."

"Hi." She shook her head like she was trying to rid herself of words and emotions and intentions. Clay couldn't grasp the idea that she was really standing there. Right in front of him. He'd imagined it a thousand times over the years.

"Can I come in?" She was inches from him. Clay looked down. Noticed her feet standing at the threshold. Noticed his on the other side. His heart beat frantically inside his chest.

He thought of Amber—that sweet face of hers, so trusting and innocent. But so was Kelly, before Clay had got ahold of her. She'd had the most engaging personality and gorgeous, sparkling eyes—eyes that always reflected a sincerity Clay thought impossible for himself.

No, he shouldn't let her in. He wanted to make things right, but there wasn't a way to do it. Not in the plan he had for his life.

Sometimes plans changed, though.

Despite himself, he stepped back, nodded, even as guilt stabbed his heart.

Kelly walked in and smiled at him, the same smile that had caught his attention when she'd first walked up to him all those years ago, on a loud, riotous South Padre Island beach during a sweltering Bolivar spring break trip where he and Brad had picked up a last-minute gig.

Kelly set the wine down on the coffee table and slipped off her coat, dropping it to the couch. Her clothes were simple but draped across her in the most beautiful way. Clay shut the door, paused there, his hand still on the knob. She was across the room, watching him.

"I'm sorry," he said, the emotions bubbling to the surface with those two simple words. It was what he'd wanted to say to her over and over through the years. He'd picked up the phone to call her but never dialed. He wrote her three separate letters but never sent them. He'd prayed for her some but at the same time didn't want to think about her. Or maybe wanted to think about her too much. Eventually he had to forget about her. He'd dropped her out of his hands just like he'd dropped the commandments to the ground.

"Clay, you don't have to—"

"I do." He nodded, his back against the door. "I should have a long time ago, Kelly. What I did was . . ." It was unspeakable. There weren't really words to describe it.

"I'm not angry. I just wanted to see you again," she said softly. She stepped around the coffee table, closer to him now but still far enough away. "It's been so long. And I'm . . ." She choked up, shook her head. "I've had a rough year."

For a long time they both stood there, looking at each

other, a familiar easiness settling between them as Clay felt himself being absorbed by everything he had always loved about her. His knuckles were bloodless now, white as cotton, as he held the doorknob.

"Kelly, it's just that . . ."

"Yes? What is it?" She was genuinely asking as she always did. She was genuine in every part of her life, with every question she asked, with everything she ever sought out.

He closed his eyes and turned, his head resting against the wood. Right here, standing in his living room, was everything he'd wanted and nothing he should have.

What was he doing?

And then he felt her behind him. Her hand touched his shoulder, slid underneath his arm. Her cheek rested against his back.

He turned to her, his beautiful girl, the one he let get away. She was a decade older now, and her youthful eyes had dulled slightly with a train-wrecked life—a life he'd helped create.

Kelly reached up and touched his face, wiping away . . . a tear? He hadn't even realized he was crying. He trembled against her, scared and helpless, wanting to make right all that he had done wrong while fully understanding how wrong it would be to try.

Her fingers swept through his hair, over his neck, down his back. She held on to him tightly and he moved his arms around her, protecting her from whatever had happened since . . . him.

She looked into his eyes, tears rolling down her face. She had been the only one he'd ever really loved. But by the time he'd figured it out, she was pregnant by another man. Then married. Then gone.

Clay squeezed his eyes shut, remembering Kelly standing next to him one cold winter night on a small wooden bridge built a century ago, staring over frozen creek waters.

She was the one who convinced him God loved him. She was the one who told him he could be saved. He resisted it at the time. He wanted her but not all the baggage that came with what she believed. She kept telling him he could change, but he didn't want to change. He didn't believe he needed to.

"Clay," she said that cold night, entwining her fingers with his, "you can't tell me you're happy. That all of this makes you happy." By then, his and Brad's gig was growing nonstop.

"You make me happy," he said, grinning at her, pulling her tightly against him.

But she wouldn't be distracted.

"I'm serious," she said as they shivered together. "Clay, I see something in you. Something bigger than all this nonsense you and Brad do together. You're intelligent. You're funny. You've got this passion, this fire inside you that can make a difference in people's lives." God would use him, she always said. God had a plan and a purpose for his life.

"I only want to make a difference in your life," he told her. He'd kind of known at that moment that he was falling for her because for the most part, he hadn't cared much whether he made a difference or not, to anybody. He cared only for himself. Maybe part of him was attracted to her because, of all the women he'd been around, she seemed to be the only one who could resist him.

Now, inside Clay's home, under the cover of darkness, Kelly drew closer to him, nudging her face into the hollow of his neck. He pulled her in against his chest, his lips sweeping her hair, and drew a deep breath.

CHAPTER 17

AS MUCH AS SHE COULD, Amber walked on the grass, feeling the cool, prickly blades between her toes. Clay had taught her that: the beauty of a walk. Sometimes she was so compelled to look up that she forgot about the solid, sturdy ground under her feet. Her shoes were slung over her shoulder and her coat was wrapped tightly around her waist. She loved the sound of the crunching leaves beneath her.

The sun was lifting above the horizon now but still dimmed by the trees on the skyline. Peach-hued light sliced into the fading black sky. Even though it had not fully risen, already it was providing warmth. She smiled as she thought of Clay. She'd never met anyone like him. Not even close. To think she ran out of gas right here in this town, right at this time. It felt like more than fate. It felt like maybe divine intervention had finally come into her life.

This man, this quirky, gentle soul, with ocean-blue eyes and moppy, boyish hair—he was the goodness she'd been looking for her whole life, all wrapped up in a hoodie and faded jeans. She'd been many places and met many people, some of whom she'd call friends for the rest of her life. But none like Clay Walsh. None who had convictions that wouldn't falter, not even when she could see in his eyes that he wanted to step over the line. How could she go wrong with this guy?

So she walked until she got to his street, then combed her hair out of her face and took a deep breath. For a very long time, she hadn't put all her eggs in one basket. It was too risky. But she'd finally found the one on whom she could completely depend.

Finally.

This morning, she would make it right. She would tell him they could go at whatever pace he needed. Work through a dozen books. See counselors galore. Mark out a financial plan that would make Warren Buffett look like a slacker. Whatever. He was worth it.

She hurried along the sidewalk, eager to get to his house. As she reached the edge of his property, just behind a hedge of bushes, she saw his front door open. A flutter of giddiness told her she was on the right track. What perfect timing.

And then a woman came out.

Amber stumbled backward, behind the bushes almost by

accident. The leaves rattled and she held her breath, standing perfectly still but able to see through the gaps.

The woman was tall, thin, blonde. She looked sophisticated. Everything Amber seemed not to be. She realized who it was—the girl in the photograph she'd pulled from Clay's Bible.

Kelly.

Amber covered her mouth to keep from screaming or crying or cursing. She wasn't sure what was about to fly out.

Kelly carried a large overnight bag and wore a long, shimmery dress, like one might wear for a wedding. Not a hair was out of place. She stopped at Clay's truck, touched the window, then walked on. What? Had it all started in the truck? Some steamy make-out session on some lonely, dark street that Clay would not have dared take Amber to?

Dared? Or would not have desired to?

Just like that, Kelly disappeared into her sleek sedan and left.

Amber turned, her chest heaving with more emotion than it could hold. She had worried about a lot of things concerning Clay, but she had never worried about another woman.

How could she have been so stupid? Her stomach cramped with a stabbing pain of regret and remorse as she turned and ran, as fast as she could, her bare feet pressing onto dead, dry twigs that she never even looked down to see. The earth was not solid anymore beneath her feet.

She kept going until she ran out of breath, on a street she didn't know, lined with old, abandoned warehouses. She thought she was heading east and needed to go north, so she cut through an alley, but the shadows of the buildings trespassed the morning sun and hovered over her like dark hands.

And she found herself unable to walk anymore.

Amber slumped against an old brick wall, a couple of nearby cats watching her with little interest. Maybe this was what she deserved. But all she really wanted was to be wanted.

She put her face in her hands and sobbed.

♥

Clay rushed into the house so fast that everyone, all at once, stopped and looked at him. He searched the crowd for David. A few guests kindly nodded toward the doorway of the bedroom. There he was.

"David," he said, "I'm so sorry. I'm here. I have the ring."

David scowled, he and Brad both looking Clay up and down as Brad adjusted David's tie. "You look terrible," David said finally, letting him off the hook. "You okay?"

"I'm fine."

"You look hungover," Brad said with a suspicious grin.

"I'm fine. Really. Just overslept."

"I wasn't worried," Brad said. "I told him you were probably double-checking his wedding vows for theological errors or something. Making sure his ceremony is up to standards, without stain or blemish."

Clay tried a good-natured laugh, though it seemed there wasn't a bit of joy left inside him. It most likely came out as a grimace, but he wasn't about to look in the mirror at himself.

David shot Brad a look. "Just let him live his own life."

"It's fine," Clay said, turning away from the mirror to slip on his vest. "Like you always said, Brad—eventually I'm going to crash and burn."

"And I hope I'm there to see it."

"Maybe you're looking at it right now."

David and Brad exchanged glances, but Clay focused on getting his tie right.

Brad stood next to him and turned toward the mirror, starting with the gel in his hair. "So you guys want to know what I did last night?"

"No," David and Clay said in unison.

"For starters, the appe*teaser*, I pick up this crazy-hot chickapoo at the Brewhouse. Uber-tasty. Take her back to my room at the hotel—" Brad inserted a guitar sound.

"Don't do that," David groaned.

"Boys, it's almost time," a lady said, sticking her head through the doorway and clapping her hands as though they were children.

"Sorry," David said. "That's Lisa's aunt. She's a wedding planner, so she's taking this very seriously."

Clay walked to the window and peered out at the setup in the backyard. White chairs lined the lawn, perfectly straight like a marching band. There was a wooden arch at the back of the yard, covered in flowers. Even the grass looked to be groomed better than he was. Maybe he should fix his hair or something.

He felt a hand on his shoulder. David.

"Wow, man, this looks incredible," Clay said. "Beautiful."

"Thanks. All Lisa's doing. I just show up, do what I'm told." He grinned. "So is Amber coming?"

Clay shook his head, stared out the window.

"Okay," David said in a tone that said he knew not to ask any more questions right now.

Within a few minutes, the wedding planner/aunt had lined the guys up at the back door and led the bridesmaids in, partnering them with their groomsmen.

Kelly stepped next to Clay. She looked stunning, her hair pulled back from her face, his favorite way she wore it. They stood silently, Clay only giving her a small smile of acknowledgment. He really wished he wasn't having to do this.

The music started and Brad and his bridesmaid moved toward the arch.

Kelly slipped her arm around Clay's like she was supposed to for the walk. And in the quietest voice imaginable, under the string quartet, said, "Clay." The way she said his name caught him off guard, like hearing a favorite old love song or smelling homemade chocolate-chip cookies. The familiarity of her was his greatest temptation.

He glanced at her even though he didn't want to.

"I was pretty stupid last night," she said.

He didn't want to talk about last night. At all.

"Clay, you could've done anything you wanted." Her eyes watered and her voice trembled. "What I'm trying to say is . . . thanks for not . . . I mean, thanks for . . ." She caught her breath, looking determined to say what was on her heart. "Thanks for being a gentleman."

Relief flooded his heart. He actually smiled at her, the kind of smile that was safe and meant for friends.

She laughed a little. "I can't believe you slept in your truck. You didn't have to do that."

Her wedding ring glinted in the sun. Clay felt the full force of regret for all those years before. Loss for not hanging on to a really good, nice girl. Guilt for having caused her so much pain. Gratitude that he wasn't standing here in the aftermath of a terrible mistake made last night.

The wedding planner gestured for them to go, so they did, arm in arm, until they parted ways to stand in their places.

Little Cosie walked next, in her tiny formal dress poufed out like a ballerina's skirt, a halo of fall leaves over her head. She tossed rose petals by the handful, relishing the attention and making everyone laugh as she intermittently and randomly threw out a scowl to a wedding guest.

Then Lisa came through the back door. She looked beautiful, seeming to soak up all the sunshine. Her dress drifted around her like the gorgeous, foamy peaks of white-water rapids.

She couldn't take her eyes off David.

The justice of the peace began the ceremony, but Clay could only stare out at one lonely, empty seat in the yard. He imagined Amber sitting there, watching him, smiling at him the way only she could, giving him a look that said he looked adorable and goofy all at once in his tuxedo.

He glanced at Kelly, who smiled gently at him. It was

irony at its fullest. He'd finally become everything she'd hoped and prayed he would. But only after he'd sown such destructive seeds into her life. The best girl he ever knew was now wrapped up in sorrow and dismay, in a life she would've never hoped for herself. And it sealed their fate: they'd never be able to be together.

Clay fixed his gaze upon the grass and never looked up again.

CHAPTER 18

AMBER CLUTCHED THE CORNER of her pillow and prepared herself for another bout of crying. It would start and stop on a whim, so she'd not ventured out of her house all day. Instead, she stayed in, tried to stay busy, considered taking up four or five different hobbies. But nothing brought her peace. She'd soon end up on her bed, crying again, clutching her—

She threw the pillow down. No. She wasn't going to be *that* girl. She had to be strong.

But she wasn't. She wasn't strong at all. That was the point of the money jar, wasn't it? To run when she couldn't face things anymore? As she lay on her side, she looked at it, sitting innocently on her bedside table. Sometimes it seemed to call her name.

She hopped up from her bed, scorning herself. "Get a grip!"

As she dried her face and put her most comfortable and snuggly pajamas on, Amber noticed the Bible she'd bought, sitting on the counter, barely cracked open. She didn't know a lot about religion, but she did know that book wasn't going to do much good unless she read it. It had seemed, once or twice, to call her name too.

She got comfortable on her bed and started flipping through it. Her eyes roamed over the words, for hours it seemed, searching for something, anything that would help her. It was all so confusing, so . . . heady. And so much of it didn't make sense. A talking donkey? What was all this? Where were the passages on love? She needed something to hold on to, something that told her she wasn't alone.

Clay loved this book. But why? What made him read it every day? What made him want to become a good person—the best person—despite everyone making fun of him? What kept him that way? There had to be something in here that had caused his change of heart.

Eventually Amber found herself reading more of the back of the book than the front, studying the words written in red—she figured out that the red was when Jesus spoke. And she wanted to know this Jesus, but He talked about cutting off hands and poking out eyes and it all seemed so bizarre to her. Except she knew there was *something* to it.

Further in, she read a lot about holiness by a guy named Paul, who was apparently writing a lot of letters to people from prison. And she found a passage on what love is supposed to be. Kind. Patient. Hopeful. But even though she wanted all that for herself, and wanted to give it too, it seemed impossible. How could she ever be this good? Do all the right stuff, all the time? Be good enough to deserve someone's love?

She was about to shut the book and put it away when one last line grabbed her attention. As she read these words, her heart swelled with a hope she'd never had before. A peace, so palpable it felt like her soul had been warmed by fire, caused her to grow very still. She had never felt anything like it, had never known a time when there wasn't a worry that pricked her heart in some way or another. She read the words again, out loud, though even when she'd read them silently she could clearly hear them as if they were being spoken right in front of her.

"'Never will I leave you; never will I forsake you.'"

That was what she'd wanted to hear from Clay—from any of the men in her life. *Those* were the words. Clay had never said them, but here was someone who was saying it to her, right now, right here in the dark, candlelit room of her apartment.

"Never will I leave you; never will I forsake you." The words burst through her heart, a soundless, underwater wave. Her whole body relaxed. Her mind calmed to a standstill. And she knew something immediately, a wordless truth that was so real it was as if God had come down to stand in front of her and proclaim it. Was this what love was supposed to be? *How* it was supposed to be?

This man. This Jesus. He would come after her. He would chase her. She knew instantly that He'd been chasing her for a long time.

And tonight she would let Him catch her.

Amber stood, compelled to go draw water in her tub. She climbed in and slid down, water the temperature of peace resting at her chin. And then, without taking a breath, she let it swallow her whole.

When she emerged, she felt light. And clean. She felt new. Delighted in.

Something enormous had changed in a place within her that she was never really sure existed.

For a long time after her bath, she sat on her bed, wrapped in blankets, and smiled. She'd been forgiven of all that she'd done in her life. Instantly. It amazed her. *He* amazed her, this man who knew all of her and still wanted her.

Minutes passed. Then hours. She dwelled deeply in her thoughts with God, talked openly with Him as if He sat right there in the room with her.

After a while, she knew what she had to do. Before she could really move on, she had to make things right with Clay. She had to forgive him, even if she didn't understand him. It was easier to forgive when your own debts had been paid.

As Amber drove to his house, the emotions she felt for him returned with each corner she took. Only God knew what she'd find when she got there, but Clay deserved to know what he meant to her. So he'd messed up. There was forgiveness. There was mercy. He had introduced her to this

Bible, to these words. She had to say thank you at the very least. But she wanted to say more.

It was early evening when she knocked gently on the door. There was no answer.

"Are you there? Open up." She knocked again, leaning against the door the way she'd dreamed of leaning against his chest. "Please open this door." Her knock was barely a tap now. "Please . . ."

Nothing.

Amber felt her chin trembling with everything she needed to say. It came tumbling out even though all that stood there to receive it was a wooden door. "I don't want normal. I want you." She pressed her forehead against the door, tears rolling down her face. "Do you know what I did on my honeymoon? I cried myself to sleep, trying to figure out why my brand-new husband was more interested in watching . . . He didn't touch me. He didn't want to touch me." She put a hand on the door. Listened for him. Then she stepped back. "And that's not your fault. You're not him."

The door opened suddenly. It was barely cracked, as if there were a safety chain holding it, but there wasn't. Clay squinted as though he were looking into midday sun. He looked awful, still wearing his wedding attire. She'd never seen him look so despondent. But here he was, and she needed to say what she needed to say. It wasn't going to be easy, fetching the truth, working through it.

"Why did you let her in?" It wasn't the best lead-in, but she had to know.

He blinked, seemingly lost.

"I saw her leaving this morning. That was Bible girl, wasn't it?"

A flicker of recognition passed over his face, but he didn't say anything. Fine. She could do all the talking.

"Was anyone else here? In the house?" That was the obvious question, wasn't it?

"No."

Amber caught her breath, tried not to show her hand. "You were alone together?"

He nodded, his eyes watering. She tried to hold on to what she'd read, about God never leaving her. But she felt left at this moment. And it was doing nothing short of wrecking her soul—even while she was trying to forgive.

"Just for a moment," Clay said, and then he smiled a little, shaking his head.

"What's so funny?"

"I slept in my truck."

Amber tried to process. He slept in his truck? Which meant . . . that was why Kelly stopped at the window of his truck. "You didn't . . . ?"

"Almost." He looked at his feet. "I thought about it."

"Do you want to be with her?"

"No." His response was more firm than she anticipated.

Amber clutched the doorframe. "Why didn't you come after me?"

His eyes watered again, which made her eyes water. She didn't like to see this man cry.

"I have a theory," she said gently. "Maybe love doesn't have to be perfect to still be worth it. And you don't have to be perfect for me to . . ." *Love you.*

"You don't know all the things I've done."

"I know more than you think. As far as I can tell, we're all big, pathetic, messy piles of . . . I won't finish that sentence in honor of you. But I've been reading that Bible you like so much." She sighed, trying to find the right words. "You're worth it. That's what I'm trying to say."

But he didn't look like he believed her.

"I am not sure if I should be with anybody. At all."

She wanted to reach out and touch him, but his body language told her that wasn't a good idea. So instead, she asked again, "Why didn't you come after me?"

"I did."

Something about the way his lips moved into a straight line and his eyes absorbed all the light away told her that he knew something.

"I went to Carol, who sent me to the Brewhouse. I ran into Trish. She told me you hooked up with some guy." Now his eyes went narrow with accusation. "Who?"

Amber stiffened. She hated the way he was looking at her. "I don't know his name. I never asked for it."

"What did you do?" he asked.

The question wounded her more than she anticipated, but she held a steady expression. This seemed like an emotional standoff, and she wasn't going to back down. "Would it make a difference?" she asked.

He just stood there, no consolation even hinted at.

"Ouch."

"Amber . . ."

"I was ready to forgive you, no matter what." Her voice cracked, but she didn't care. "That's what I'm supposed to do, right? Isn't that the whole idea? Isn't that the *Good News*?"

He looked like the most broken man she'd ever seen. "You make it sound so easy," he whispered.

"*You* make it sound impossible."

"If I had betrayed everything I said I believed in, that would make a difference."

"Maybe," she conceded. "But it wouldn't mean that it wasn't true. Just because you fell, got it wrong, made a mistake." She shook her head, realizing it was like talking to a brick wall. "You sure know how to talk the talk. What do you think I did last night? You tell me."

Again, it was like being stabbed in the gut. His expression said everything. He really wanted to know, and it was really going to make a difference to him.

She backed away from the door, from him. "Nothing happened with that guy. We left the bar. We went to his hotel room. He opened the door and I just stood there, staring at my feet. All I could think about was you. I never even went inside."

There wasn't even relief on his face. Just a hardened, broken man who lived in a black-and-white world, looking at a woman who was fifty shades of gray. She stared at him, right into his soul, the best she knew how. He had been her goodness as recently as this morning. The only goodness she'd ever known. Slowly, she was making the separation—Clay wasn't God.

But this still hurt.

Amber turned and walked away. Didn't look back once. She never wanted to see him again. And she was certain that, as soon as she could get out of town, she never would.

CHAPTER 19

MAYBE IT WAS WHAT crazy felt like, but Clay couldn't lose the voices. Night had settled over him, even before the sun went down, and all he heard were the girls' cheers and chants—giddy over the stupid, ridiculing things he said to them. They'd flaunt themselves, and he would let them. Encourage them. Somehow, with just his words and a microphone in front of him, he'd get them to take off their clothes. And then when they did, he'd treat them like trash, like they weren't even worth a conversation. Inexplicably, they'd come back. Over and over. In droves.

All night long their voices came. He sat slumped against the wall in the living room. Shafts of moonlight sliced through the shutters, casting light and dark stripes against him. He reached for the radio. Maybe white noise would drown them out. He twisted the knob randomly until he found static, and he turned it up.

If Kelly was any indication of the destruction he left, he couldn't even fathom it. Last night he'd held in his arms a lonely, crushed, lost woman. She had not been that way when they'd met. She had been so strong, so sure she could show him the path to a better life. "You're a man after God's own heart," she'd once said. "You just don't know it yet." Somewhere along the way, they really fell in love. Except the truth was, Clay Walsh couldn't deal with that kind of reality. Not back then, anyway. And so he did the meanest thing possible when she wouldn't give in to temptation. Instead of walking away like every other guy, he slept with her best friend.

He pulled his knees up, rested his head on them, remembering the confrontation, how clueless she'd been about what he'd done. She found him one night in one of his favorite bars, hanging with the guys, intoxicated into oblivion.

Kelly looked, as she always did, out of place in the midst of drunken revelry. She approached him, trying to ignore the guys at the table laughing at her. "We need to talk," she said.

He remembered looking up at her, his words loose on his lips, the idea of their consequences lost in the inebriation. "What's up, baby?"

She was trying to keep her voice low, trying to keep their conversation out of the hands of his friends. "I want to talk to you. You haven't been returning my phone calls."

The boys behind him chuckled.

"Can't we just step outside for a little bit?" Her face looked so sweet at that moment. She truly didn't have a clue, he realized, and he grew angry. Not at her, but at himself, because of the train wreck she was about to witness. But as was typical Clay Walsh, the anger didn't stay in its intended boundaries, and coupled with the alcohol, it was about to become vicious.

"Look, sweetheart, it's just that we're not really working out."

She shook her head, tears shining through the smoky air. "That's not true. We have some things to work through, that's all."

"It's over, Kelly."

She glanced at the boys. He couldn't see their faces but imagined some smirks. A couple of decent ones were probably staring into their beers.

"Let's go outside and talk. That's all I want. I just want to know what's going on."

"You really don't."

She ran a finger under the rim of one eye. "Jessica said I should come talk to you, that maybe we could work things out if we talked."

"I slept with Jessica two nights ago at your apartment while you were at work."

The words slid out so easily, as though they were traveling down an oil slick, but then they just hung there between them. He had never in his life, before or since, seen such pain and horror on a woman's face. She lost all color in her cheeks. Those bright, beautiful, soulful eyes died right there in front of him, the light instantly snuffed out. Kelly was shaking her head ever so slightly, like there was nothing that could be more untrue. Behind him, the rowdiness of the table hushed completely. He'd stunned even them.

She blinked slowly, looking at that moment like she'd suddenly stopped believing in everything she'd been trying to convince him of. And that, more than anything, he felt in his very numb heart. He realized he'd stolen all that she believed was good. Him. Her dignity. Her best friend. Her belief that God could change people. Her belief that she was worth the wait.

She would never be able to feel the same way about herself again.

Kelly had turned and left, disappearing quickly amid scores of people on the dance floor.

And now, she was a mother with a cheating husband, who possibly believed again that she was not worth anything.

Clay wasn't sure he could ever again be responsible for another human being's heart. And Amber deserved the best. She deserved someone who would never fail her.

"Hey, wake up. Romancing the Stone, get up."

Clay's eyes fluttered open, his heart rushing with confusion, his mind dizzy from the deep sleep he'd apparently slipped into. He hadn't even realized that in the midst of all the memories and voices and angst, he'd actually fallen asleep. He shielded his eyes from the glare of the sun. How was it daytime? Someone stood in the doorway of his home, but whoever it was, they were backlit. Sharp pains stabbed his temples.

The person stepped closer. David. And Cosie was with him.

David was looking around the living room, his eyes wide with disbelief. "Dude, I knew you weren't okay. Look at you! Look at this house!"

"What?" Clay groaned as he lay back down on the sofa he'd apparently moved to at some point in the night. His last memory had been of sitting on the floor. The radio was on across the room. Why was the radio on? It was giving him a headache.

"Something is terribly wrong if there is a dirty plate on the table and clothes on the floor at Clay Walsh's house." David set Cosie down.

"What's wrong with Uncle Clay?" Cosie asked.

Sheesh. He must really look bad if a two-year-old could spot it.

"What are you doing here, David?" Clay draped his arm over his eyes. He hadn't had a hangover in years, but goodness, whatever this was, it made a hangover seem like a mild cold.

"I was ordered by the *wife* to come get that tux you're still wearing. We have to turn them in today or there's a fee."

"Aren't you supposed to be on a honeymoon or something?"

"We leave tomorrow."

Brad's voice suddenly and inexplicably arrived. *"All right, welcome back, kiddies. I'm still here. Live. In the flesh!"*

Clay raised his head. The radio was, unfortunately, just out of reach. "He's already back in LA?"

"Took a flight right after the wedding."

"The Zen master of what you want, when you want it. Now, where were we before the commercial break? That's right—the rest of my crazy-hot-chickapoo-at-the-wedding story. From time recently served in flyover country. Yes, sir, I did my duty, but alas, as I was saying before the break—" he broke into a guitar sound—*"it was not meant to be. She never even uttered a single word. Just turned a one-eighty, walked away, gone, out of my life forever. Nothing but a tease. And I thought we had something special."*

"Ugh. David, get that, will you? Just turn it off," Clay groaned.

"So what else could I do? After facing such rejection, I did the only thing that any respectable man could do. I went down to the hotel bar to redeem myself."

Clay peeked out from his arm, wondering what David was doing. He'd taken a seat in the living room chair and was still listening to the radio.

Now he fished a picture book from a small box of toys Clay kept for Cosie's visits and handed it to her. "Sweetie, go look at this for a few minutes, okay?"

"Okay, Daddy." Cosie grinned widely and then disappeared. David turned back to the radio again.

"The night took a luscious turn toward the demented. My plan was to find some lonely, insecure, last-call-for-alcohol mama

to tend to my wounds, help me forget my recent and catastrophic loss. But instead, oh, this is so good."

Clay lifted his head, watching David. His typical cheery demeanor had turned solemn as he seemed transfixed by the radio.

"I didn't find anything. Nope. She. Found. Me. That's right. I finally met my match, man. I kid you not. And she would not be denied. Believe me. It was glorious. Details? You want juicy details? Want me to play show-and-tell, do you? Huh? Share my goodies with the rest of the class? Is that what you want? Is it? Well then, strap yourselves in—"

David lurched forward and hit the switch. The radio went silent.

He looked toward the kitchen, where they could hear Cosie talking to herself.

"Look, go be with Lisa," Clay said. "I'm fine. I'll drop the tux off at the store myself."

"You're not fine, Clay. From one man to another, I think we both know why."

"It's complicated."

"You think you have the corner on the market for complicated? It's all complicated." He scanned the disheveled room. "Love is sweet, but it's never simple."

Just then Cosie came out from the kitchen. David burst out laughing. Clay turned his head to see what was so funny. Little Cosie had gotten into the Scotch tape. She had it wrapped all over herself, around her forehead, into her hair, across her shoulders, around her waist, back up over her face.

She looked dreadfully guilty, walking over to Clay and handing him the tape dispenser, still attached to the tape she wore. "I sorry."

Clay sat up, broke the dispenser free, took her in his arms. "It's okay. I'm not mad."

He looked at David, who was shaking his head and laughing all at once. He stood and lifted Cosie into his arms. "We better get going."

"I'll take care of the tux."

"Take care of you." David went to the door, Cosie still in his arms, Scotch tape dangling from her elbows and her chin.

"Good luck explaining that one to Lisa," Clay laughed.

David opened the screen door, then turned back. "You know, I can only hope that she grows up to find a man half as good as you."

Clay watched them leave, Cosie buckled in her car seat, waving out the window at him.

♥

Amber climbed out of the bath. The fourth bath in twelve hours. There was something about candles and water and warmth that had always helped her think more . . . freely. As she dried herself off, there was an uncanny feeling around her. Not spooky, but weirdly present. It felt like the missing piece of the puzzle that was her life had finally been found. When she'd read the Bible yesterday, those words—*"Never will I leave you; never will I forsake you"*—they'd seemed alive.

Like they were spoken right to her, right then. She couldn't explain it, but that didn't mean she didn't believe it.

With her hair still dripping wet and a towel secured around her, she walked to her bulletin board. Last night she'd taken everything off it, packed the pieces away like usual, ready to flee. Only the board still hung. Bare naked, kind of like her soul. Her life. Her heart.

But as she studied it now, it didn't seem so much stripped as it did . . . what? She stood silently, wondering. *A clean slate.*

Amber turned to her money jar, stuffed to the brim, the tops of dollar bills hanging over the edge. "You, my friend, have a new job."

Thirty minutes later, she was dressed, out the door, and on the steps of the Bolivar University administrative building. She reached to open the door just as a group of students came out, and she stepped aside to let them pass. A few of the girls grinned at her like she was one of them. A guy a couple steps behind took the time to say hi to her.

With a deep, steady breath, she walked in and found the admissions office. The secretary directed her to the desk of Corinne Burns, a jolly-looking woman with a blouse buttoned too tightly and gaping in all the wrong places. But Amber hardly noticed because Corinne was smiling brightly like something special was about to happen to Amber.

"What can I do for you, honey?" she asked.

Amber handed her all the transcripts she'd kept. She hadn't figured she'd ever really use them again. They were a little dusty. Corinne thumbed through them, nodding and making verbal notes as she went. Amber handed her the admission form she'd filled out too.

Finally Corinne set the paperwork aside. She put her arms on her desk and leaned closer to Amber, gesturing toward the money jar. "We take checks, you know."

Amber looked down at the jar. She was clasping it so tightly that her fingers were going white. "It's a long story."

"I gathered that from your transcripts. You're a smart girl, you know that?"

"I've recently had some . . . life experiences . . . that have made me realize I need to finish what I start. Not run so much."

"What's his name?" Corinne said with a wink. "Or is it the name that shall not be uttered?"

Amber smiled. "Something like that. He's actually a really good guy. He's kind of the reason I'm here. Doing this. Because of him, I've got someone sticking by my side now."

Corinne nodded. "Well, I'm going to have to crunch the numbers, Amber, but I think you're going to qualify for some partial scholarships."

"Really?"

"Yep. We'll have to see. But I think it looks promising." Corinne opened her hands, gesturing for Amber to hand over the money jar. "Let's start counting."

CHAPTER 20

"I WANTED TO MAKE SURE I made my point," Aunt Zella said as they drank tea together.

"You did. I'm here," Clay said. On the table was the large box of tea bags she had shipped to him. Forty-five of them.

"You can set that jar down, you know. It's not going to run away."

Clay stared into it, cupped in his arm. It had been left on his doorstep a couple days after the wedding. All the money emptied out. When he first saw it, he'd been overcome with sadness, believing she'd run again. But there was a note inside, written on a paper place mat from the diner, that simply read *Home*. As he stood on his porch holding its emptiness, he'd wondered if maybe that was the point of it all—to empty himself rather than to fill himself up. He'd held the glass jar up, and it magnified and purified the sunlight in extraordinary ways, spraying it here and there, capturing it and then releasing it as he turned his wrist.

"Hmm?" Aunt Zella tapped her fingers on the table. "What's on your mind?"

"She believed in me" was all he could think to say. It hurt his heart to even think about her.

"In you?" Aunt Zella said with a sarcastic tone and a raised eyebrow. She waggled her finger at him. "If you don't chase after that girl, you're nowhere near the person we thought you were."

Clay glanced at the picture of Lloyd on the counter. Lloyd seemed to be staring right at him, agreeing with Aunt Zella.

"She's better off. I'm damaged goods. I don't deserve—"

"My Lord, if you were any more self-absorbed, you'd be a dot."

"So you agree, I should be alone."

"Probably."

They sipped tea again for a little while.

Finally Aunt Zella said, "I'd like to wring your neck. I'd like to wring his neck, Lloyd. Look at you. The high-and-mighty. You expect the whole world to stand up and, what? Do the wave for you? Give you a trophy for being good? And when they don't . . ." She mumbled something under her breath. Probably something Clay didn't want to hear anyway.

The words, especially coming from Aunt Zella, stung. If he didn't have goodness to stand on, what did he have?

"So help me," she continued, "if you lock yourself away for another nine years . . ." She shook her head, looking up like the answer might be hanging from the ceiling. "You think that will make you holy?"

"I wish I—"

"I, I, I!" Aunt Zella was more fired up than he'd ever seen her. She could be snarky to say the least, but he'd never seen her enraged. "Stop twisting it! Wake up!" She lightly slapped him upside the head. "Get over yourself. You and your pain. Stop. And stop trying to use the grace of God as a brick wall. Do you get this upset over children starving? Anyone else's suffering?"

Clay looked down at the jar, trying to keep his emotions in check. This hurt. But maybe it had been too long since anyone had dared speak this kind of truth to him.

The two of them settled a bit, and finally Clay smiled slightly. "Go ahead. Dispense the wisdom."

She took his hand in hers, gently cupping it. Her knuckles were swollen and hot. "I admire you so much, Clay. In all my days, I've never seen anyone work harder at being good."

"Define *good*," Clay said. At this point, he wasn't sure if he really could.

Her eyes twinkled with a lifetime of wisdom, all zeroed in on him. "There is no such thing as goodness without mercy. No virtue without forgiveness."

His dull, lifeless heart tapped weakly against his chest. He could do nothing more than just sit there and listen.

"And I'm not talking about Amber forgiving you. Or you forgiving Amber. None of this is about any of that."

"Then what?" It only came out as a whisper.

"The way you carry ancient, crusty, useless guilt. Like a spoiled pet poodle you want to show off." She let go of his hand and stroked an imaginary pet in her lap. "Like an excuse, right, Lloyd? Let it go. What are you waiting for? How long?"

Clay swallowed. He didn't know. Was there even enough of a lifetime left for him to make up for all he'd done?

Aunt Zella's hand reached for him again and then for the glass jar. She tapped her fingernails on it. "You are loved. You are so loved."

Uncertainty came out swinging at her words.

"Oh, my child. You are. Listen to me, Clay."

He looked at her kind face.

"Enough. We never fully arrive this side of heaven. You could stay hidden in that house of yours for a hundred years. Isolated. Detached. Bury yourself. Warm and cozy, safe and snuggly with all your sorrows. Your sordid past." She made a snoring noise. Clay laughed a little. "Woulda, coulda, shoulda. Never see another face. What a shame that would be." She stroked his hand again. Her touch felt warm, just like her gaze. "You would miss out on sharing it all with a bunch of other confused nitwits. Some of whom inexplicably care about you a great deal."

Then Aunt Zella rose, walked to where her wedding picture sat on the counter. She took the pewter cross, the one that had been draped over the frame for as long as he could remember, and placed it firmly in his hand, drawing his fingers closed over it.

"Playtime is over. Be a man."

Clay sat still, pondering her words, trying to reconcile all that she'd said. It was what he thought he was doing for so long—being a man. Owning up to what he'd done. Wasn't that what he was doing?

"This is the day the Lord has made, Clay. It's the day that you start trusting Him more and you less." She tilted her head toward another picture of Lloyd nearby. "As Lloyd tells me every day—be a good steward of your pain."

Another walk, but this time it was different. Before, he'd taken them to isolate and maybe insulate too. Now, though, it was like he was exposed, out in the open, vulnerable to anything and everything.

Clay walked to the park where they'd sat on the swings. He watched them sway slightly in the breeze.

A father went by, his young son trailing him. As the father extended his hand back for his son, the little boy reached for it but missed and fell. Giggling, he got up and reached again but missed.

Had Clay been reaching for his Father's hand and missing? Or not reaching for it at all?

At home, Clay picked up his house, swept and dusted. He put everything in order. But there was one thing that remained broken. The Ten Commandments. He sat on the couch, holding the frame in front of him. At what point had he started bowing to this and stopped bowing to the One who made it? The One who made him?

Next to him sat the Scotch tape. He remembered Cosie, all wound up in it, stuck from head to toe. He wondered if that's what he looked like to God: a broken mess taped together by grace—grace that until now he'd rejected. Just like the law had been given to show him his sin, maybe the cracks stayed there to show him God's grace. Hadn't he seen the Leonard Cohen lyrics on Amber's bulletin board? *"There is a crack in everything. That's how the light gets in."*

He set the frame on his lap and started taping. Tears rushed to him again, but this time they were the summation of all that he was releasing, all that he was letting go of. His cracks were seeping with God's love. God was able and willing to do for all those whom Clay had hurt exactly what he'd done for Clay. He let go of them, released them from his heart, unshackled them one by one, as he continued to tape.

He felt so . . . light.

The window he'd opened earlier was ushering in a gentle breeze. On the table, where his Bible sat, the pages flipped one by one as if by an invisible finger.

Finally he hung the commandments back on the wall, tape and all. And draped over the frame was the pewter cross—what made it possible to be broken and whole all at once.

CHAPTER 21

ON TOP OF THE HILL in that old cemetery where George had buried Helen, Clay sat on the grass. From here he could see virtually the whole town. The late-November wind was brisk but not unbearable. Behind him, the dirt of Helen's grave had settled into only a small mound. The headstone had not been placed yet. A single flower lay over the dirt, a few days old, nearly dead but clinging to its last stages of life. He wondered how often George came by here to visit her. In its wilted state, the flower seemed to say everything about how Clay's life once was. But now, things were different.

"A cemetery?"

Clay smiled as he heard the footsteps approaching, crunching leaves in their wake. She was breathing hard.

"I knew you were weird, but this is weird even for you, and that's saying a lot. *A lot.*"

She grumbled all the way until she was at his side. He patted the ground next to him and she sighed her aggravation loudly. "What is this, a séance?"

"Thanks for coming, Carol."

She took her sweet time getting to the ground, still mumbling and scowling. Then she said, "I'll shoot straight with you. I'm meeting you today totally out of morbid curiosity. And here we are. At a cemetery. I won't lie to you—I'm a little frightened that I might end up on *Dateline*. I'm murdered by the straightlaced guy—because there's always got to be irony—at a cemetery." She sighed again. "So what do you want?"

"I'm sitting up here on this hill, in this cemetery, because I buried someone."

Carol appeared truly scared as she slowly turned her head to look at the dirt pile behind them.

"Don't worry. That's Helen. She died of natural causes," Clay said, enjoying the moment a little too much. "Here's the deal, Carol. I've buried the old guy. The old me. The one you always thought was so . . ."

"Weird? Sideshow-circus-act weird?"

"Isolated. Legalistic. My convictions were right but my approach was perhaps a bit faulty."

"Right."

Clay took a deep breath. "I love her."

Carol blew out her own breath. "Oh, boy. I gotta give

you props for the symbolism of the whole . . ." She gestured at the tombstones. "But a grave is only so deep. It can only hold so much."

"I know I've made a lot of mistakes. Too many to count. But she means everything to me. Everything. And I believe in love with all my heart. A guy I know, who married a girl named Helen, made me believe true love is also in the working out of the differences, to start as two and end as one." He glanced at Carol. "Is she . . . is she doing okay?"

"Busy. Studying like crazy. Men falling at her feet. She's had eight dates in four days. . . . I made that last part up to make you jealous because she's a fantastic girl who deserves a lot of attention."

Clay nodded. "I know she does."

"Well, listen, if you want my advice, I'd say stop being so . . . uptight. I mean, there's stiff as a board and then there's stiff as dead, and then there's you."

Clay pulled at the grass. "I'm already working on that."

"I can see that by the way we're meeting at a cemetery, which oozes with coziness. Secondly, you've got to show her. I mean, really show her. Pull out all the stops. This is going to take more than dinner and a movie."

"I've been working on that too." Clay reached into his pocket and pulled out a black velvet box.

Carol's eyes widened. "Please tell me this isn't an ankle bracelet." She took the box from him and slowly opened it. "You picked this out? By yourself?"

"You think she'll like it?"

"Good heavens, man. She's going to faint from shock. I expected something like a chastity belt with the word *morality* stitched on it."

"I wanted to ask your permission."

Carol's gaze left the ring.

"I know, I know. I'm old-school. But the way I see it, you've looked after her since she got here. You're like family to her. And she doesn't have a dad. So I wanted to know . . . if I could have your permission to marry Amber."

Carol's mouth dropped wide open.

"And just so we're clear," Clay added, "this is way more terrifying for me than asking a father."

Her eyes teared up and she slapped him on the back. "Clay Walsh, you never cease to amaze or surprise me."

He kept watching her, hoping for any sign she might agree.

She handed him back the ring. "You don't need my approval, honey. The truth is, as weird as you are, you're the best thing to happen to that girl in probably her whole life." She looked out over the city. "You're a good man. Decent. Kind. *Reliable.*"

Clay laughed.

"She'll be lucky to have you."

"So that's a yes?"

"Go get 'em, tiger."

"Thank you."

"And listen, I'm no expert on the Bible. God knows I haven't cracked that thing open since I hollowed one out to hide a gun in it. But if I'm not mistaken, I believe the whole idea of the thing is that man couldn't ever save himself, no matter how hard he tried." She shrugged. "That's the point, isn't it?"

Clay put his arm around her shoulder. "That's the *whole* point."

Carol stood. "Now can we get outta here? This place is freaking me out."

Clay stood too. "Not quite yet. I have one more favor to ask of you."

CHAPTER 22

BOOKS AND PAPERS were strewn across the kitchen counter, table, and bed. She had note cards pinned up everywhere, including her bulletin board. She'd already been to study group this morning and would have another one tomorrow before work. Carol had been kind enough to help her by scheduling her hours around her school needs. And though she was disappointed, Trish understood that late-night partying was out of the question. Amber was focused— Bolivar had generously admitted her late, and she had a lot of catching up to do. She wanted this.

College life ended up suiting her. She was older than most of the students, but she'd made friends—though she'd been strong enough for once in her life to resist the attentions of some very cute guys in her class. She'd been asked out three times in as many weeks. Two of them were hotties, but she didn't want Trish's claim that she was a "cougar" to stick. Besides, she'd grown up. She'd tasted the best wine and didn't want anything less. She didn't know who God had in mind for her, but she knew the qualities to look for. For that, she would always be thankful to Clay Walsh.

She rarely saw Clay. He wasn't at his shop much, and when he was, he stayed inside. She missed him terribly, knew he was a man with a lot of skeletons and a lot of healing to do. She wasn't the one who was going to be able to bring that healing—she had her own to contend with.

But she had someone to run to now, and she'd been enjoying getting to know Him. He was interesting to her, not always clearly showing His hand at the times she wanted it, but making her realize it was there in an unexpected way the whole time. She found herself praying more and worrying less. There was a defined peace inside that called her attention when her heart fluttered with dismay or disappointment. And it often did. Sometimes she got lonely. Sometimes she got restless. Sometimes even bored.

Amber shook her head, trying to get her mind back into her studies. She had work to get to. And a lot of it.

Outside, there was a noise at her doorstep. Her door was open, with the screen shut. She didn't see anyone, but then she thought she heard footsteps going down the stairs. Mr. Joe jumped off the couch to investigate. Then she heard a car horn, except it sounded old, almost like a warped record.

She opened the screen door. Below was George, at the bottom of the stairs, standing by an old car. Was that the vintage Rolls-Royce he'd been working on? It was gorgeous. And he was dressed like an old-time chauffeur.

He pointed to her stoop. She looked down, and at her feet was a small envelope.

Amber grabbed it and opened it, hardly able to contain her excitement. It was a handwritten note from Clay, a short attempt at some pretty bad poetry—a quote for her bulletin board.

The car horn honked again, and George hustled to the other side to open the door for her. He stood like a perfect gentleman. "Come on. Your chariot awaits."

She should probably lock up or change into something a little more . . . Her head was spinning like crazy. She clutched the card and ran down the stairs, straight into the Rolls-Royce. It was gorgeous inside. George gently shut her door and hurried to the driver's seat.

As they pulled away, Amber glanced up at Mr. Joe, who stood at the screen door wondering what was going on. She was wondering too.

She saw George put a CD in, and through a very nice sound system came the song she and Clay had danced to in the field. She couldn't help the grin that nearly reached both ears. When she woke up this morning, this was the very last thing she'd expected. If this was his best effort at a romantic date, he'd already far exceeded her wildest expectations.

But . . . what *was* this? Surely more than just a peace offering. She knew him too well.

The Rolls-Royce stopped on Marvin Street, off the town square, where shops lined brick walkways. George was out of the car in a flash and opened the door for her, smooth and debonair. She looked at the sign above her. LuLu's Nail Salon.

George, with the mannerly formality of a footman, gestured that she should go in.

Inside, Amber found a woman waiting for her. "I'm Jenny," she said. She looked to be midthirties, but it was hard to tell—her nails were long and bright green, her lipstick hot pink. Feather earrings dangled all the way to her shoulders and her eyes were lined in aqua. "Come, sit." She patted her nail desk and went to the other side to sit down, then took Amber's hands. "Lovely hands, dear. Just lovely. Those long fingers! And beautiful nail beds." Jenny stroked her hand as she said, "So what would you like done today? Your choice. It's completely paid for. Reach for the stars. Whatever you'd like."

Amber studied her hands for a moment. "Just make them look nice. Simple." She smiled. "Clear polish."

Jenny almost looked insulted. "Clear?" She gestured toward the wall of colors. "We have everything you could ever want. Some of them even glow in the dark. Also, I'm very good at the art. I can paint tiny flowers or zebra stripes. I once painted the entire alphabet on a teacher. We had to use her toes, too, but it was cute."

"Clear."

"Maybe a French manicure?"

"Clear."

Jenny finally relented and started buffing and shaping Amber's nails. "So . . . clear. That's kind of boring. You don't strike me as the boring type. In fact, if it were five decades earlier, I think you and I might be hippies. But I couldn't do the earth tones," she said, waving her nail file at Amber's outfit. "I'd be tie-dye." She continued buffing, her hand gliding effortlessly over the nail beds. "And you don't really strike me as a girl who'd wear or not wear a color to satisfy the tastes of a man."

"These days, true."

"So you just like . . . plain?"

Amber shrugged. "I guess it's kind of symbolic."

"Oh? I love symbols. I can do flags. Peace signs. No-smoking symbols."

"Have you ever had such clarity that even when nothing in your life was making sense, you trusted that it would all fall into place? That all your suffering was molding and shaping you into a person you never dreamed you'd be?"

"You mean like a Pilates class?"

Amber smiled. "Yeah. Like that. But for the soul."

"Oh." Jenny gently shaped each nail. "You're one of those kinds. A deep thinker."

"I've had a season of great disappointment," Amber said, "which led to many things becoming . . . clear."

Jenny appeared to be following. "Well then, I guess that

makes sense. Especially if you consider the hottie that came in and paid for this whole gig a couple days ago."

Amber smiled. "Cute, right?"

"Girl, smokin'. In that light-blue shirt with those eyes . . ."

"Light-blue shirt?"

"What?"

"No, I mean . . . it's just that he doesn't really do color. He wears a lot of . . . black."

"Ah. The goth type."

"And white."

"Amish?"

"No, no. He's just very simple in his tastes. I'm surprised, that's all. I didn't even know he owned a blue shirt."

"So, this one—I'm impressed. Comes in, buys his girl a manicure. Now that's romantic. Most guys enjoy the scenery but don't help plant the trees."

Amber laughed as Jenny grabbed the clear polish. She was going to have to visit Jenny more often. "He's a good guy. We've had our ups and downs."

"Hard to find, you know," Jenny said. "I've been with this guy Ted for three years. He's cheated on me four times, but what do you do?"

Amber leaned forward. "You get out, Jenny."

Jenny looked at her, a curious interest in her eyes. But it flamed out in a moment and she shook her head. "I couldn't ever leave Ted."

"Why?"

"You know. He's . . ." Her words trailed off. "Nobody has

stayed with me very long, and Ted, you know . . . he's stuck around."

Amber touched her hand. "You deserve more than a guy who just 'sticks around.'"

"I don't know that I do." Her smile stuck like a press-on nail. She lifted Amber's hands. "Well, it's not fancy, but there it is, clear as day. Are you sure you don't want some kind of pink wash over it? Or polka dots?"

"They're beautiful, Jenny. Thank you."

Jenny sighed. "All right." She glanced out the window at the Rolls-Royce. "Looks like you're in for a fun evening."

"What's your schedule next week?" Amber asked.

Jenny grabbed her book. "Pretty open. Especially on Tuesday."

"Book me for ten."

Jenny grinned. "Really?"

"Yeah. And I'm doing neon pink all the way."

Jenny waved her hands in the air. "Yes, ma'am!"

"I want to tell you about someone I think you're going to want to meet. Someone who sticks by you without condition. Just because He loves you."

Jenny looked flattered. "No kidding. I'm all ears. Until then . . ."

"Until then."

George held the salon door and then opened the car door. Amber hurried inside, so eager she could hardly contain herself. But George drove only a half block before stopping again. Amber peered out the window and saw it immediately:

the beautiful green dress she'd spotted on one of her walks with Clay.

Inside the dress shop, a statuesque woman greeted her and introduced herself as Gloria, with such sophistication Amber wasn't sure if she should respond. She looked around at the store. Plush white carpet and light-pink walls with cocktail dresses hanging on every one. The dressing rooms had thick, velvet curtains in place of doors. The chairs looked too expensive to sit in.

Gloria took her hand and observed her with a sharp eye, gauging her from head to toe. "A size four?"

Amber nodded.

"And a size-seven shoe?"

She nodded again.

"Right this way." She was led into one of the dressing rooms. Gloria brought her the green dress, along with some matching strappy slingbacks. Amber quickly slipped on the dress and shoes. When she emerged, Gloria held out the tiniest emerald earrings, literally sitting on a silver platter.

"Wow, these are . . ."

"Yours." Gloria smiled.

"Mine? But these are—"

"Extravagant?"

"Very."

Gloria only winked and sent her on her way. Back in the Rolls-Royce, George continued to drive, three blocks this time. He stopped in front of the flower shop but didn't get out.

Carol bolted out the door so fast that Amber wondered if something was on fire. But at the excited look on Carol's face and the bouquet carefully cradled in her arm, Amber couldn't help but grin.

She rolled her window down with a slight squeak that made George frown. The smell was intoxicating. "Irises," Amber said, closing her eyes.

"Especially for you. Courtesy of Mr. Clay Walsh."

Amber looked suspiciously at her. "Carol, that's the first time I've heard you say his name without it sounding like a cussword."

"He's still weird. But apparently in a very romantic way." Suddenly Carol's eyes diverted to George, and she was grinning just like Amber.

George had turned in his seat, charm oozing from any orifice it could squeeze out of. "You like this face or what?" he asked.

Amber gently cleared her throat. She was getting antsy to see this romantic Clay Walsh, the one who'd embraced color and impulsive spending.

"Yes, ma'am," George said with a gentleman's flair, but it was unclear who he was talking to. Amber and Carol were both smiling.

"See you soon, darlin'," Carol said as she stepped back and waved.

Rolling up the window again with another little squeak, Amber held the flowers close, stroking their petals and letting the scent envelop her.

George watched her in the rearview mirror. "Hey. Carol. Great figure for a woman her age."

"George, we are going to have to work on your pickup lines."

"What does she like?" George asked, unfazed.

"Chocolate."

"My middle name! You gotta put a good word in for me."

Amber laughed. "Well, this car is going to score you major points right off the bat."

George clutched his heart. "You know just how to make a man weak in the knees."

Then George drove her in silence, and it felt like Amber entered a dream. As the car zoomed toward its unknown destination, the last of the autumn leaves on the road scattered into the air, exploding in a breathtaking performance of colorful spins. She turned to watch them through the back window as they floated softly to the ground. The sun, bulbous and orange, was setting behind her, awash against the horizon.

She had the fancy car, the perfect dress, the groomed nails, the gorgeous flowers, the striking earrings . . . She had it all, except the one thing that really mattered. She couldn't wait to see him, though she had no idea what to expect. This was not the Clay she knew, but it was the one she always suspected was in there somewhere, locked away and hidden until he could make amends for his past. Yet that was the thing she was beginning to grasp. There wasn't enough penance in her or him or whomever to make whole what all of them were capable of utterly shattering. So if it wasn't penance, then what?

Love.

Above her, newly hung Christmas lights lined the street, reflecting through the window as she gazed at them. They rounded a corner and she felt the car slow. Then she saw the oddest thing: an antique traffic light sitting right in the middle of the grocery store's empty parking lot—the grocery store where they'd shopped together.

It was glowing. Not red. Not yellow. Green. The most inviting and luminescent green she'd ever seen.

George stopped the car and opened the door. Amber stepped out in wonderment, staring at this traffic light, this emerald-green symbol. And signal, perhaps? It said so much standing there by itself in the dusk, greeting her, beckoning her. She looked at George, not even sure she could speak. George seemed to sense the depth of the moment, quietly observing the stoplight himself.

Then he pulled something out of his pocket and held it up in front of her, displaying it like a great treasure. It was a necklace. Made of wagon wheel pasta.

Amber laughed as George tenderly placed it around her neck. She touched it, shaking her head. She couldn't even imagine what was coming next.

With measured flair, George gestured toward the front door of the grocery store with a smile. "Have fun."

She took a careful step forward, but George said, "Oh. Take your shoes off."

Amber didn't even hesitate. Yeah, she liked these shoes, but whatever was waiting in there for her, she was certain she would like it way more. She handed the shoes to George and continued on.

At the front of the store, the automatic doors swished open, blowing her hair back. The grocery store was eerily dark but for a faint and distant glow. As her eyes adjusted, she noticed candles. Dozens. Maybe hundreds. They were tiny, like stars in a dark sky, flickering and winking. And they seemed to be her guide on a path. She took a few steps and began to feel sand under her toes. She wiggled them, keeping a slow pace. She didn't want to miss a thing. Not one single moment.

Ahead, a quartet, maybe a jazz band, started playing. She recognized the store manager playing the clarinet. The music reminded her of the record she'd put on the first time she walked into the Old Fashioned antique store, before she'd ever set eyes on Clay Walsh, when she was still running from a life that never seemed to settle for her.

She kept walking, slowly, carefully, peeking down each aisle as she passed. But she couldn't see him.

And then, there he was, halfway down an aisle. Her breath caught in her throat. He was dressed in a suit, a tie, and . . . a fedora. Amber laughed and held her heart. He'd never looked so handsome. It was like a movie poster.

Clay smiled at her and she just then noticed the grocery cart in front of him, overflowing with stacks of cased bottled water. Not neat stacks either. They looked like they'd been tossed in there, along with a few boxes of wagon wheel pasta.

She started to walk toward him, unable to take her eyes off him, until something caught her eye.

Baby food.

They were on the baby food aisle? She wanted to take it all in—each part had so much meaning attached, it was like trying to swallow a steak whole.

She looked at Clay, questioning, but those beautiful blue eyes beckoned her with a casual, strong confidence that she couldn't have resisted if she'd tried.

He took off his hat and smiled at her. "Hey there, pretty girl."

"Hey there, stress boy."

"I love you."

Amber blinked, her lashes wet with tears she didn't realize were there. "Say it again," she whispered.

"I love you."

She glanced around. "The baby food aisle?"

With a single finger, he nudged a jar out of alignment. She took a step closer to him and nudged it back into place.

"A little on the nose?" he asked.

"Very romantic. And I love you too." She smiled. *"Te amo! Te amo!"*

Clay reached into his pocket, where he normally stuffed his hands when he didn't know what else to do with them. He pulled out a tiny, black velvet box and drew it open with nimble fingers, like she was watching a magician. And there, cushioned in white satin, was the most dazzling ring she'd ever seen. It wasn't flashy. It was quite simple, in fact. An antique, of course.

Amber looked into his eyes, her heart bursting. Her entire body started trembling and she squeezed her hands into balls and pressed them against her cheeks.

Then Clay hitched up a pant leg and started to go down on one knee.

"Yes!" she exclaimed.

"You didn't let me—"

"Yes. Yes!" She pulled him up by the lapels. Close to her. Both of them swept into a moment like no other, entangled in each other's arms.

"It won't be easy. . . ."

She held out her hand, spreading her fingers. "Yes."

He slid the ring on her finger, making her skin dance at his touch. She threaded her fingers through his and looked down at their feet. There was no threshold. Just sand. So for good measure, she stepped closer until her toes rested on top of his black leather wingtips.

For once, he didn't look terrified. Just mesmerized. It was all that she'd wanted—to mesmerize him.

He leaned in, their lips dangerously close. Was he going to actually kiss her? Was this a test? Amber looked into his eyes, barely able to think.

He smiled at her in a way he never had before. She returned the smile, a little mischievously, and drew her lips closer to his—as close as they could be without touching.

And then she turned her head and tapped her cheek.

But suddenly his arms fully wrapped around her and she lost her breath. He pulled her body close to his, the way she'd always wanted him to, and cupped her face with his hand, turning her toward him. She saw it in those beautiful eyes—she meant everything to him.

Never before and never since has there been a more purely passionate, innocently sexy, beautiful kiss on any girl's cheek.

The ~~end~~ beginning

about the authors

RENE GUTTERIDGE is the award-winning and best-selling author of twenty-two novels, including her latest releases, *Misery Loves Company* (suspense), *Greetings from the Flipside* (comedy), and *Heart of the Country* (drama). Her recent suspense titles also include *Listen*, *Possession*, and *Escapement*. She has novelized six screenplays, including *Old Fashioned*. *Never the Bride*, a romantic comedy with screenwriter Cheryl McKay, won the Carol Award in 2010 for best women's fiction.

Rene's indie film—the comedy *Skid*, based on her novel—is in postproduction and due to release in 2014. Rene is a creative consultant on *Boo*, a film based on her beloved novel series, which is in development at Sodium Entertainment with Cory Edwards attached as director and Andrea Nasfell as screenwriter. Rene is also a cowriter in a collaborative comedy project called *The Last Resort* with screenwriters Torry Martin and Marshal Younger.

Find Rene on Facebook and Twitter or on her website, www.renegutteridge.com.

RIK SWARTZWELDER is a writer-director-producer whose films have screened at more than 145 film festivals worldwide and garnered over 50 major awards, including a Crystal Heart Award (Heartland Film Festival) for his 35mm short *The Least of These* and a student Emmy for his highly acclaimed graduate thesis film, *Paul McCall*. Other accolades include two CINE Golden Eagles, a CINE Special Jury Award, four ITVA-DC Peer Awards, and the Sprint/PCS Filmmaker of the Future Award. He earned his MFA in motion picture production from Florida State University and is invited regularly to teach and speak on film, including the honor of an invite by the Heartland Film Festival (Indianapolis) to lead the very first workshop offered ("The Craft of Film Directing") when they launched their Heartland Truly Moving Pictures Institute.

discussion questions

1. We know that Clay Walsh holds old-fashioned views about dating. Are there other areas of his life where he is old-fashioned? Do you see his views as good or bad ideas?

2. As she drives into town, Amber says to her cat, "See how the road winds, and then off it goes, through the trees? You don't really know what's around the bend, see?" How do you approach a bend in the road? With fear? Excitement? Nonchalance?

3. To an outsider, Brad, David, and Clay seem to have very little in common, yet they remain close friends. Why would they stay in relationship if they have grown so different from each other? Are there friendships that have endured in your life despite similar changes?

4. Clay believes dating only trains people to be good dates in superficial relationships. Do you agree?

What benefits do you see in the dating model of contemporary culture? What are some of the dangers or drawbacks?

5. If you were in Amber's position, what would you think of Clay's relationship philosophies? Would you go along with his rules and "dating" process? Why or why not?

6. Clay thinks of Amber as "just the opposite of who he'd always imagined might draw his attention," and several characters throughout the story comment on how different Clay and Amber seem to be. In your experience, is it true that opposites attract? How much similarity do you think is necessary for a couple to be compatible?

7. According to Clay, some of the boundaries that used to exist to protect us have been removed. Name some boundaries that you believe fall into this category.

8. One of Clay's customers tells him, "Well, if you're going to leave a legacy, you can't be merely an observer, son. You gotta get a little beat up, like this old rocker." What does Bert mean by this? Have you lived as an observer, or have you been beaten up? Explain.

9. Amber keeps a list of all she's done to live a life of giving. What would be on your list? Or, if you wanted to start living that way today, what goals would appear on your list to create a life of giving?

10. Betty from the diner says to Clay, "Marriage is kind of like a tea bag. You don't know how strong it really is till you get it in some boiling water." Have you seen any real-life examples to confirm this? What steps do you think can be taken to strengthen a marriage before the "boiling water" comes along?

11. Amber and Clay come up with some unconventional activities for their dates. Which of these sounded the most fun to you? Which was the strangest? If you were to fill a shoe box with ideas for creative outings, what would be in it?

12. On one of her dates with Clay, Amber finds herself longing for "the simple fun of being chased." What's the difference between being chased and being test-driven? What role do you think pursuit should play in establishing a romantic relationship?

13. At one point, Clay fears he'll never be free of the chains of his regrets and his past life. Have you ever struggled to be free of similar chains? What advice would you give to someone trying to be free of their past?

14. Clay's wise aunt Zella chides him to "Get over yourself. You and your pain." Do you think this is good counsel? Why or why not? What does it mean to "be a good steward of your pain"?

15. Disappointed by Clay's reaction to her confession, Amber thinks, "He had been her goodness as recently

as this morning. The only goodness she'd ever known. Slowly, she was making the separation—Clay wasn't God." Have you ever found yourself elevating another person too highly or expecting them to take the place of God in your life? How did you make the separation?

Rene Gutteridge Interviews
Rik Swartzwelder

RENE: The latest statistics show that 1.89 billion people have a screenplay to pitch. How'd you beat the odds and get your movie made?

RIK: That's a question you get asked by other filmmakers quite a bit. Everyone wants to know how you pulled it off . . . that or the names and numbers of your investors. Here's the thing: ask a hundred different directors with a finished film that question and you'll get a hundred different answers. Personally, I've had films almost get made at least a dozen times over the years.

Even with *Old Fashioned*, it almost got set up several times before things actually clicked and we got the green light. You really just have to keep moving forward, keep your head above water, keep believing in the impossible. Okay, confession time: I'm a huge *Rocky* fan (go ahead; mock me), and like he says, "It's about . . . how much you can take and keep moving forward." No one can answer that question but you.

Outside of divine intervention, persistence and tenacity

trump just about everything else in this business—in a lot of things in life. So staying alive long enough . . . that's the trick. You have to fight the creative battle because you love it. Because you can do nothing else. Because it's what God wired you to do. You may struggle for years and never see results. Or you might be an overnight success. We don't often get to call those shots. Dream. Hope. Create. Let the chips fall where they may.

All of that's probably not the answer you or any aspiring filmmaker out there was hoping for, alas. I wish I could give a checklist or a point-by-point how-to that could guarantee results, but I can't. All of our journeys are different. And there are many paths to success. What I can say, without question, is this: the impossible . . . isn't.

As writer, director, and lead actor in this film, did you ever get confused and start yelling, "Cut!" when you were supposed to be delivering your lines? Or are you pretty good at managing your split personalities?

That's funny. At least I can laugh about it now. During production however, it wasn't easy; that's a fact. There were certainly many times I wish I could have yelled at the director or the actor playing Clay.

You put your finger on something that makes acting and directing in the same film such a tricky proposition—the hat of "actor" and the hat of "director" are very, very different, and managing those "split personalities" requires a good plan and the support of your creative team.

The one thing we did that made it much more feasible was have a longer than usual (for an indie film) period of pre-production. We spent several months on the ground in Ohio and had things mapped out pretty well before any cameras started rolling; that made a big difference. Also, I had some key people, whose eyes I trust, help keep me from going off the rails, as they say. I'm grateful to have a lot of extremely talented and generous friends and cohorts.

Some of where this film was shot has special meaning to you. Why was the location important to you, and what was the experience like filming in a place where so many people know you?

Tuscarawas County, Ohio. I grew up there, and to this day, I consider it one of the most beautiful stretches of land in this country—especially in the autumn. Am I biased? Of course! But that doesn't mean it isn't true.

The right locations can make all the difference in a movie—and even more so when you don't have a lot of money to spend on building sets and art direction and all that good stuff. When your means are modest, it's imperative that you find existing locations that are uniquely visual and alive and help tell your story without having to add much to what is already there. As much as I love that area, it wouldn't be the perfect place to shoot every movie. However, it was the perfect place to shoot *Old Fashioned*. The stunning fall foliage, the town squares, classic Americana architecture, and variety of landscapes all lent themselves perfectly to what our story was about. Further, at an even deeper level, I knew that I had an emotional connection with the places and people there that would heighten my senses and, hopefully, provide a heightened sense of intimacy and immediacy to our film. I wasn't disappointed in any way. Plus, I actually ended up seeing more of the area than I ever had growing up there, which was cool.

The big surprise to me was just how much the community rallied around us. I figured we'd have decent support, but what we got was an avalanche of love and enthusiasm that really helped turn our modest budget into much, much more. It meant a lot to many of the locals that we thought the region was worth being in a movie. There was one elderly lady—I'll never forget—who came up and took my hand and thanked me, tears in her eyes, for coming home and acknowledging what a special place the county is. I almost lost it.

One of the things that drew me to the script was how funny yet deeply emotional it was. As a filmmaker, how hard is it to find actors who can do both in one film?
Not every actor can play both, that's true. But just like casting for any type of film or character, you look for the actor who can do what you need most naturally. Also, whenever possible, having potential actors read together and play off of each other during the audition process is a big help. Sometimes actors just click, especially with humor, and you really don't want to wait until you're on set to see if there's chemistry or not.

You have to keep digging right up until the moment you

simply run out of time. To beat the same drum yet again—don't rush preproduction, especially on a low-budget film. We spent many months auditioning well over a thousand people (both nationally and in the local region) trying to find just the right mix.

When you're casting a film, what are some qualities you look for beyond an actor just "looking right" for the part?
Above all else, you have to try to find an actor who simply *is* your character . . . even if that means he or she doesn't look exactly like you imagined the character in your head.

Case in point: Amber. When I was writing the script, I always imagined Amber with long black hair and dark-brown eyes. Now, one of the very first actresses to audition for the role of Amber was Elizabeth Ann Roberts. No doubt about it, Elizabeth has a great look—but she doesn't have black hair or brown eyes. So even though I saw her audition and was completely blown away by her talent and how much she embodied the essence of Amber, I kept looking . . . and looking . . . and looking . . . for an actress with black hair and brown eyes who could make the character come alive the way Elizabeth did. No one ever even came close. And the more I searched, the less the hair and eyes seemed to matter. Elizabeth was Amber; she was from the very beginning.

I won't call the additional casting sessions for that role a complete waste of time because I learned a lot in the process, but it was a long journey to come back around to where it began. I think you have to have an idea of what you're looking for in a character, but it's risky to lock into specific physical characteristics in advance—especially if you're the writer as well. You need to stay open, look for connections beyond just the physical—look for the emotional, the spiritual.

What is your favorite scene in the movie?
That's like asking which of your children is your favorite. Even if there is an answer to that question, you can't really give it. And every scene serves a different purpose, you know? A scene that might seem less important or powerful may actually be planting the seed that provides the "great" scene with all its resonance. Take away one piece of the puzzle and it's incomplete—it's the whole that matters. Just for kicks, however, I can say this: my favorite scenes in the screenplay are not necessarily my favorite scenes in the movie. But that's as far as I'll go.

Which scene was the hardest to film and why?
Again, it's hard to compare. Some scenes are tricky for emotional reasons; some are more difficult from a technical perspective. Generally, any of the scenes with more people—the bar stuff, the party at David and Lisa's, the bachelor party—require a little more time and effort. The ending in the grocery store definitely raised the bar for all the departments and had a lot of moving pieces, but in that case, the extra work was more in the prep. The actual production went pretty smoothly.

In fact, to the credit of the cast and crew, there were very few hiccups during production. Outside of the standard production challenges, there really weren't any major disasters.

And that's a testament to the countless hours of prep and commitment to excellence by many.

On the emotional side, the raw and heartfelt moments with Clay and Amber were hard . . . but not in terms of execution, more in just the process of experiencing all of those feelings. Those were the days when all those hats I was wearing really took their toll on me. It's not easy to rip open your soul and then immediately shift and go check the monitor for playback.

This is one more reason (of many) that I thank God for Elizabeth Ann Roberts playing the role of Amber. First and foremost, she is a committed actor who does all of her home- work and really knows how to dig deep and bring it when it matters most—and that brought out the best in everyone else. The value of that is immeasurable. But equally impor- tant—to me, personally—was how supportive she was of the unique and daunting situation I was in as a writer-director- actor. She bent over backward to lessen the pressure and strain I was under. I will always be grateful to her for that.

What prompted the idea for *Old Fashioned*? And when you get an idea, what qualifications must it pass to get it to the next level of actually writing it? In other words, what do you look for in an idea that makes you more carefully consider it and decide if you want to dedicate the next ten or so years of your life to it?

The writing of *Old Fashioned* was birthed out of a lot of fac- tors and ideas all culminating at a very specific moment in my own spiritual journey. It covers a lot of years and experiences and could really fill up a book on its own—I will spare you that. Actually, we cover the answer in greater detail in *The Old Fashioned Way* (yes, that's a shameless plug for our companion book), but to boil it down to a single idea here—I'd say I believed there was a story that wasn't being told at all and I felt compelled to try.

Compelled. That's a good word in regard to the second part of your question. If I can't ignore or shake loose an idea or a thought or sometimes even just an image—that's how I know. Usually, I'll jot down notes on anything I can find. (I have notebooks, boxes, and folders full of scribblings on napkins, old plane tickets, store receipts, etc.) Once enough of those random thoughts start collecting around a single theme or character(s), then I might go away for a few days and see if I can cluster them together into something worth pursuing.

In terms of time . . . as I write this, we are still in post-production on *Old Fashioned*, and I have already been through many months of editing, multiple rounds of test screenings, extensive conference calls and feedback sessions, etc. I'm telling you, if I wasn't absolutely in love with the core idea of *Old Fashioned* (and surrounded by a committed group of folks who love the idea as much as I do, if not more), it would be very hard to keep pushing forward with the passion and enthusiasm that filmmaking demands.

And of course, as we get a little older, the value and preciousness of time begins to settle on us a bit—at least it has on me. Life is far too short and sacred a thing to exhaust your time or talent—or any gift from God—on something you don't believe in or is less than the best you have to offer at that moment. So for those projects that we initiate, the ones that we bring into being from the deepest reaches of our souls . . . well, as someone once said, we should consider the cost.

The first time we spoke on the phone was during a conference call with all the parties involved, and I promised you I'd take care of your "baby." It must be pretty terrifying to trust another writer, in an entirely different medium, to do justice to all aspects of your story. Yet I find filmmakers are way more trusting about the interpretation of their work than most novelists. What makes you so trusting? And what was it about your story that made you think it would make a good novel?

Although I'm not sure if screenwriters are any more trusting than novelists, I do think the collaborative nature of filmmaking helps prepare screenwriters to accept—if not always embrace—the realities of "team" creativity.

Once this idea of a novelization started to gain traction, I remember making the choice to approach it just like production. A screenplay is a template for production—the realities of which all but guarantee there will be changes, adjustments, slight detours along the way. Same thing for turning the screenplay into a novel. You have to maintain the integrity and "blueprint" of the script, but just like production, you have to be open to the realities of the process and accept that certain twists and turns will be necessary.

Having you as a collaborator made all the difference, Rene. And this is another parallel to filmmaking: having the right collaborators is essential. It is much, much easier to hand off a screenplay to a producer or director who really "gets" the material and is committed to it. Same thing with the novelization.

From our very first chat, it was obvious to me that you genuinely understood what we were trying to do with the film and what the heart of the story was all about. You cared about the characters and you had such respect for the interconnectedness of all the elements of the screenplay. I knew you were trustworthy. And your work verified that trust.

And finally, what was it about the story of *Old Fashioned* that made me think it would make a good novel? That's a great question. I wasn't sure at first, honestly. But clearly the folks at Tyndale saw something there—saw the potential. And the more I thought, the more I saw it too. I also saw the possibility of expanding and enriching the story in certain ways—especially in regard to the character of Clay.

Clay doesn't say a lot. He doesn't do a lot. His struggle is very internal. These are challenging characteristics for a film protagonist, where visual representation is so crucial. In a novel, since we can so much more easily get in a character's head and unpack the baggage a little more directly and explicitly . . . that's a real advantage for a character like Clay.

At the end of the day, *Old Fashioned* is about ideas, and the novelization was a way to dig deeper and mine those ideas even more. You did so with such precision and artistry that the book really does stand alone and, in many ways, improves and helps illuminate the source material. Thanks again for that . . . for sharing your unique and elegant voice in the telling of this story.

So what does it mean to do things *The Old Fashioned Way*?

Inspired by the motion picture *Old Fashioned*, this book will show you how to reclaim the lost art of romance by introducing you to romantic love as God intended it. Regardless of your past experiences, where you've been, or where you are now, you can find and create a love that will last a lifetime.

AVAILABLE NOW IN BOOKSTORES AND ONLINE.